JENNIFER S. ALDERSON

Death by Bagpipes

A Summer Murder in Edinburgh

First published by Traveling Life Press 2020

This novel is entirely a work of fiction. The names, characters and incidents portrayed in it are the work of the author's imagination. Any resemblance to actual persons, living or dead, events or localities is entirely coincidental.

First edition

ISBN: 9789083001180

This book was professionally typeset on Reedsy.
Find out more at reedsy.com

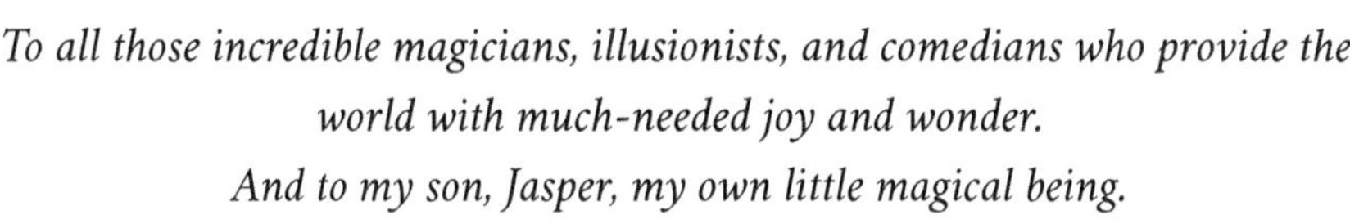

To all those incredible magicians, illusionists, and comedians who provide the world with much-needed joy and wonder.
And to my son, Jasper, my own little magical being.

Contents

1

Welcome Home

August 8—Seattle, Washington

"Lana Hansen, would you move in with me?" Alex Wright was down on one knee, holding a small box in his outstretched hand.

Lana gasped as she stared at the key nestled inside.

"Wow, I didn't see that coming." She dropped onto her couch, and her cat, Seymour, sprung into her lap, sensing she'd want the comfort of his soft fur while processing this shocker. She and Alex had been dating for three glorious months, but she hadn't even considered moving their relationship to the next level.

Alex stood up and snapped the box shut before running a hand through his wavy hair. "I thought you would be pleased."

Lana took his hand and pulled him down onto the couch next to her. "Gosh, I am, trust me. It's just that things are going so great between us right now. Why do we need to rush into living together?"

"Being with you feels so right, I don't see the point of waiting."

Lana brushed her nose against his. "You are the best thing that's ever happened to me, Mr. Wright. Could you give me a few days to digest your offer? It's been pretty hectic lately with back-to-back tours, and I'm not even certain which time zone I'm in. I was hoping we could enjoy a stress-free week together, before you have to fly out to London." Lana had just returned from five weeks of leading tours through Germany, Denmark, and Norway and was drained.

"Sure, okay." Alex smiled as he rested his forehead against hers. "I guess that's why I decided to ask you now instead of waiting until we're both back home from our next assignments. I wish you could join me in London. But the training sessions and networking functions run from early in the morning to late at night. I'm afraid I wouldn't have much time to be with you, even if you did."

"It's the same for me," Lana admitted. "I wish you could come to Spain with me, but we're visiting several cities on this tour and are going to be on the road more than usual. It doesn't seem fair to ask you to come and then not be able to spend time with you."

"I guess it's the nature of our jobs," Alex conceded as he snuggled against her neck.

As much as she would miss him, Lana couldn't wait to visit Spain. Ever since her fellow Wanderlust Tours guides had told her about the Andalucía trip and shown her their pictures, she had been bugging their boss, Dotty Thompson, to let her lead one of those tours.

Lana breathed in Alex's scent, as he moved his mouth up to hers and kissed her tenderly.

"Why don't you fly over to Seville after your job is finished? We can spend a few hours together before my tour starts. It's not much, but it would be wonderful to share some authentic Spanish tapas with you," Lana suggested after she recovered her breath.

Alex brightened up. "I would love that."

"Let me talk to Dotty first. I'm certain she won't have a problem with you being there, but I should let her know what we are thinking before you change your ticket."

"That sounds great. But first, I sure have missed you. We have some catching up to do." Alex pulled her in for another passionate embrace.

"Dotty can wait," Lana murmured as she relaxed into his arms.

A booming voice called out from outside her front door. "Lana, honey? Are you home?" It was Dotty Thompson.

Or perhaps not, Lana thought.

2

Tour Switcharoo

August 8—Seattle, Washington

Alex and Lana flinched before pulling apart. "That's spooky. Did she hear us talking about her?" Alex whispered.

Lana opened her door to find her boss holding a sleeping pug in one arm and a squirming Jack Russell terrier in the other.

"I apologize for yelling like that, and for interrupting your date." Dotty blushed when her eyes fell upon Alex. "But I need to ask you something work-related, and it can't wait."

Dotty poked her head around Lana. "Could I borrow your girlfriend for a few minutes, Alex?"

Lana lifted the wriggling Jack Russell terrier out of Dotty's arms, cuddling him tight. "Chipper, you silly boy, were you jealous of Rodney?"

"I swear, I cannot pick up one without the other one whining for attention, so it was easier to hold them both," Dotty explained as she began rocking her snoring pug. "Rodney is feeling poorly, and the medication his veterinarian prescribed knocked him right out."

Lana gently stroked Rodney's short black fur. The little pug's bright pink tongue whipped out and licked her finger, yet his eyes remained closed. Lana wasn't certain whether he was an excellent actor or simply dreaming.

"I should go, anyway." Alex squeezed Lana's shoulder as he walked towards the door. "Can I pick you up later and take you out to dinner?"

"That sounds great. I'll see you at seven."

This time, their kiss was more of a peck on the cheek, considering Dotty's presence. Alex kissed her cheek on the way out, too, getting a titter out of the older woman.

Once he'd exited their backyard, Lana turned to her boss. "What can I do for you, Dotty?"

"Would you mind if we go upstairs? I want to put Rodney to bed."

"No problem." As Lana started to pull her basement apartment's front door closed, Seymour bolted outside and stalked around their patch of grass and fruit trees, surveying his territory. Lana watched as he suddenly flattened down to the ground, then slowly pushed one paw out in front of his body before pulling himself forward. An unsuspecting bird pecking the ground for worms was in Seymour's crosshairs. Unable to allow that innocent robin to be murdered, she clapped her hands, scaring the bird away. The look that Seymour gave her made clear that her actions were not appreciated.

Lana chuckled as Seymour stalked off in search of new prey, then released Chipper from her arms. The Jack Russell terrier tore off for his owner's front door. Not only was Dotty Thompson Lana's employer, but she was also her landlord and occupied the top floors of their farmhouse-style home in the Fremont district. After Dotty got Rodney settled in bed and had tucked a flamingo-pink blanket over his little round body, she led Lana into the kitchen and put on the kettle.

"Hon, I am in a bit of a pickle and need your help. I know how much you want to go to Spain, but I need to switch you out onto a different tour. Please don't be mad at me."

Lana frowned and leaned against Dotty's countertop. "That's too bad, but I assume you have a good reason."

"I do, and I promise I'll make it up to you. A longtime client asked me to arrange a last-minute, week-long tour of Edinburgh and the Scottish Highlands. He is being honored at a dinner in Edinburgh next week and wants his extended family to join him for it. The thing is, he is so used to being pampered that he wants two guides to join them. He can be quite finicky, which is why I would prefer to send at least one experienced guide along."

Lana paused to consider the group dynamics as she grabbed two cups from the cupboard. "It will be different being with one family instead of several strangers, but it's only for a week. I'm sure it will be fine."

"There is another reason I am asking you to be one of the guides…" Dotty's voice trailed off as she turned away and began filling the cups with twigs of mint.

"You've got my attention," Lana said, encouraging her boss to continue.

"This client knows that I am currently hiring more guides and is convinced his grandson is a shoo-in. So I met with the young man yesterday. He claims to have extensive experience in the tourism and hospitality industry, but frankly, I didn't get a good feeling about his abilities. He seems pretty flaky, and I'm afraid he isn't organized enough to do the job right. The problem is, this client has been coming on my tours for so long now that I consider him a friend. I felt bad about saying 'no' outright, so we came to a compromise."

Lana's gut began to sink as Dotty turned to face her again.

"His grandson will be the lead guide during the trip. I'm sending you along to help train him and assist when needed, as well as get a feel for his abilities. If he does well, I will hire him. But if he messes up, then I can gracefully say no to my client without hurting his feelings. As charismatic and charming as my client is, I don't want to get stuck with a guide who isn't capable of leading a tour. I trust your opinion implicitly and know you won't lie to me in order to spare my feelings."

Lana gulped as she realized what she was getting herself into. "So I'm going to be holding this grandson's hand while he leads his own family on a tour? If you really want me to go along, I'm happy to do so, but this feels strange. Why do they need a guide on a family trip, anyway? Just how picky is this client of yours?"

"As far as his family goes, from what he told me, they are not close and rarely get together as a group, so in a way they are strangers. I do know they are flying in from all over the world because I arranged their tickets."

The kettle began to scream for attention. Dotty pulled it off the burner and filled their cups. The earthy scent of fresh mint filled the kitchen.

"My client is a special fellow. He's quite successful and is used to first-class treatment, which is why he prefers to have Wanderlust Tours deal with all the travel arrangements, transportation, and meals, instead of his personal secretary. He really can't stand unnecessary delays and has a quick temper—I better warn you about that now. And he did request several day trips and excursions that required reservations."

Dotty stirred honey into her tea, then handed the pot to Lana before continuing. "This is also a good way to see if this grandson can handle himself under pressure. My client is expecting the typical Wanderlust Tours treatment, but if he can't figure out how to get the group from point A to point B, they are going to miss out on something, and he'll get upset. I don't want this boy's incompetence reflecting back on Wanderlust Tours in any way. You know how important those five-star reviews are to me."

Lana listened to Dotty, trying to keep an open mind. "It sounds like an interesting challenge, and I have always wanted to see Scotland. It does look quite beautiful, in a stark and desolate kind of way."

Dotty looked so relieved. "Thank you, child." Her landlord enveloped her in a hug, before adding, "There is one little thing I want to warn you about, before we make this official."

Lana chuckled; with Dotty there was almost always "one little thing." Usually it ended up being something rather large. "What is it?"

Dotty bit her lip as she mumbled, "The client in question is a magician— and a famous one, to boot. Seeing as your ex-husband was a magician, I wasn't certain if spending the week with a legendary one would conjure up too many bad feelings."

Lana tapped her chin as she considered Dotty's question. Nine months ago, right after their divorce was finalized, spending a week with a magician would have been a painful reminder of her ex-husband, Ron. But so many positive things had happened since then that she was starting to feel well and truly over him.

"No, I don't see why it would. If anything, it might be fun talking with your client about his performance and acts. I don't miss the lifestyle, but being onstage was quite fun. What's his name?"

"Gary Craighead but he prefers to be called by his stage name, even when he's not on tour. It's Presto—Presto the Incredible, I believe. Have you heard of him?"

Lana about choked on her tea. "Presto the Amazing, you mean."

"That's it! Do you know him?"

"You could say that. Though we have never met," Lana said as she wiped her chin dry.

Dotty cocked her head. "Do I have to drag it out of you?"

"Sorry, no, he and Ron had a long-standing feud that ended badly—for Ron. I don't know Presto personally."

"Uh-oh. Maybe this isn't such a great idea."

Lana thought back on the lawsuit her ex had attempted to file against Presto, only to be told by his lawyer that it was a waste of time and money. Ron had stood no chance at winning; Presto was too famous and Ron's evidence too flimsy.

"No, it's okay. The incident happened before Ron and I met. Presto wouldn't know who I am."

"If Ron won't mind…"

"Why would he?" Lana snapped. "Ron left me, remember? And we aren't in contact anymore. Not since…" She stopped abruptly, unable to finish her sentence. Shortly after their divorce was finalized, in a moment of weakness, Lana had called Ron to say hello and see how he was doing. However, the woman who took her place had answered his phone, and she had never dared to call back.

Lana downed her tea before squaring up her shoulders. "When does the tour leave?"

"In four days."

"Excellent; I better do laundry and check the weather reports in Scotland."

Lana started to turn away when Dotty grabbed her arm. "I'm so sorry for making that remark about Ron. You are absolutely correct—you two aren't together anymore, and his opinion has no bearing on your life."

"Thanks for that, Dotty. It hasn't been easy, but having this job and meeting

Alex has made life infinitely better. Speaking of which, Scotland is a whole lot closer to London than Seville."

"That's right! Alex is off to the UK next week, isn't he? If you're willing to help out in Edinburgh, I'll fly you down to London after your tour and pay for your hotel. It is an expensive city."

"That sounds wonderful! Thank you, Dotty." Lana kissed her boss on the cheek. "After my screw-up this morning, it will be good to surprise Alex with this at dinner."

"What do you mean? Did you two have a fight? He didn't seem upset to me."

"He asked me to move in with him," Lana responded, realizing too late that she was not only talking to her friend, but also her landlord. "Oh, Dotty, I said no," she rushed to add. "Don't worry; I won't up and leave you."

"Why would I worry?" Dotty asked, a frown on her face. "If moving in with Alex is what you want to do, then you should. Heck, you can move out tomorrow, as far as I'm concerned."

Lana's eyebrows shot up. "Really? I figured you would be upset if I did."

"I sure would miss playing with Seymour and our spontaneous chats, but you have to think about your future. Alex is pretty wonderful, and you aren't getting any younger," Dotty stated matter-of-factly.

"Thanks for that shot of encouragement!"

"All I'm saying is that you should do what's best for you and not worry what about anyone else thinks. Granted, you two have only known each other a few months, but the older you get, the less time you need to know if it's right. Trust me on that. Heck, my sixth husband and I only knew each other for a week before we tied the knot. And although all of my husbands were wonderful, God rest their souls, he might have been the best of the bunch."

Lana nodded in understanding. "Ron and I only knew each other a few months before we got married. I guess after that fiasco, I'm a little more cautious than I used to be."

Dotty started to reprimand her, when Lana added, "And Alex and I are both away so much because of work, we haven't spent much time in the same city since we started dating. I honestly don't know whether moving in so soon is the right thing to do. But I can't see dating him for years, either. He turned forty last month, which probably motivated him to ask me now."

"That is a milestone birthday. I can imagine it got him thinking about his future and who he wanted to spend it with. You should feel pretty lucky that he asked you. But you shouldn't feel pressured into saying yes, if you aren't ready. Maybe you should hold off on making a decision until you get back from Edinburgh. That will give you a chance to mull it over."

"Thanks, Dotty," Lana said, hoping her boss was right and that Alex would wait that long for an answer. "I think that's a great plan."

3

Meeting the Family

August 12—Day One of the Wanderlust Tour in Edinburgh, Scotland

Lana stared up at the magnificent Edinburgh Castle as she caught herself humming Ed Sheeran's *Castle on the Hill*. Even though she knew this wasn't the fortress the Irish singer was referring to, it could have been. The imposing citadel loomed over the city center from its perch high atop a mountain of rock.

She pressed her face up to the window, watching the dark, soot-covered architecture fly by. Her taxi was one of those classic London cabs, and it was super luxurious. Her only complaint was feeling as if she was being swung to and fro whenever her driver whipped around a corner.

Edinburgh was much larger than she had expected—and much darker. It seemed as if the entire city was covered in a layer of black dust. Lana had read that the stain was a remnant of the Industrial Revolution, but she hadn't realized how pervasive it was.

Luckily the stain couldn't suppress the grandness of the architecture; in fact, it somehow accentuated its beauty. There were gothic spires and turrets everywhere she looked, and in combination with the color, they made Lana feel as if she were driving back into medieval times.

As they rode past the steep slopes of the Royal Mile, Lana stared at the plethora of tourists and busking performers jammed onto it. August was festival month, and there were three taking place this week alone. The energy wafting off the crowd was palpable and invigorating. Lana couldn't wait to walk down that famous stretch later today.

She stifled a yawn with the back of her hand, wishing she'd slept better on the plane. Considering it was still early in the morning here in Scotland, Lana knew she had a long day ahead before she could take a nap. Her first priority would be finding a cup of coffee, once she arrived at the house Dotty had rented for Presto, his family, and their guide.

Because the trip was planned at the last minute, and it was so busy in Edinburgh, finding ten rooms at the same hotel had proved impossible. Lana was a little nervous about being under the same roof with one extended family for a week, so she hoped the house would be big enough that they could give each other space during their down time. Not that they would have much time to be lounging around at the house. Dotty had packed the week full of excursions, guided tours, and day trips—at her client's request. It seemed Presto wished to show his family as much of Edinburgh and the surrounding environs as humanly possible, given their time constraints.

Lana hoped Presto was in good physical condition. She'd looked him up online after her initial chat with Dotty and was shocked to see that he was quite a bit older than Ron. One of the more recent results was coverage of his seventieth-birthday party, held six months earlier, at which Presto announced he was retiring—effective immediately.

At first, he gave no explanation for his unexpected and shocking decision. According to multiple news sources, he was one of the highest-paid entertainers working in America at the time—and certainly one of the most beloved. When rumors of him being gravely ill surfaced in the newspapers soon after, he had come forward and stated that he was fit as a fiddle, but after twenty wonderful years of performing for sold-out crowds around the world, it was time to step aside and give the new generation a chance to shine.

His heartfelt statement was even more appreciated by his fans when he announced that he was in the process of choosing a successor to entrust his world-renowned magic acts to—someone he found worthy of the name

Presto the Amazing. In the article, dated two months earlier, he stated he would soon announce this young magician's name. But as far as Lana could tell, he had not yet revealed their identity.

Whatever the reason, based on the articles she had found, Presto seemed to be a witty, charming, and flamboyant public figure. If he was the same in person, this was going to be a fun week. Lana wondered whether his family would be as colorful and engaging as Presto appeared to be.

Thunderous bells and chimes rang out from nearby clocks and towers, marking the eighth hour of the day. Lana hoped the family she was about to meet was already awake and not feeling too jet-lagged.

As she rode through the streets of Old Town, Lana tried forcing her mind to concentrate on the views, in an attempt to suppress her growing nervousness about meeting Presto's grandson. Would he welcome her with open arms? Or be suspicious of her watching over him? Lana was about to find out.

She hoped the young man was up for the job and that she wouldn't have to tell Dotty not to hire him. Not that it would be in Lana's best interest to lie. If she did fib and Dotty hired the grandson, she might get stuck with him on a later tour. Messing up in front of your family was one thing; forgetting to arrange a cab or confirm a reservation when strangers had paid thousands to be there was a whole different story.

To make matters worse—at least, in Lana's mind—Presto was apparently quite fond of Edinburgh and had performed regularly at the Fringe Festival, meaning he would be far more familiar with the city than she could ever be.

Thinking of Presto brought Ron to the forefront of her mind. Riled up by Dotty's remarks about her ex-husband, she hadn't told her boss the full truth about the two men's relationship and feud.

Before creating his own magic show and persona—The Great Ronaldo— Ron had worked at a Seattle theater as a set designer, the same spot Presto began his career at. After Presto's show began growing in popularity, he hired Ron as his full-time assistant. What exactly happened between them the world may never know, but her ex swore to this day that he'd thought up and devised the props necessary to make the Rainbow Walk work—the same act that ultimately rocketed Presto to international stardom.

Did Presto steal Ron's idea and run with it? Or had Ron given his boss permission to perform the trick, only to regret it later? After Presto made The Rainbow Walk famous, Ron tried to sue for compensation, claiming he had thought up the act and thus that it was his intellectual property. Unfortunately for her ex, he could never prove it in a court of law.

Whatever really happened, the world knew Presto the Amazing as the mastermind behind the jaw-dropping act, not The Great Ronaldo. The Rainbow Walk was Presto's ticket into the largest theaters around the country and, later, the world. While his shows quickly sold out the largest halls available, Ron had trouble filling the side lounge at most bars and casinos.

How Ron used to curse Presto's name. Yet Lana sincerely doubted that Presto would remember The Great Ronaldo or know the name of his first and now ex-wife. That was the only reason why Lana had said yes to leading this tour. If she had suspected that Presto would recognize her, she wouldn't have flown to Scotland.

As her cabbie took her farther out of the city center, the tree-lined streets were increasingly populated by stately homes and regal apartment buildings. He pulled up in front of an elegant brownstone that bordered a small park. Lana retrieved her luggage and rang the bell. Moments later, she heard heels clicking on tile. A plump, older lady dressed in a tweed suit opened the door.

"Hello, there. You must be Lana Hansen. Do come in."

The woman stepped back to let Lana pass. Her voice was as friendly as her face and smile. Lana felt immediately at ease.

After closing the door, the woman held out her hand. "I'm Betty, Presto's personal secretary."

Lana was glad the woman used her client's name right off the bat. She hadn't been certain whether he preferred to be called by his birth name, Gary, or his stage name—despite Dotty's reassurances that he always went by the latter.

"We arrived an hour ago from London and are still getting unpacked," Betty explained as she clip-clopped down the hallway. "The family is squished into the bedrooms on the upper floors. I saved you the room downstairs, so you can have a little privacy. Why don't I introduce you to them, then I'll take you to it?"

Lana smiled and nodded, thankful for Betty's warm welcome. Dark wood paneling and heavy wooden furniture lined the long hallway, most of which seemed to be antique and well cared for. A large vase filled with gorgeous flowers added a much needed burst of color to the entry. A grand staircase rose up one side, a carved wood railing marking its path.

When they entered what Lana assumed was the formal living room, her eyes were immediately drawn to the thick burgundy curtains tied back with braided gold cords. Gracing the walls were beautiful paintings of idyllic landscapes, still-life florals, and castles in ruins. Sitting in a chaise lounge close to the door was an older woman, her arm thrown over the back as if she was posing for a portrait. She was intently watching a younger man with flaming red hair who was shuffling a deck of cards in his hands.

The older woman's hair was teased out with too much hair spray, and her makeup was quite dramatic. Lana wondered whether she worked in the theater. Whatever she did, she must be successful, the older woman's silk blouse probably cost more than Lana earned in a month.

Behind them were two more young people, both reading magazines—she about art history and he about sports. Standing behind the art lover was a man old enough to be her father. He leaned over the wingback chair as if he was reading along with her, his head so close to hers that it almost touched the young woman's hair. Lana shivered a little; it would make her nervous having anyone but Alex breathe down her neck like that—family or not.

A few feet behind them was an older man sitting well apart from the rest. Judging from the crook of his neck, he had fallen asleep. Locked in his hand was a glass of whisky. Based on the puddle on the floor, some alcohol had already dribbled out. Lana hoped she wasn't responsible for cleaning up after the family, as well.

"Everyone, this is Lana Hansen, the guide from Wanderlust Tours," Betty said.

"Thank goodness, the cavalry has arrived," the sports lover quipped as he stood up, letting his magazine fall to the ground before walking towards

Lana. He was quite tall, yet as skinny as a pole.

Betty clicked her tongue as she crossed paths with him and picked up the magazine.

Apparently he noticed Lana's perturbed glance because he chuckled when he held out his hand. "I'm teasing you. The name is Terrance Craighead. I'm Presto's grandson."

"It's nice to meet you," Lana said as diplomatically as she could. "Dotty said I'm to help out wherever I'm needed."

"Considering this is my family, I doubt your services will be necessary." Terrance ran a hand over his slicked-back hair. "But enjoy the free vacation, nonetheless."

Lana felt a knot forming in her stomach as she swallowed a snarky reply. "I'm sure you're right. But if you have any questions, please let me know."

"Sure," he sneered as he walked back to his chair.

Before Lana could find her tongue, a resounding voice drew her eyes to the door.

"Welcome, Lana!" A tall, fit older man strode over. He was wearing a three-piece suit cut from purple paisley with a bright yellow square sticking out of his jacket pocket. His leather shoes were so shiny that they reflected the chandelier's many lights as he walked.

"I'm Presto the Amazing." He bowed dramatically before taking her hand and kissing it, maintaining eye contact the entire time.

Lana felt herself blushing at his touch and gaze, now understanding why Dotty found him so charming. Presto was definitely not lacking in confidence. But then again, he was arguably the most famous illusionist in the world and had been at the top of his game for twenty years. According to most newspapers and magazines, the man was a national treasure.

When he released his grip, her hand fell limply to her side as if he had sucked up her remaining energy.

"You can call me Presto. I am so glad you could come over on such short notice. It will be good to leave our trip in your capable hands."

When Terrance started to grumble, he hastily added, "And those of Terrance, of course."

"The pleasure is all mine," Lana said. "It is an honor to be working with you. Dotty holds you in high regard."

"She's a doll, isn't she?" He turned quickly, his coattails swinging around his legs as he gestured towards the rest. "Have you met the family?"

"Not quite everyone, but I just arrived—"

"Where are your manners, children?" Presto scolded his kin. He pointed to the woman stretched out in the chaise lounge. "This is my daughter, Ursula. She is quite a talented actress. You might know her from *Weatherly Lane*."

Lana shook her head slightly, embarrassed to admit she didn't recognize the show's name.

"She was nominated for an Emmy for her role," Presto added.

"That's impressive. It's good to meet you."

The woman offered a limp hand, mumbling *enchanté* when Lana carefully shook it. Lana couldn't tell how old she was on account of the thick layer of makeup covering the older woman's face, but figured she must be in her late forties or fifties.

"It's alright, darling. *Weatherly Lane* was a popular costume drama in the eighties, but I suspect you were a teenager then and wouldn't have been interested in such a serious show," Ursula laughed, to Lana's relief. "Some say the writers of *Downton Abbey* used our show as inspiration. You'll have to watch for me in Michael Engler's next film. I'm playing the lead." She patted her hair and resumed her pose.

"Oh, wow, congratulations! That must be exciting," Lana gushed. She had never been a big television or film person, but would look up her guest's career later anyway.

"And this is her son, Harry. He wants to be a magician." Presto pointed to the young redhead with cards in his hands. To Lana, Presto didn't sound as enthusiastic as she would have expected, considering his grandson wanted to follow in his footsteps.

Harry frowned at his grandfather. "Presto means I *am* a magician. I just finished a month-long tour on the West Coast. Have you heard of Harry the Magnificent?"

Lana shook her head, and the young man's expression soured. "That's my stage name. Look out for me; I'll be performing again in Seattle before you know it."

The young art lover walked over and held her hand out. She was so thin and waiflike that in her floor-length floral gown, she seemed to float across the room. "I'm Viola. It's a pleasure to meet you. Granddad does love to travel with Wanderlust Tours."

"That's nice to hear. My boss has put together a wonderful tour of Edinburgh and the Highlands for us. I think it's going to be a week to remember."

"That's right—Granddad said we would be taking a trip out of the city later this week. I hope we'll be visiting some of those famous castles along the way. I bet their art collections are to die for."

"If you want a copy of the itinerary, let me know."

Viola chuckled. "I have one somewhere; I keep misplacing it. It doesn't matter; as long as you remember to call me to the bus, we'll be fine."

Presto slung an arm over her shoulder. "My Viola is an art expert. She's helping me get my private collection in order and is even trying to talk me into opening it up to the public."

"It's no joke, Grandpa. A private museum bearing your name would be a wonderful asset to culture lovers everywhere."

"Or at least to those in the greater Seattle area," Presto teased. "It's more of a mishmash of what I like rather than a well-thought-out collection, like the ones you usually see in a museum."

'Trust me, Grandpa, you have excellent taste."

"Hello there, I'm Kurt." A male voice accompanied the burly hand that was thrust into Lana's face. The older man who had been sneak-reading Viola's magazine was now standing right in front of her.

"Hi Kurt, it's good to meet you." *How did such a large man move so silently?* she wondered.

"If you're speculating as to why you see no resemblance between me and the others, it's because I'm not family," Kurt said, chuckling at his own joke. Lana laughed along politely.

Presto slapped him on the back. "I've known Kurt so long that he does feel like family to me. He's also my personal physician, but he's not on duty during the trip," the magician said, wagging a finger at his friend.

"If anyone gets hurt, don't hesitate to bring them over to me, you hear?" Kurt squeezed Lana's shoulder so hard, she was afraid he might shatter it. The man was incredibly strong, in spite of his age. Judging by the crow's-feet and laugh lines, Lana figured Kurt was pushing sixty. He was also a close talker, a trait that had Lana leaning back in order to create more personal space.

After briefly examining Kurt, Lana looked at rest of the family and realized none of them were similar in appearance. Whereas Viola was a waiflike blonde, Harry was solidly built and had a flaming red mane. Ursula was hard to place. She was tall and reasonably thin, like Presto, but her hair had obviously been dyed a dirty blonde.

It was hard to tell what kind of body type the man sitting at the back of the room had. While the family introduced themselves to Lana, Betty had been shaking the whisky drinker's shoulder, clearly trying to get him to wake up. If he hadn't been snoring so loudly, Lana might have been concerned for his health.

After several attempts, the man woke with a start and shielded his face with his arms, as if he was being attacked. "I'm good for it!" he bellowed.

The man spoke with a slightly British accent. Lana wondered whether he was also a family friend. After he sprung up and noticed that no one was trying to assault him, he straightened his jacket over his rather large midriff, then fell back into his chair.

"Zach, you are the only one of us not suffering from jet lag, so you have no excuse," Betty admonished. "Can you try to stay sober, at least until after dinner?"

Though she spoke in a soft, motherly voice, her words carried across the long room. The rest of the family was silent, carefully watching how Zach reacted.

Betty seemed to notice the rest studying them and added loudly, "Zach, the guide is here. Why don't you stand up and introduce yourself?" The way

Betty spoke to him, one would have thought that Zach was a young child, not a forty-plus-year-old man.

Zach again rose out of his chair, holding onto the arms to steady himself, before grabbing his drink from Betty's hand and stumbling over to Lana. He was quite tall and broad-shouldered with a gigantic belly hanging over his belt. His clothes looked quite expensive and well-tailored to his oddly shaped body. She could smell the whisky on his breath even from a few feet away. Lana wondered whether she was going to have to hide the liquor during the trip or be expected to keep it stocked up.

The man offered a hand. "I'm Zach."

Betty smiled up at him as if she was a proud mother. "This is Presto's son. He's a famous theater-maker."

Presto snorted at her comment, making both Zach and Betty bristle.

"We were just in London to see one of his plays." From his sarcastic tone, it was clear that Presto was not as impressed with his flesh and blood as Betty was.

"I liked the play, Presto," Betty said as she patted Zach's shoulder. "The music might have been more bombastic than I'd have expected from a romance. But the final scene—when the hero stripped off his clothes, put on that blindfold, and dove into the sea of blood—was quite symbolic."

Zach nodded enthusiastically. "Falling in love is akin to taking a blind leap of faith. Some critics adore it."

"It's too bad most of the reviewers didn't see what Betty did, isn't it?" Kurt added in his boisterous voice.

"It really is," Presto chimed in. "You could use a few more financial backers."

"Yes, well, my plays aren't for every man," Zach answered.

"More like no man…" Lana heard Harry mumble, garnering him an evil glare from his mother.

"That's not polite. There's a stranger present," Ursula scolded.

Zach's cheeks flushed to a burgundy deeper than the curtains hanging behind him. "What is your stage name, again?"

From his snide tone, Lana figured Zach wasn't asking to be polite. Harry didn't seem to notice his uncle's tone.

"Harry the Magnificent," the young magician said, his chest puffing up with pride.

While Presto rolled his eyes, Zach sniggered. "Real original. You're just ripping off the old man's tricks and his name. At least I don't steal from others or dumb down my act to cater to the masses."

"That's enough, you two. I invited you all here so you can get to know each other again, not squabble." Presto stepped in between the two men. "With me being on the road most of the year, I wasn't around much when you were younger, and I'll always regret that. Unfortunately, I can't turn back time and make it up to you, but I can share with you the spoils of my hard work. And being here together and exploring our family's native Scotland sounds like a great way to begin."

"I didn't even know we were Scottish," Viola said.

"Me either, but that explains Harry's red hair," Ursula laughed.

The longer her guests chatted, the more Lana felt like an intruder at a family reunion. As they began sharing increasingly personal stories about their lives, Lana began slowly backing up towards the door.

Suddenly, Betty was at her side. "Shall I show you to your room? After such a long flight, I can imagine you want to freshen up."

"That would be great, thanks."

Betty picked up Lana's backpack, shooing away her hand when she tried to take it from the older woman. "I might be pushing sixty, but I'm as strong as I ever was. However, I will let you take your suitcase. I don't think I would make it down the stairs with that."

Lana followed her to the end of the hallway where another set of stairs led downstairs. This one was less grand than the front staircase and much narrower. The basement was darker, and the ceiling seemed to be lower, as well. They passed a massive kitchen full of copper pots and pans, then several storage rooms. Betty used a key to open the last door. When she did, the door smashed against a single bed filling the space. A free-standing armoire was at the foot of the bed, but Lana assumed it was for decoration only. There was so little space, she doubted that she could actually open the doors. Shoved into one corner was a chest of drawers that did seem to be accessible.

"I do apologize for giving you the smallest room," Betty stammered. "Unfortunately, all of the bedrooms on the upper floors are being used by the family. I know this is the servant's quarters, but it's not a reflection on you. If you prefer to stay in a proper hotel room, I'm certain we can make other arrangements."

"Don't be silly. It's nice to have a little privacy. Besides, I won't be in this room much; I am here to work," Lana said diplomatically. Betty looked so concerned, she almost felt bad. "It will be fine, really."

After Betty rejoined the others upstairs, Lana wrestled to get the drawers open, breaking off a knob in the process. This certainly wasn't typical of the rooms she had stayed in on other Wanderlust tours, but then, Lana had a sneaking suspicion nothing was going to be normal on this trip.

4

Dotty Calls to Say Hello

August 12—Day One of the Wanderlust Tour in Edinburgh, Scotland

Lana was almost finished unpacking when her phone rang. A smile sprung to her lips when she saw that it was her boss calling. She glanced at her world clock and noticed it was a few minutes after midnight in Seattle—far later than Dotty usually stayed up.

"Hi, hon, I'm glad I caught you," Dotty exclaimed as soon as Lana answered. "I couldn't wait to see how things are going. What's the family like? How is Presto? Has he asked about me?"

Dotty sounded like a schoolgirl in love. Lana couldn't bear to hurt her feelings, but didn't want to lie to her boss. "He seems like a nice guy and is quite charming. I've only talked with him briefly because I only arrived a few minutes ago. Once I'm settled, I am certain he'll want to know everything you've been up to lately. When was the last time you saw him, anyway?"

"Gosh, it's been at least a year, maybe longer. He had just broken up with his last girlfriend and wanted to get away to forget about her. I guess I offered a good shoulder to cry on," Dotty tittered. "If he wants to chat, tell him he can always call on me. Anytime."

Lana covered the mouthpiece with her hand to prevent her boss from hearing her giggle. No wonder Dotty was calling so soon; she was pining for the old magician.

"I will let Presto know."

"Day or night."

"Gotcha, Dotty," Lana replied, then cleared her throat. "Say, I was checking the itinerary, and it all looks quite straightforward, except for the Highlands trip. That's a long drive for a two-day visit. Would it be better to fly up to Inverness and take a bus from there?"

"I know it's a long road trip, but Presto specifically requested they travel by touring car from Edinburgh because he wants to get lost in the desolateness of the Highlands. Plus he wants to visit Stirling Castle, which is on your route."

"Excellent, one of Presto's granddaughters has already mentioned wanting to see the interior of a Scottish castle."

"She's guaranteed to love this one. Now tell me, what's the house like? Is it as pretty as it looks on the website? I don't usually rent entire homes for our guests, but it was more cost-effective than I expected, when you consider there are ten people staying there. I might have to do this again, if it's fancy enough. Let's see your room."

Lana turned her phone so Dotty could see the interior, adding, "My room is not indicative of the rest of the house. I think this is the servant's quarters. I'll have to take pictures of the upper floors for you—they do match the website."

Dotty took in the cramped space, empty walls, and bars over the single window. "The bedrooms looked so pretty on the website. Why did you choose this one?"

"I was the last to arrive, and it was the only one left."

"That's strange; I thought there were eleven bedrooms in that house, meaning there should be a spare."

Lana hid her smirk behind her hand as Dotty confirmed her suspicions. Yet, as much as she would prefer a more comfortable room, she would rather rough it downstairs if it meant having more privacy during the week. She'd only just arrived and was already feeling uncomfortable about sleeping under the same roof as this family.

"It doesn't matter, I won't be here much. Besides, you are paying for my weekend in London after this trip, which is a good reason to let this slide." Lana laughed.

"Are you certain you don't mind staying there? I'm sure I can find a single room in a hotel close by."

"Presto's personal assistant said the same thing. It's really no bother to sleep down here. And this way, Terrance can always pop by to ask a question if he needs assistance."

"What do you think of the grandson? Is he excited about leading the tour?"

"It's hard to tell. He doesn't exactly seem pleased to see me."

"That's too bad. I wonder what Presto told him about you being there. Why don't you stop by Terrance's room and go through the itinerary with him? It's a good way for you two to get to know each other better before the trip begins, and you can give him a quick rundown of what is expected of him. He has worked in hospitality before so I'm sure he'll know the basics. I do hope you two can find a way to work together."

"Don't you worry about a thing. I'm sure we'll get along fine," Lana said while crossing her fingers behind her back.

"Great! Glad to hear it. Now you go and enjoy Scotland. Have some haggis for me," Dotty cackled, then hung up.

5

Catching Up With Terrance

August 12—Day One of the Wanderlust Tour in Edinburgh, Scotland

"Hi, Terrance. Do you have a minute?"

The young man glared down at Lana from his bedroom's doorway but made no move to let her in.

"I thought we could talk about the tour and decide how to split up the duties," Lana pressed, standing her ground.

Terrance stepped back to let her in, yet kept his arms tightly wrapped around his torso. She paused a moment as she crossed the threshold, shocked by the enormity of his room, as well as the four-post bed, antique dressers, and tasteful artwork decorating it. Dotty would be pleased to hear the upper floors matched the photos she had seen online.

He closed the door and turned to her. "I thought you were here to grade me, not actually help out on the tour."

Lana kept her facial expression as neutral as possible, hoping he couldn't read her mind. That was exactly why she was here, though Dotty asked that she not admit that to Terrance.

"What? No, of course not. I'm here as your backup. There are always at least two guides on a tour, so if someone is injured or has a problem that needs addressing, one guide can deal with it while the other keeps the rest entertained. If you want to lead tours, you'll have to get used to working in pairs," she reasoned, hoping her logic would make sense to him.

Unfortunately, Terrance's frown didn't lessen. Lana pushed on.

"I know this is an odd situation because you are all family and not strangers. Normally, part of a guide's job is helping their guests get to know each other. But in this case, there's no need. Which is why Dotty asked me to be the second guide on this trip, in part to free up your time. She figured you would want to spend time sightseeing with them, instead of catering to their every whim, as you normally would on a tour."

Terrance began to nod slightly, encouraging Lana to lay it on a bit thicker. "Think of me as your assistant. Why don't you reconfirm our transportation and bookings, and let me worry about the meals and the day-to-day handholding."

The young man relaxed visibly and allowed his arms to fall to his sides. "Okay, that sounds good. And so you know, the family isn't as close as you might expect. Presto was always on tour, and they never got together as a group. Most of them haven't seen each other in years."

Lana's brow creased at his word choice. It sounded as if he didn't feel like he was a part of this family. She felt bad for the young man. "That is even more reason for me to be here, so you can spend time getting to know them again."

Terrance cracked a smile, bringing joy to Lana's heart. There was still hope that they could work together as a team, instead of working against each other. "All of the phone numbers and contact information you'll need are in the tour planning documents Dotty sent over. If you have any questions about the day trips or how to reconfirm a booking, let me know. I'm only a floor away," Lana said, trying to infuse her tone with enthusiasm.

"Yes, I know. Betty and I put you in the servant's quarters." A smile played on Terrance's lips.

Just when things were looking up, she thought. Based on Terrance's grin, she wouldn't be surprised if they put her downstairs to reinforce the fact that she was not one of them. Not wanting to start a fight with the young man, Lana ignored his jab and turned to leave.

Terrance grabbed her arm. "Please wait. I'm sorry about being so rude.

My grandfather is putting a lot of pressure on me to get this right. Like I told your boss, I've never done anything like this before. If Presto hadn't forced me into this role, I never would have volunteered for it."

His response caught her off guard. "Wait a second, I thought you wanted to be a guide."

"No way. I want to get my punk rock band back together. We were pretty successful but couldn't afford much studio time. If Presto helps finance our next album, I'm certain we'll be able to hire a great producer who can get us airplay."

"Oh, so you don't really want to be a guide. That's good to know. I'll tell Dotty there's been some confusion." *Great, so he's snotty and unmotivated,* Lana moped in her mind. Being around this young man for a week was going to be a challenge, she realized.

Terrance leaped in front of his door. "No! You can't do that. If I don't lead this tour, Presto won't let me stay at his house anymore. And if he kicks me out, I'll never be able to wear him down enough to fund my band."

What am I getting myself into? Lana wondered. She'd promised Dotty that she would judge him objectively. Now she was going to feel pressure to approve him as a guide, if only to ensure the young man had a roof over his head.

"Well, let's do everything we can to help you succeed, shall we?" Lana put on a brave face, hoping against hope that the family got along well and would be forgiving of any mistakes. Terrance's chance of success would increase substantially if that was the case. "Do you have any questions about the itinerary or the tour notes?"

"Oh, um, I misplaced my copy. Do you have another one?"

Lana bit her tongue as she opened her bag and pulled out a second copy of both documents. Because Dotty had warned her that Terrance came across as flaky, she'd brought her reserve copy along, even though she'd hoped it wouldn't be necessary. "Certainly; here you go. Why don't we look through them together?"

Terrance held up the itinerary. His lips moved as he speed-read the text. When he looked up at her again, he said, "No, I don't have any questions.

Now, if you don't mind, I'm going to lie down. The jet lag is starting to catch up."

"Wait, that was only the overview of locations. It would be good if you read up on what we will be seeing today, before the tour begins. And we do have a guided tour of Edinburgh Castle starting in an hour."

"Darn it, that's right. I guess it'll have to be a short nap," Terrance said, as he nodded towards the door.

"Sure, okay, I'll get out of your hair. Sleep well."

Once Lana was back in her room, she flopped onto the bed and stretched out. Despite its narrow format, it had a comfortable mattress. Though she still had her doubts about Terrance's abilities and attitude, Lana was glad that it was easy enough for them to come to a truce. The last thing she needed was to be locked in battle with him the whole trip. The fact that he needed the job to keep his home was worrisome, but Lana hoped it would motivate him to do his part, so she didn't have to lie to Dotty about his abilities.

Now that she had one crisis resolved, it was time to call Alex. She only hoped he would still not be upset about her hesitance to move in together so soon. She'd promised to tell him her decision the next time they were both home, but she could tell that he wasn't happy that she needed more time to think it over.

To help decide what she should do, on the flight to Scotland Lana had counted the days they'd spent together since they started dating. During their three-month-long courtship, they'd only spent seven weeks in the same city. The rest of the time, one or both of them had been on the road for work.

Yet the brevity of their relationship wasn't the only thing holding her back. She did love the surprise flowers he brought her, the candlelight dinners, and flirty text messages that often made her blush. If they moved in together now, would he still feel compelled to sweep her off her feet? She was only thirty-seven years old, not sixty-seven. They had plenty of time to get to know each other better before living together. She only hoped Alex would see it that way, as well.

6

Striving for Perfection

August 12—Day One of the Wanderlust Tour in Edinburgh, Scotland

At precisely eleven o'clock, Presto pulled open the living room door and called out, "Hey, Harry—catch."

Lana looked up from her map to see a bowling ball flying through the air towards Harry's head. Instinctively, she screamed, "Get down!"

Before the young man could duck, the ball hit him in the chest. Lana feared the worst as it impacted his rib cage.

Yet instead of releasing a blood-curdling scream, Harry began laughing loudly when the ball exploded into a burst of confetti.

"How the?" Lana mumbled as Ursula clicked her tongue at her father and went back to reading a fashion magazine. Betty immediately began picking up bits of colored paper.

"That was great, Grandpa," Harry gushed as he held a piece of the tissue paper bowling ball up to the light and examined it intently. "How did you get the paper to remain strong enough to hold its form?"

"One of my many secrets," Presto said with a wink.

"Which will soon be passed onto Harry, so why not share it with him now, Dad?" Ursula asked.

"This isn't the time to teach Harry tricks—we have a visit to Edinburgh Castle and a walk along the Royal Mile," Presto said, a scowl already forming on his face. Lana swore she heard irritation in his voice, as well.

Why is he so upset that Harry is interested in learning more about his craft from his grandfather? Lana wondered. She couldn't understand why Presto wasn't more proud that Harry wanted to follow in his footsteps.

"When will it be the right time? You announced your retirement months ago, and yet you haven't officially announced Harry as your successor," Ursula whined.

Presto ignored his daughter and looked around the room at his offspring and their children. Lana did the same. Ursula was again spread out on the chaise lounge, and Zach stood next to one of the floor-to-ceiling windows, watching the cars and pedestrians go by while sipping a drink.

Kurt and Viola sat next to each other on one couch as they watched Harry practice what Lana assumed was a new card trick. From what Lana had seen so far, the young man was still working out the kinks. Harry's presentation was quite stiff and lacking charisma, but the trick did have potential. Betty hovered around, picking up bits of confetti, empty glasses, and any magazines or coasters that had fallen onto the floor. The family seemed to ignore her completely.

"Where is Terrance?" Presto asked.

Lana groaned internally as she sprung out of her chair, wishing Terrance hadn't decided to take a nap. This was not the right way to start off the tour, especially considering his living situation and dreams of being a musician were probably dependent on getting things right during this trip.

"He was having trouble with jet lag and wanted to lie down. He must not have heard his alarm go off. Why don't I check on him?"

Presto nodded curtly. "Thank you, Lana. Again, I do appreciate you flying over here to help us out. I think we're going to need it."

She smiled as warmly as she could and then raced upstairs. Behind her, she could hear Betty admonishing Presto for being too hard on Terrance.

Before Lana reached the second floor, she heard a door closing.

"Am I in trouble?" Terrance asked when Lana rounded the corner.

"No, not yet," she laughed. "But I'm glad you're already awake. Everyone else is downstairs and ready to go."

He must have slept in his clothes, Lana thought, noting the many wrinkles in his shirt and pants. She wondered whether the young man had even looked in the mirror after rising from his nap—and, considering how stylishly dressed the others were, whether Presto would say anything about it. She opened her mouth to comment but closed it immediately. It wasn't her place to judge his apparel choices, and she didn't want to get on his bad side again by pointing it out.

As soon as they entered the living room, Lana could tell that she had chosen poorly.

"You look like a bum, Terrance. Go change your clothes. You're twenty-four years old; I should not have to tell you that," Presto scoffed. "And hurry up; we don't want to keep the taxi waiting."

The young man's face drained of color before he sprinted back up to his room. While she agreed with Presto that Terrance was a grown man, belittling him wouldn't help matters. Dotty did warn her about Presto's temper, but Lana hoped he would cut his grandson some slack, otherwise this trip might end in disaster.

After Terrance fled the room, the previously lively conversations dimmed to a mumble. Zach and Ursula didn't seem to care about Presto's dressing down, but Viola, Harry, and Kurt were clearly gossiping about it. Suddenly Lana realized something was wrong. She counted the number of guests in the room and then double-checked the touring car reservation.

"Presto? Dotty thought there were nine guests on this trip. Is someone sleeping in, or did she get it wrong?"

He blushed as he leaned in close to Lana and said softly, "There is another guest joining us tomorrow."

Ursula looked up from her magazine. "Who then?"

"It's a surprise, my sweet." Presto took his daughter's hand and kissed it lightly. "You'll have to wait and see."

"Oh, Daddy, you know I hate surprises."

Terrance sprinted back into the room, now dressed in crisply pressed slacks and a colorful button-down shirt.

Presto nodded in approval. "Good. Now get us to the taxi."

Terrance ran to the front door and held it open for his grandfather.

"What is on our agenda today?" Viola asked after she climbed into the back of the mini-touring bus and slid the door shut.

"We shouldn't have to ask—our guides should be keeping us informed. Isn't that right, Lana?" Presto called out from the front seat as their driver pulled into traffic.

Lana started at the sound of her name. "Yes, of course. Today we are going to visit—"

"No," Presto interrupted. "I want our lead guide to fill us in. Terrance, if you want to be a tour guide, then you have to start showing more initiative. I don't want you to end up like your father."

Lana figured it was a good thing Presto was sitting in the front. The young man's face grew darker with every word of the magician's dressing down. If looks could kill, Terrance would be arrested for murder.

Lana felt so bad for the young man, as well as partially responsible. If she had known Presto was expecting the full Wanderlust Tours experience from his grandson, she would have urged Terrance to skip the nap and instead bone up on their destinations. Tonight she would have to pull him aside and explain in detail how a tour worked, if only to avoid more of these embarrassing situations.

Instead of inspiring Terrance, Presto's speech demotivated him even further, it seemed. The young man kept his mouth shut and his eyes locked outside.

"I tell you what, let me introduce the first stop, and then Terrance can take over," Lana said.

Presto turned towards his grandson and began to say something nasty, but Lana was ready to defuse this situation, so she talked over her client.

"Our tour begins with probably the most impressive site in Auld Reekie, Edinburgh Castle."

"Auld Reekie?" asked Ursula. "What are you talking about?"

"That is Edinburgh's nickname; it's Scottish for Old Smokey," Lana explained, unsure whether she had pronounced the Scottish words correctly.

"Oh, right, like London is the Big Smoke," Zach said.

Lana smiled encouragingly. "Yes, exactly. The castle grounds are quite extensive and include several important monuments and a famous church. We will have three hours to explore it all before we head down to the Royal Mile for a special meal."

"I want to see the gun salute. Dotty said it was at one o'clock, which is why this is today's first stop," Presto said.

"Great, we'll make certain we don't miss it," Lana responded.

"I want Terrance to worry about it, not you. It's time he pulled his own weight for a change. Otherwise…" Presto's voice trailed off, leaving his threat unspoken.

Terrance bowed his head in shame or anger; Lana wasn't entirely certain which.

"Leave him alone, Dad. We can't all be as perfect as you," Ursula called out, making everyone turn to stare at her. So far, she and Viola seemed to be Presto's favorites, or at least he indulged them the most.

"If he doesn't try, then he'll never amount to anything. We all have to make our own way in life, not leech off others," Presto responded, apparently not bothered by the fact that the entire family was listening. Lana looked away, embarrassed for the young man.

"You're one to talk." Ursula's laugh was bitter. "As if you did everything yourself. How many assistants did you borrow from before you finally became successful?" she said, using two fingers to emphasize the word "borrow."

"That's enough, Ursula. My acts are just that—mine. You were too young to remember anything correctly, anyway," Presto growled at her, then turned around to stare out the taxi's front window.

Lana felt a chill go up her spine. Was Ursula implying that Presto had stolen ideas for magic acts from his assistants? She had always thought that Ron was stretching the truth about what happened between him and Presto out of jealousy, figuring he had helped to improve one of Presto's existing acts and wanted credit for his ideas. She couldn't believe a magician would steal an assistant's idea outright.

7

The Castle on the Hill

August 12—Day One of the Wanderlust Tour in Edinburgh, Scotland

Before her mind could process what Ursula's comment might mean for Ron, their cab slowed to a halt. Lana took in the castle rising up before them. It was exactly what a fortified castle should look like, she thought, except for the absence of the moat. Its location—on the top of an extinct volcano, high above the city—more than made up for that missing feature, though.

"The entrance is straight ahead," their driver said as he pointed to a massive port on their right. As they crossed the broad Esplanade, Lana noticed that the castle's dark walls seemed to be made of orange and grey stone. Flags topped the many towers and walls of the castle complex. They entered through a port that was easily three stories tall. Lana wondered how heavy the fortified doors were and how many men were needed to open them.

Thanks to Terrance's tardiness, they were almost a half hour late for their guided tour, but the woman leading it was quite relaxed about their delay. She hurried them through the massive castle grounds at a rapid pace, recounting its extensive history as she went. Lana took in the solid towers, turrets, and cutout walls, large empty squares for soldiers to assemble in, and plenty of small windows from which the keepers of the castle could keep an eye on their surroundings. She expected a knight in shining armor to round the corner at any moment.

As they passed under Portcullis Gate, Lana shivered as she took in the spikes lining the base of the mesh-like screen.

"After the Lang Siege of the sixteenth century, this fortified gateway was built. It included three heavy wooden doors and the deadly portcullis we just walked underneath," the castle's guide stated while continuing towards a staircase curving around an imposing stone turret. Their guide briskly climbed the seventy steps of the Lang Stairs, which was apparently also the original entrance to the castle, as she led them to the summit of Castle Rock.

When they approached Saint Margaret's Chapel, their guide stopped and surveyed the long line of visitors waiting to go inside. "This chapel was built by King David I in 1130 in memory of his mother, making it the oldest building in Edinburgh. We need to push on, but if you get the chance to return later, the ornate arches and stained glass windows are worth seeing."

Their guide then directed their attention to a massive cannon placed close to the chapel's entrance. "This is Mons Meg, a six-ton siege gun. When it was made, it was considered cutting-edge military technology and could fire a gunstone two miles into the distance. Stones were used as shot before iron cannonballs were invented," their guide explained.

Lana half listened as the woman told them about Mons Meg's uses and history, preferring to enjoy the stunning views of the Old Town. She marveled at the soot-covered spires and carved stone facades of the many tall buildings and churches. It was quite beautiful, yet slightly dreary at the same time. Even on this bright and sunny day, the dark structures seemed to suck up the sunlight. In the distance, Lana could see gently rolling hills and what appeared to be a lake.

"What a glorious day!" the castle's guide exclaimed after she wrapped up her spiel about Mons Meg. "It's so clear we can even see Forth Bridge," she said, pointing the long, red suspension bridge out to her guests. "That body of water is the Firth of Forth, and there is Bass Rock."

"Why are all the buildings in Old Town so dark?" Ursula asked, running her hand across a nearby wall. "Is it a special black stone?"

The guide chuckled. "No, most of the buildings in Old Town were constructed from native Scottish blond or red sandstone. Unfortunately, during the Industrial Revolution, Edinburgh was thick with furnaces belching smoke and soot into the air, and that seeped into the pores of the stone facades. The Clean Air Act wasn't passed until 1956, meaning most of the classic Gothic and Georgian buildings got a thick coating of residue and stain."

"Couldn't someone have cleaned them since then?" Viola asked.

"Many Scots agreed with you, at first, and several cities began doing just that in the 1960s. But it's a devil's dilemma, getting that soot out. The sandblasting and power washing removed the stain but damaged the sandstone, which weakened the structures and disfigured the facades of historical buildings with horrid pockmarks. Luckily Edinburgh lagged behind with its cleaning efforts, which most locals are now glad for. But it does mean that most of the city center is permanently dressed in black."

Their guide checked her watch again. "Let's see how long the line to the crown jewels is." She hurried them farther up the top of Castle Rock. Lana could tell which building held the jewels before the guide pointed it out. A long line of impatient-looking tourists were already waiting to view the Honours of Scotland—the crown, sword, and scepter—and the Stone of Destiny.

"Oh my, we are not having much luck today. With it being festival season, all of our historical sites are extremely busy. And the room in which the jewels are displayed is rather small. I'm afraid you'd better come back closer to one o'clock. The line usually thins out around then."

"Add it to the list, Terrance," Presto called out.

"Sure, got it," the young man replied without looking up from his smartphone. It must have been a generational thing, Lana figured, because both Harry and Terrance were constantly checking their social media.

"Let's see if we can get into the Great Hall. It's just around the corner." As their guide rushed them on to their next destination, Lana found herself walking next to Zach.

"Are you enjoying the tour so far?" she asked.

"Oh, yes. The history and architecture are fascinating and quite a bit different than London."

"That's right, you live in London. Why did you move there?" Lana asked.

Zach laughed. "I was twenty-five years old and felt invincible. One of my plays had a successful run at several theaters on the West Coast, so I decided to go all-in and moved to London, with my sights set on the West End. It took almost twenty years, but I now have several productions running each year. It's a dream come true."

"That's incredible—good for you! It must have taken a lot of money and time to break into the scene, especially as a foreigner."

"It was quite a challenge, at first. It helped that I married a successful English theater agent soon after moving over. She really did open many doors for me, though of course, it was my talent that got us to the West End. After she left me last year, things got a little hairy. But I'm still at the top of my game. It'll take more than a few setbacks to get rid of me!"

"Of course," Lana responded, worried she may have unintentionally offended him with her comments. "What a wonderful life you lead. What do you have coming up next?"

Zach's cheery demeanor wavered. "If all goes well, my next show will open this Christmas. It's a contemporary adaptation of Romeo and Juliet, with refugees playing the lead roles. I'm waiting to hear back from a few theaters about their dates and availability. You do have to book these shows several months in advance."

"That must be exciting. I can't even imagine what it takes to get such a large production off the ground."

"Lots of manpower and wealthy sponsors go a long way. If you're ever in London, you'll have to see one of my shows," he said jovially. "I'll even give you a backstage tour."

"I would love that. Thank you," Lana said. She had no intention of telling Zach that she would be heading south after this trip was over. Even though London was her next destination, she was flying down to spend a weekend with Alex, not to hang out with one of her tour members.

Their guide was already standing in front of the Great Hall, waiting for her clients to catch up. Luckily, there were only a few tourists gathered around the entrance. As soon as they entered, Lana was immediately overwhelmed by the size of the hall and bright red color of the ancient walls. The sturdy wooden roof reminded her of the hull of a ship curving down towards them. Lances and spears were fanned out on the walls as decoration, and highly polished suits of armor stood guard behind velvet ropes. A stone fireplace as large as Lana's living room dominated the far wall.

"What do you think of the display techniques, Viola?" Presto asked.

"Paintings are my specialty, but this is quite impressive. I love how they display all those weapons of death as objects to be admired for their carvings."

Presto took his time examining each suit of armor, asking their guide extensive questions about their use, history, and worth. Lana was less keen on the armor and weapons, choosing instead to take in the magnificent views of the castle grounds and city below.

A beeping noise soon drew her attention. Lana automatically reached for her phone, but it was silent. Instead, the castle's guide pulled out her phone and turned off the alarm. "I do apologize for leaving you so abruptly, but I must meet my next tour by the entrance. Can I walk you back down, or do you wish to stay here a while longer?"

"I'd rather stay. Thanks for sharing your knowledge with me. It's fascinating stuff," Presto said.

"It was a pleasure chatting with you today, sir."

"The pleasure was all mine." Presto took her hand and kissed the back of it.

She blushed as he released it, then sped off to meet her next group.

"What do you want to see first, Grandpa? The jewels or the church?" Terrance asked.

Before Presto could answer, a loud explosion made them all jump.

"What was that? A terrorist attack?" Zach asked, panic in his voice.

Lana looked at her watch, and her stomach sank. "It's one o'clock. That must have been the gun salute."

"Terrance!" Presto's rising voice made everyone turn. "I told you I wanted to see the gun salute. Doesn't your watch have an alarm on it? Lana, is that a requirement for tour guides?"

"I usually set an alarm on my phone, but Terrance didn't know that. We didn't have much time to talk about how these tours work." Lana cursed their first conversation and her decision not to push him to prepare better.

"A little common sense goes a long way," Presto said dismissively. "Terrance shouldn't have to be told every little thing he is supposed to do. How many times do I have to say it—show some initiative, man!"

"I thought Lana would warn us when it was time to walk over," Terrance sulked.

Presto shook his head. "I told you to keep track of the time, not Lana. Why can't you take responsibility for your own actions? Now we're going to have to come back. Lana, could you see if we can squeeze in another visit?"

"Sure, Presto, I'll take a look. The itinerary is pretty full, but I'm sure we can find a free morning."

"We shouldn't have had to return, but I do appreciate your efforts," Presto said. "Now, Terrance, can you follow the signs to the Half Moon Battery? I want to take in the views."

When Presto stormed off, Terrance smirked at Lana, then followed his grandpa.

Lana started after him, wanting to make clear that she was unwilling to be his scapegoat for this trip, when Betty touched her arm.

"Don't worry, Presto knows it wasn't your fault. Terrance is a lost soul, and we are trying to help him find his way."

Betty's tone knocked the force out of Lana's anger. "What do you mean?"

"Terrance's father, George, was Presto's oldest son. They had a falling-out on George's twentieth birthday, and he left home, never to return. Apparently he died of cancer nine years ago, but no one informed Presto. Terrance had been living with his mother in Nevada and didn't know he had family in Seattle. After she died in a car accident a few months ago, Terrance found out about Presto and tracked him down."

"That must have been quite a shock for Presto to find out he had another grandson."

"It was an enormous shock, yes, and one he had trouble accepting at first. But Terrance had a copy of his birth certificate, as well as several early family photos that he could have only gotten from George. Presto didn't even have copies of them anymore."

"And how are he and Terrance getting along?"

"Like oil and water. After touring full-time for twenty years, Presto isn't used to being home and stuck in one spot. Since retirement, he's been restless and cranky. And he's certainly not used to having young people living in his house. They've been butting heads for most of the time. I'm afraid Terrance has inherited the Craighead stubbornness gene, meaning neither will back down without a fight."

"That's got to be difficult for both of them."

"It really is. But Terrance didn't have a very good life, so we are trying to help him, not judge him. Apparently his mother barely broke even by waitressing in a bar outside of Reno, so he dropped out of high school to work odd jobs and help pay the bills. Presto still feels quite guilty about how things ended up with George and felt like he had to make it up to Terrance. So he let him move into his mansion in Seattle's Capitol Hill while he was finding his feet again."

Betty bit her lip and looked out over the skyline before continuing. "Because Presto is so wealthy, Terrance seems to think he doesn't have to work—or do anything, really. We have been trying to help him find a job or study he is interested in, but the boy doesn't want to do anything but play video games and go bar-hopping. Presto is a workaholic and expects everyone around him to have a strong work ethic, as well, so he is trying to instill one in Terrance. Personally, I think what the boy really needs is for Presto to take an interest in him."

Lana nodded in understanding. "That makes sense. Though I don't know if asking Terrance to be the guide on a family trip was such a hot idea. It might make him feel like he isn't part of the family."

Betty nodded emphatically. "That's exactly what I said. I'm afraid Presto didn't think it through, but made a spur-of-the-moment decision. He had your boss on speaker phone when he was booking the trip, and I heard her ask if Presto wanted one or two guides to accompany us. Before you know it, he's recommending Terrance for the job. Granted, the boy says he has worked in a lot of different bars and cafés over the years, but I suspect more as a dishwasher than waiter. Terrance isn't exactly forthcoming about his previous lifestyle or occupations. Unfortunately, me calling Presto out on his decision only made him even more resolute that Terrance should be our guide."

Lana tried to control her emotions as she processed what Betty had said. It was becoming increasingly difficult to recommend Terrance to her boss, even if it meant the young man might lose his right to live in Presto's home.

Before she could think up an appropriate response, Betty exclaimed, "I don't know why I'm telling you all this! I guess because you're here to see if Terrance would make a good tour guide. He's gotten off to a rough start with pretty much everyone, but I hope you'll cut him a little slack."

"Thanks for sharing this, Betty. I'll be sure to take his personal history into account," Lana promised, knowing she couldn't overlook the young man's shortcomings if it meant shifting Presto's problem onto Dotty's shoulders. But the trip had just begun; there was still plenty of time for Terrance to redeem himself as a guide. Especially once it finally sank into his thick head that his grandfather wasn't going to let him slide by anymore.

"Do you think Presto will be able to let Terrance be, so he can get to know his family? They have been fighting constantly since I arrived."

"Unfortunately Presto is not a very sympathetic person," Betty said. "His nitpicking isn't making it any easier for Terrance, I agree with you about that."

Lana looked over at the young man, trying to engage Zach and Kurt in conversation. Neither seemed interested in what he had to say. A feeling of shame rolled over Lana for disliking the young man. His deep-seated desire to fit in with this family explained his snootiness and attempts to shift the blame onto her. She would have to do as much as she could to help him succeed.

"Is this the first time Terrance is meeting everyone?"

"Yes, well, except for Kurt and Viola. He and Kurt seemed to have butted heads, as well, and they tend to avoid each other. Kurt is convinced that Terrance isn't Presto's grandson, and he isn't shy about expressing his opinion. Viola usually comes over to Presto's house on her days off so she can document his art collection. She and Terrance get along alright, though he doesn't have an affinity for art and that's all she wants to talk about," Betty laughed.

"Ursula and Harry live in Los Angeles and usually come up to Seattle for Thanksgiving. Zach lives in London, and he and his father used to meet up whenever Presto was there on tour. So Terrance hadn't met them before this trip. And the rest of Presto's kids are spread out all over the United States and rarely come to Seattle."

"What do you mean, the rest?"

"Ursula, Zach, and George were born in wedlock; Presto has one more daughter and four more sons born out of wedlock—one of which is Viola's dad. But those children were raised by their mothers, and he rarely sees them. Presto only got to know Viola because she moved to Seattle to study art history around the same time he was home nursing a twisted ankle. Honestly, I couldn't even tell you all of those kids' names without looking them up first; it's been so long since he corresponded with any of them."

"Has Presto had many relationships?" Lana asked, unable to stifle her curiosity.

Betty blushed and averted her gaze. "I guess you could say Presto loves the female species, perhaps too much. He had his eight children by six different women, which is why two of his sons are only a few months apart."

Lana looked away to keep Betty from seeing her shocked expression.

"Presto truly is a rolling stone. He's always had trouble settling down in one spot, let alone with one person. I do wonder what retirement is going to do to him. These past few months, he's been flying back and forth to Las Vegas almost every weekend, even though he's not performing there anymore. I think he's having trouble letting the showbiz life go. Although he's been so secretive about what he's been doing on his trips, I wouldn't be surprised if he announces at his dinner tomorrow that he really isn't retiring, but is kicking off a new tour. Presto is that kind of guy."

"So you've been working for him for a long time?" Lana asked.

"Twenty-nine years and counting. He hired me before he got famous. I suppose I'm the only woman who's been with him through thick and thin,"

Betty said, while patting her bob of gray hair. "Though if he truly does retire, I don't think there will be much more for me to do. Since he's stopped touring, I've been working part-time on administration for his charities. But with no tours to book or publicity events to organize, there's not much more for me to do," Betty said. Her tone was conversational, but the forlorn expression on her face betrayed her true emotions.

"After this trip is over, I'm going to talk with Presto about my retirement. My sister lives in Florida, and there are always new vacancies coming up in her apartment complex. I've never been a fan of the long winters in the Pacific Northwest."

"Are you married? Or—" Lana clapped a hand over her mouth, shocked by her own poor manners. There was something about Betty that made her feel as if she was chatting with an old friend. She couldn't forget that the woman was a client.

"No. I was on the road with Presto so much that I never had a chance to meet someone special. Presto's life was my life for so long, it's going to be strange not to be with him on a daily basis," Betty said, as she wiped away a tear.

Lana bit her lip to prevent her mouth from dropping open. Was Betty actually infatuated with Presto? Lana knew she shouldn't be shocked if she was; Betty had been at his side for almost three decades and knew the man inside and out. Though they weren't married, it sounded like they had shared as much as any married couple did, except for the physical intimacy. Did Presto know how Betty felt about him? Lana looked towards the magician, wondering whether he had ever considered Betty to be anything more than his assistant.

8

A Killer View

August 12—Day One of the Wanderlust Tour in Edinburgh, Scotland

Terrance led the group up the long ramparts towards the Half Moon Battery, charging ahead as the rest paced themselves to avoid overheating in the hot midday sun. The castle grounds were quite extensive, yet it was definitely worth walking around the entire site. Its snail-shell-like design meant that around every corner was a surprising new viewpoint or architectural element to take in and admire.

As she rubbed at her calves, Lana was pleased to see Presto bouncing around spryly as he gestured towards several buildings in the distance, telling stories about shows he'd performed in each of those monuments over the years. *He is in great condition for a seventy-year-old,* Lana thought.

Despite Dotty's claims that they didn't see each other often, Lana thought the family was getting along quite well. Ursula walked with her arm hooked through her father's, both clearly entranced by the old brickwork and colorful weapons decorating the turrets and walls. Kurt and Viola also walked arm in arm, chatting easily about the artwork and decorations they had seen on their whirlwind tour of the castle. Harry and Terrance seemed the least interested in the tour or monument, preferring to hang back and show each other funny videos on their smartphones. So far, Harry seemed to be the most interested in Terrance, Lana noticed, which made sense considering how close they were in age.

After they reached the top of the tower, Presto pointed to a church located at the base of Castle Rock. "That's Saint Cuthbert's Church. I've performed there four times now, and each show was spectacular. It's an incredible venue and beautifully lit."

"I know that name. The Tiffany Glass Company created a window for it, one depicting David going out to meet Goliath. It's one of only two Tiffany glass windows in the United Kingdom. I can't wait to see it," Viola said.

"I've heard of that church, too," Zach piped up. "Agatha Christie married that archeologist there. Oh, what was his name?"

"Max Edgar Lucien Mallowan," Viola responded.

"That's true, for her second marriage," Presto said, suddenly lost in thought.

"I saw her *Mousetrap* again last week. It is such a divine mystery. Did you know it's the longest-running theater production on the West End? I can only hope that one of my plays will enjoy such success," Zach said dreamily.

"I wouldn't hold my breath," Presto mumbled, loud enough for Zach to hear. His son's shoulders slumped. "Anyway, we are going to visit Saint Cuthbert's Church later this week. It holds a special place in my heart."

"Why is that, Dad?" Ursula asked.

"For many reasons. It was one of the first venues I performed at during the Fringe Festival, for starters. And it is the parish church for this castle and many soldiers are buried in its cemetery. I've spent time there looking over the gravestones and reading the heartbreaking inscriptions. It's quite a unique place, actually." He stared down at the building, adding softly, "But after this week, it will have even more significance in my life."

"What do you mean, Grandpa?" Viola asked.

"It's a surprise, my dear. When we visit it, everything will become clear." Presto started to hook his arm into Viola's when he paused and gently grabbed her wrist. "That is a beautiful watch. Are those diamonds circling the face?"

As he turned her arm in the air, the watch seemed to sparkle in the sunlight.

"They are. My secret admirer loves to surprise me," Viola said, her cheeks flushing.

"He is certainly a keeper if he's giving you such wonderful gifts." Presto turned to his grandson. "Terrance, I want to see Saint Margaret's Chapel now. Can you lead us to it?"

"Sure, Grandpa," Terrance responded, his voice full of confidence as he checked his map, then took the lead.

Presto pulled Viola forward, ahead of the rest. Betty and Harry followed Terrance, while Ursula hung back, blocking the path of Kurt, who was coincidently standing in front of Lana and Zach.

"Why do you think the old man is so emotional about that church?" Ursula asked Kurt.

"That remark about the soldiers' graves was rather morbid," Zach said.

Ursula gasped and placed a hand over her mouth. "You don't think he wants to be buried there, do you?"

Lana took a step back, feeling out of place.

"I don't know. Maybe. He has been making strange decisions lately," Kurt admitted.

"But why would he choose a church in Edinburgh? He hasn't been in Seattle much, I'll give you that, but this whole Scottish roots thing is a joke. He's never been interested in learning about our ancestry before; in fact, he's always hated dredging up the past. Do you think he might be seriously ill, like cancer or ALS?" Ursula asked, then tapped a manicured nail against her chin. "That would explain why we had to join him in Edinburgh this week, more so than simply to be present at that dinner honoring him."

"I don't know what is going on," Kurt admitted. "He did have a physical last month, but he used another medical team. I only found out because the doctor he saw had a few questions about medications I'd prescribed for him in the past. And he's steadfastly refused to share the results of the tests with me."

"It's not like Dad to shut you out. Betty said he's been acting really odd, as well. Since he retired, he's been lying to her about what he does during the day, and he keeps sneaking off for long trips without telling her where he's going. And every time we talk on the phone, he babbles on about different projects he's planning on funding through his charities. It's like the world's problem have become his own. Dad never cared about where his charities' monies went to before; he only set them up for the tax write-off. I wonder what is going on with him," Ursula said, watching her father and Viola, now quite a bit farther up the path. "Say, Kurt, last week I talked to a lawyer about having Dad declared mentally unfit."

"You what!" Kurt pulled her closer as Zach moved in to better hear them. "You won't stand a chance. He's of sound mind and body. I sure hope he doesn't find out. With that temper of his, he'll probably cut you out of his will completely."

"I don't know. My lawyer thinks if his personal physician agrees with Zach and me, we stand a chance at being named the executors of his estate."

Kurt started to protest again, when Zach touched his arm. "We are simply asking you to think about it, that's all. We wouldn't want to have to do anything that might put you in an uncomfortable position, like mentioning your relationship with Viola."

Kurt turned bright red as he shook his head violently from side to side. "We aren't involved. You've got it all wrong…"

Zach leaned in close to his father's doctor. "Doth protest too much, methinks. But don't worry, your secret is safe with us. Right, Ursula?"

"Of course. We're friends, and that's what friends do. Protect each other. Think about it, Kurt," Ursula said as she crooked her finger towards her brother. They walked off, leaving Kurt to consider their proposition in silence.

Lana stayed frozen in place, shocked by the family's conversation. Presto must be worth a fortune if they were plotting against him. Should she say something to him about his children trying to have him declared mentally unfit? No, it was not her place to repeat what she'd overheard. Besides, their chances of success were virtually null, as far as she could tell. For a seventy-year-old, Presto seemed quite spry and nimble. She figured it was his many years on stage that kept him fit. From her experience touring with The Great Ronaldo, she knew how dexterity and limberness were crucial traits, and any injuries that limited your movement meant you weren't able to perform. And as far as his mental capacities went, he seemed as sharp as a tack. Lana couldn't believe any legitimate doctor would declare him incapable of handling his own estate.

But what was Zach implying about Kurt and Viola? They did seem quite close, but then, they were the only two who saw each other on a regular basis. Well, except for Terrance, but neither Kurt nor Viola seemed to have warmed to the recently arrived nephew.

No, whatever Ursula and Zach were planning on doing was certain to backfire. As far as Lana could tell, Presto might just outlive them all.

9

Running Into an Old Friend

August 12—Day One of the Wanderlust Tour in Edinburgh, Scotland

Saint Margaret's Church was indeed worth visiting, as their guide had promised. The ornate arches and stained-glass windows were heavenly. Lana was touched by the fresh flowers on the altar, brought in daily by members of the Saint Margaret's Chapel Guild.

As they exited the church, Lana found herself walking next to Betty again. It was the perfect time to sate her curiosity. "Why is the dinner honoring Presto being held here and not in Seattle?"

"He loves the Fringe Festival. He's performed here every year since 1984. Some of his best friends are artists he met here, which is why this dinner is taking place during Fringe. Most would have been here anyway, to perform."

"That's really sweet of them to honor Presto in this way. It's too bad I missed seeing him perform live. I'll have to check out his acts online."

Betty moved closer and whispered, "You're in luck. Presto is going to perform as the evening's finale. But please don't tell his family yet. It's supposed to be a surprise."

"Oh, that is really exciting! What is he going to be doing?"

"The Rainbow Walk. It's his most famous act. Have you heard of it?"

Lana could feel the blood draining from her face. She knew it intimately, even though she had never seen it performed live. It was the same act her

50

ex-husband claimed that Presto had stolen from him. It took her a moment to find her voice. "Uh, no, I've never seen that one."

"It's spectacular. And this time he has added a twist that I bet will rock his family's world," Betty said as her expression grew dark. Lana looked around in confusion, until she saw that Betty was glaring at Harry and Ursula.

"What do you mean?" Lana whispered conspiratorially.

"I can't ruin his surprise. But trust me, you'll want to watch the family's reaction when he gets up on stage. Especially those two." Betty smiled sweetly at Presto's family just as Lana's telephone alarm went off.

She and Terrance had already agreed that getting them from the castle down to the Royal Mile would be her job. His ability to read a map was sadly lacking, as were most of the skills required to be a guide, Lana thought ruefully.

She noticed the family was gathered close to the railing, looking out over the city's New Town. That Georgian-style neighborhood of lightly colored stone and brick was a strong contrast to Old Town's soot-covered facades.

She approached her group and called out loudly, "Okay, folks, it is time to head to the Royal Mile. It's a short, yet steep, walk down the hill, so you might want to grab hold of a loved one," Lana joked.

Ursula rushed to take her father's arm. "I've got you, Dad."

Presto looked at his daughter as if she was crazy. "Got me? I only retired six months ago. I'm still quite agile."

"It's just, you're getting older, and you never really did explain why you stopped performing so suddenly..." Ursula's voice trailed off.

"Because I was tired of performing the same tricks. I've been in the game for forty years; it's time to do something else with my life," Presto explained, adding, "And I'm going to live at least another twenty years, so don't start spending your inheritance yet."

Lana couldn't help notice that Ursula, Zach, and Viola all reacted strongly to Presto's last remark. Considering the magician had been one of America's top-earning performers for several years running, Lana could imagine there would be a lot of money and properties to be divided up once he did pass on.

"So Lana, are you leading us down to the next stop, or is Terrance? I want to get this show on the road!"

Lana scurried ahead. From the castle it was a downhill walk along Castlehill and Lawnmarket streets to High Street—a pedestrian-only zone popular with street performers during the festival season. The many celebrations and events drew two million visitors and performers to the city each year. The "Royal Mile" was in fact a series of streets that led from the castle to the Holyrood Palace. As they descended along the cobblestoned streets to their destination below, the crowd noise grew substantially louder. A mix of tourists, singers, performance artists, and musicians lined the vast street, all competing for the many tourists' attention.

She navigated through the thick crowds while keeping her eyes on her guests as she went. When they were about two blocks away from the restaurant, Lana turned around so as to better address her group. "Folks, our restaurant is just ahead, on the left-hand side. It shouldn't take us much longer."

"Terrance, can you handle it?" Presto asked.

Lana closed her eyes to avoid him seeing her roll them. Why couldn't Presto give the kid a break?

"Sure, Grandpa, happy to do so." Terrance skipped forward to head up the group. Lana handed him the map and pointed to the restaurant, circled in red, then quietly added, "It's two blocks ahead."

"Got it," he whispered back.

She walked to the back of the group and stood close to Betty. "Terrance wanting to take the lead is a good sign," she said softly.

Betty nodded in response and leaned in to answer when a loud noise made them both jump. A busking bagpiper standing a few feet behind them had begun bellowing out a melancholically song. Betty clutched at her heart, and Lana's was pounding so hard that she could almost feel it bonking against her rib cage.

"Good gravy, that about gave me a heart attack," Betty panted.

Lana nodded in agreement as she yelled back, "I had no idea they were so loud."

The piper's kilt swayed in time with the music. He was dressed in a tall furry hat and had a fur-covered pouch hanging over his crotch. Lana wondered whether he was wearing underwear.

It was fascinating to watch him work the intricate instrument, though Lana wondered what the locals thought of the almost deafening noise. She got her answer when a woman poked her head out of a window two stories above and shook her fist at the piper.

"The police told you to move on!" she raged but the man didn't react.

Lana doubted he could even hear her complaint. She looked to the rest of her guests and saw that Ursula was yelling something to Zach, who was gesturing animatedly at the piper. Curious, Lana moved closer to the pair, in time to hear him finishing a story about a group of bagpipers he once used as a live musical soundtrack in a performance.

"After they finished, they would lift their kilts and flash the audience. That always got a round of applause," he said in a loud voice.

Ursula chuckled along, until Presto called out, "What are we waiting for?"

"The piper, Dad. Unlike Zach, I've never seen one up close, let alone heard one play." She began swaying in time with the drawn-out melody. "Is that *Amazing Grace*?"

Zach listened intently. "By golly, I think you're right!"

He twirled his sister around, then pulled her in close for a slow dance. Harry and Viola clapped along, and after a moment's hesitation, Terrance grabbed Betty and spun her around, too. Presto's assistant beamed with joy.

The magician watched his kin with disinterest. "Pipers are a dime a dozen in Edinburgh, especially during the festival season. Come on, it's time to eat."

Lana watched Presto storm off alone, wondering again why he'd asked his family to join him. Despite his claims to Dotty that this trip was to get to know them again, he was being quite hard on most of them and didn't seem interested in actually talking with them, only in ordering them around.

She knew from experience how difficult it was to be estranged from your family, yet she also knew that it was never too late to reconnect. After ignoring each other for ten years, Lana and her mother had recently found each other again. Though they still butted heads sometimes, Lana was glad they had both made the effort to be a part of each other's lives.

It is the first day of the tour, Lana scolded herself, *perhaps I'm being overly sensitive and too hard on Presto.* Regardless of his intentions, it was apparent that the rest of the family was getting along quite well. It was hard to believe that Zach hadn't seen his sister Ursula or his nephew Harry in five years, or that Terrance had only met them a few days earlier. The wannabe rock star seemed to be bonding with all of them, with the exception of Kurt. Presto's doctor lingered on the periphery most of the time, and usually around Viola. Maybe it was because she was often at Presto's home and thus knew Kurt better than the rest. Though Terrance did live there now, Lana realized. *What happened between the two men to make them avoid each other?* she wondered.

Lost in contemplation, Lana barely registered Presto's angry shouts. When she looked up, her group was far ahead. Through the throngs of tourists, she could see Terrance gesturing apologetically to his grandpa.

Presto grabbed the map out of his grandson's hand and barked at him. Whatever he had said clearly upset Terrance, who reacted by crossing his arms around his torso and glowering at his grandfather.

When Presto stopped to examine the map, Lana noticed a middle-aged man rushing towards him. When the stranger began jabbing a finger into his chest, pushing the magician backwards, she ran forward to help her client.

Yet when she caught sight of the attacker's face, Lana froze in her tracks. "Ron?" she whispered.

Her ex-husband was so intent on attacking his prey, he didn't hear or see her. Ursula screamed as Ron's last shove brought Presto to the ground. Zach grabbed his arms, but the pudgy theater director was not strong enough to restrain her ex-husband.

"Oh, no," Lana moaned as she raced over to her client. Her ex-husband stood over Presto, now crouching on the cobblestone road. "I found the proof, Gary. Not even your fancy lawyer will be able to talk his way out of it this time," Ron raged, emphasizing Presto's real name.

"Let him up!" Harry yelled as he rushed over to his grandfather. He shoved

Ron's shoulder, yelling, "Why don't you pick on someone your own age?"

When Ron turned to him, Harry's fist froze in midair. "Wait, aren't you The Great Ronaldo?"

Ron's expression softened immediately. "Why yes, I am."

Harry held out his hand. "I'm a big fan. Your Cannonball Drop act is mind-blowing. I'm still trying to work out how you do it."

"Pulleys," Presto said from his position on the ground.

"Why, you—" Ron pulled his leg back as if to kick Presto, when Zach tackled him, throwing her ex off-balance. Unfortunately for Zach, Ron was in much better condition and easily recovered his equilibrium before throwing his attacker to the ground. Ursula pulled her father up just as Zach went down.

Harry brushed the dirt off of Presto's pants. "Are you okay, Grandpa?"

"Are you related to this thief?" Ron asked. When Harry nodded in affirmation, his expression turned to disgust.

"Leave us alone or I'll call the police. You have no right to push me around or harass my family," Presto said, sticking his chest out.

"I can do whatever I want; this is a free country. And if you don't settle this out of court, my lawyers will take you to the cleaners," Ron said. Lana had never seen him look so determined.

"Mine will make mincemeat out of you," Presto countered as he surged forward and swung out a fist.

Presto's aim was far off, but it did trigger a younger woman lurking behind them to grab Ron and try to pull him away.

"Let the lawyers deal with it, Ronnie. He's not worth your time."

Lana bristled at the woman's choice of words. "Ronnie?"

When her ex-husband turned to face her, his eyes about popped out of his head. "Lana? What are you doing here?"

She grabbed onto his other arm and pulled him away from her group.

"I'll be right back," Lana called out to Betty, now concerning herself with Presto's well-being.

Harry rushed over. "Do you need help, Lana?"

"No, I've got this. Take care of your family."

The young magician looked to her, then Ron. "Do you know each other?"

"You could say that. I'll explain in a minute. Don't worry, Harry, I can handle him."

Once Presto's grandson was out of earshot, Lana turned to her ex. "What are you doing here? And why are you physically attacking old men?"

"I found my proof, and now he's going to pay. This confrontation was the pre-show; interrupting his dinner is going to be the main act."

Lana shook her head. Of course Ron would have known about this dinner honoring Presto; the world of magic was quite small and gossipy. And for Ron, the attention Presto was receiving for his contribution to the craft would be extremely painful to watch. She could easily imagine that her ex couldn't let it go.

"What do you mean, you found the proof?"

"Remember I told you that I took a picture of myself with my sketches and a newspaper the day I finished it?"

"How could I not, Ron? You told me that story so many times I can recite it from memory. But you tore up the photograph after you saw that he'd performed your act."

"I was so angry, I thought I had destroyed the only photo. But I forgot that I'd put a second copy of it in my copy of Harry Houdini's *Magician Among the Spirits*. We moved a few weeks ago, and the photograph fell out of the book! Can you believe it? Presto can't ignore me any longer. My lawyer is convinced he is going to have to pay me a hefty sum for stealing my trick and profiting off of it for all these years," Ron said before staring defiantly at the target of his anger.

The famous magician was surrounded by his family, who were all staring at Lana. When Ron turned back to her, there was confusion on his face. "What are you doing here?"

"I'm leading Presto and his family on a private tour of Scotland."

Ron looked as if Lana had slapped him. "How could you? After all he did to me?"

"Why should I care about you, Ron? You left me, remember? And Presto is my client, nothing more."

Suddenly Lana remembered the woman standing behind her ex. "Is that the floozy you replaced me with?" She had been confined to bed, recovering from her shoulder injury, when Ron hired her replacement—the same woman who eventually stole his heart—meaning she had never met his new girlfriend. And though mutual friends had told her about Ron's new assistant, they apparently had spared Lana's feelings when describing her. She felt a wave of jealousy wash over her as she realized her replacement was much younger and quite a bit prettier than any of her friends had mentioned.

"That's Candy, yes." Ron's expression softened when he answered.

"Eye candy is more like it," Lana mumbled.

"Excuse me?" He turned to his new girlfriend and held out his arm. She walked tentatively over to him and wrapped her arm through his. Lana's eyes narrowed to slits as Candy's dropped to the ground.

"Ron, leave Presto alone, okay? He's here on vacation, not to perform."

"No, he's here to be honored as a hero of our profession—thanks to a trick he stole from me! There is no way that I am going to leave that miserable jerk alone. Neither you nor Presto has seen the last of me. I guarantee you that," Ron said loudly, attracting the older magician's attention, as well as that of his family surrounding him.

10

Who Is That Awful Man?

August 12—Day One of the Wanderlust Tour in Edinburgh, Scotland

"Who is that awful man?" Ursula asked.

"A nobody, that's who. A magician who never made it and can't accept that he doesn't have what it takes," Presto answered stridently as Ron and Candy stormed off.

He turned to Lana and stared her down. "How do you know that man?"

"He performed his magic show in a theater I used to work at," Lana said. It was not entirely a lie; they had met when she was selling tickets at the theater he performed regularly at. Given the two men's history, Lana doubted Presto would want her to stay on the tour if he knew she was Ron's ex-wife.

What did it matter anyway? Lana told herself. Her relationship with Ron was none of Presto's—or his family's—business. The past was just that—the past. And Ron had clearly moved on.

"I saw The Great Ronaldo in Reno last year. He does a few illusions that are quite well thought out. Didn't he start out as one of your assistants, Grandpa?" Harry asked.

Presto bristled. "He was, until I caught him stealing from my cash box. He might have thought up a few good acts, but he doesn't have the charisma to truly break through," Presto said while gazing into his grandson's eyes, as if he was trying to tell him something.

"Is he performing at your dinner, as well? I didn't see his name on the lineup," Harry asked, seemingly oblivious to the deeper meaning of his grandfather's remark.

"Certainly not! If he tries to enter, I'll make sure security throws him out. Terrance, I'm hungry. Have you learned to read a map yet, or should I ask Lana to take over again?"

"The restaurant is down there," Terrance responded through gritted teeth while pointing to a narrow alleyway leading down the steep hill.

Lana was glad he responded, instead of trying to shift the work or blame onto her again. She needed a moment to let Ron's presence—and the reason for it—sink in. They hadn't seen each other since their divorce was finalized, and it was a shock to run into her ex, especially with his new girlfriend in tow.

Simply seeing Ron conjured up a mixed bag of regret, pain, anger, and longing. Despite the bitterness she felt towards him for leaving her, they'd had nine wonderful years together, and she couldn't make the joyous memories vanish from her mind.

And despite the fact that they were divorced, Presto's cutting down of Ron didn't sit well with her. Her ex had sworn up and down that Presto fired him so he could steal his act. Though the incident had occurred several years before they'd met, Ron had always maintained that he had thought up the Rainbow Walk illusion, not Presto. The array of wires he had devised, along with the pulley system used to make the act work, were his designs and inventions.

Unfortunately, he hadn't thought to copyright them or submit them for a patent before showing it to Presto. All he had done was photograph himself with his sketches and the day's newspaper. And though his overall design was unique, the components used were all readily available and could be assembled by pretty much anyone handy with a screwdriver and welding kit.

Yet, if what her ex-husband always claimed was indeed true, than Presto's signature act was in fact one of Ron's earliest creations. One that should have made The Great Ronaldo a household name, not Presto the Amazing.

Lana looked to Ron, already halfway down the Royal Mile with his head snuggled close to Candy's, and any sympathy she felt for him flew out the window. Ron's concerns were no longer hers; he could sort out his own problems.

11

Sampling Haggis

August 12—Day One of the Wanderlust Tour in Edinburgh, Scotland

The restaurant Dotty recommended was a quaint little café located halfway down one of the steep staircase-alleys running off of the Royal Mile called "closes." Lana wondered whether they were called that because you had to walk close to others when traversing the narrow pathways. The restaurant was quite old and, based on the low ceiling height, was apparently built for persons of a smaller stature. The men in her group all had to bow their heads when entering and watch out for low-hanging lamps when walking to their table at the back.

A friendly waitress brought them all a "wee dram" of the house whisky with their menus, then held a pen to paper as she waited for them to decide. When Lana saw what the house specialty was, she wondered whether Presto had requested they come here or whether Dotty figured he would expect a traditional Scottish meal on their first day.

"Haggis? Are you kidding me? I am not eating that—you know they make it out of pig intestines, right?" Viola stated resolutely, apparently not caring that the waitstaff heard her protests.

"No, they cook it in sheep's intestines. I hope you all will open yourselves up to new experiences during this trip. I always loved sampling new cuisines while on tour, and haggis certainly fits the bill," Presto said.

"I'm game," Terrance said and set down his menu.

"Me, too," Harry added as he watched another waiter deliver two plates of haggis to a neighboring table.

Betty looked over the menu, then up at the waitress. "I'm going to order a side salad. I'm sure the haggis is delicious, but the ingredients don't suit me, either."

"Chicken," Presto scoffed, then turned to Lana. "Are you going to try it?"

"Of course, I wouldn't miss the chance to sample the real deal."

"Good girl! Waitress, we'll take seven servings of your house special, one side salad for the lady at the end, and whatever Viola wants to order."

"I'm going to join Betty with the salad," Viola said, refusing to meet the waitress's eye as she flicked her menu onto the table.

Lana raised her hand, drawing the waitress's attention. "I did have one question—I see the haggis is served with 'neeps and tatties.' What are those?"

"Turnips and potatoes, love," she replied before returning to the kitchen.

"Hey, Grandpa, check this out." Harry pulled a deck of cards out of his pocket and fanned them out on the table. "Pick two cards and hold them in your hand so that I can't see them."

Ursula clapped in delight. "Ooh, I know this one. It's great. I still haven't figured out how Harry does it."

Presto, however, seemed less enthused. He did as his grandson asked and watched as Harry folded the deck back together and held it up to his temple. The younger man closed his eyes in concentration before exclaiming, "The two cards in your hand are the three of diamonds and jack of spades!"

Presto showed his audience the two cards, guessed correctly by his grandson. "That's great, kid. Try loosening up your shoulders and working in a little more hand movement to help engage the audience and keep them guessing."

Harry frowned at his grandfather's words. "Oh, okay, thanks. You do know that I sold out most of my shows last year without your help."

"You sold out a few rooms in community centers, not real theaters. You've got to think big if you want to make it big."

Before Harry or Ursula could respond, three waiters returned with steaming hot plates of the daily special. Lana was grateful for the quick service and hoped that Presto's grumpiness was a result of his hunger.

She looked down at her serving of a ground-beef-like substance and mashed potatoes, wondering whether she had made the right choice or not. When she tentatively tasted the haggis, though, she was surprised by the delicious mix of spices and quickly finished her portion. Slightly embarrassed that she had eaten her lunch so quickly, she looked around at her guests' plates and noticed that most of them were done, as well. Only Viola seemed to be having trouble finishing her meal.

"Is the salad tasty?" Kurt asked.

Viola shrugged her shoulders and pushed out her lower lip, as if she was seeking his attention again. *Isn't Kurt a bit old for her?* Lana wondered. Viola was probably half his age and beautiful, to boot. She could get any man she wanted. Despite Zach's comments earlier, she couldn't believe the two were really dating.

"Presto, do we have time to stop by the Elephant House?" Betty asked.

The magician blew out his cheeks. "I know you're obsessed with Harry Potter, but would you mind visiting it during your free time? I'm not really a fan of kids' books."

"They're incredible tales of good and evil. Your family should read them—they might learn something," Betty mumbled so softly that Lana wondered if she was the only one who'd heard her.

"What did you say?" Presto asked.

"They're for anyone with an active imagination, regardless of age," she grumbled more loudly while stabbing at a tomato.

As soon as Zach finished his meal, he began regaling them all with stories about the theater scene and London's West End. It seemed as if he was on a first-name basis with every famous actor who'd performed in the city's legendary theater district during the past twenty years. He was a born storyteller and made his life in London sound incredibly delightful and exciting. Lana couldn't wait to see some of the sites he mentioned with Alex, after this tour ended.

When Zach was describing a party at Dame Helen Mirren's home, Presto clinked his fork against his glass, calling them to attention.

"Okay, folks. Coming up next is a guided tour of the Holyrood Palace, Queen Elizabeth II's official residence in Scotland, and then dinner at The Kitchin. They've been named the best restaurant in the United Kingdom, so expect a delicious meal. I hope your feet have had time to rest; we've got to get moving again."

He sprung out of his chair and walked over to pay the bill, without asking whether they were ready to leave.

Everyone stood up without protest or question and made their way back outside. Presto was clearly used to telling them what to do, and they seemed content to follow his orders without comment. Lana still found their way of communicating slightly odd, but then again, every family had its own quirks. If it hadn't been for a trip to the Netherlands a few months earlier, she would probably still be estranged from her mother. Who was she to judge Presto and his kin?

12

A Mouse In The House

August 12—Day One of the Wanderlust Tour in Edinburgh, Scotland

After a lovely tour of the Holyrood Palace and an incredible meal of barbecued monkfish tail, Lana helped Terrance find two taxis to take their group back to the rented house.

As soon as they returned, the family gravitated towards the living room, each plopping down onto the many plush armchairs and velvety couches spread around the vast space. Ursula uncorked a bottle of red wine as soon as she'd taken her jacket off and poured herself a full glass. Zach's drink of choice was again whisky.

"What a busy day," Ursula said as she lay out on the chaise lounge, one hand resting on her forehead.

"But a fun one," Viola added. "Thanks, Grandpa."

Presto blushed. "It's my pleasure. I'm glad you enjoyed it—and that you were all able to come over at such short notice."

Lana poured glasses of wine for the rest, including Terrance, who had reverted to family mode and was happily chatting up his cousin Harry and uncle Zach. Considering what Betty had told her about Terrance's past, Lana was glad anyone in the family showed interest in him. *It must have been rough growing up without an extended family, especially since his parents died too young,* she thought.

Betty watched Terrance for a moment, a smile on her face, then stretched her arms over her head and yawned loudly. "I'm all pooped out. I'll see you tomorrow. Good night."

Presto waved to his personal assistant in acknowledgement, but the rest of the family didn't seem to notice her departure.

After Lana finished serving her guests, she poured herself a half-glass of red and sat at the back of the room, content to sip her wine and let her eyelids droop. It had been a busy first day, with a few surprises, and she was glad it was over.

"So, Grandpa, what exactly do you have planned for us this week?" Viola asked.

"Didn't Terrance give you a copy of the itinerary?" Presto glared at his grandson.

"He did, but I lost it. Besides, I want to hear it from you. This is your trip, after all." Viola rested her chin on her folded hands, turning to give her grandfather her full attention.

"We are going to visit several of my favorite places in Edinburgh, as well as a nature reserve, loch, and castle. The country is too big to see in a week, but if you enjoy it, perhaps you can come back and visit."

"I've always wanted to see Loch Ness. We might even get lucky and see the monster!" Ursula exclaimed.

"I do love your imagination, child," Presto tittered.

Ursula's brows knitted together. "I was being serious, Dad. There were eighteen sightings last year alone. And in two of the photos you can see its neck!"

"How exactly are we Scottish, Grandpa?" Harry asked, ignoring his mother.

"My great-grandfather immigrated from a small village in the Highlands to America because he wanted to be a cowboy." Presto leaned back in his chair. "He grew his cattle ranch into one of the largest in eastern Washington. His oldest son, my grandfather, ran it until he retired, then sold it off and used the profits to move our family to Seattle. His son, my father, wasn't interested in our family history, so I didn't know we had Scottish roots until they died and I found a box of pictures and documents that Dad never showed me. I don't know whether Dad simply wasn't interested in rehashing the past, or if he and Granddad had a falling-out and he purposely kept them hidden away in the attic."

"But why this sudden interest in Scotland? Why didn't you tell us about our family history earlier?" Harry pressed.

"I suppose I'm more like my parents than I realized; I wasn't interested in learning more about our past. At least, not until certain recent events got me thinking about our family connection to Scotland."

Ursula and Viola gave each other knowing glances. Lana also wondered whether Presto was telling the truth about being healthy. This desire to rediscover his roots was apparently rather sudden and uncharacteristic, from what she'd heard so far. Yet Presto appeared to be quite agile and surefooted, not seriously ill.

"Even more so, now that I'm a lord," Presto added with a giggle.

"What are you talking about?" Ursula exclaimed.

"I purchased a plot of land in the Highlands, and it came with a title."

"Are you kidding me? So are we all ladies and lords?" Ursula said.

"I don't know if you can also use the title too, but I thought it would be fun to visit the site and see more of the Highlands on the way. There are several castles in the neighborhood."

"Ooh, that sounds wonderful. I can't wait to get a look at those royal art collections. It will be good to see how they present their artwork, as inspiration for our museum," Viola oozed.

"We are going to visit Stirling Castle on the way over; it's the biggest in Scotland," Presto said. Though his tone was jovial, to Lana it seemed as if he had again sidestepped Viola's attempts to get him to talk about his private art museum. Was Presto really as excited about it as Viola was?

"Lana, can you double-check that we have tickets to visit the castle's interior?"

"Of course; I'll call them tonight and confirm our dates and times."

"Why didn't you ask me to take care of it, Grandpa?" Terrance asked.

"Oh, I thought I said Lana and Terrance. You'll have to excuse an old man. The mind does go first, they say," Presto responded and winked at his grandson. He said it with a smile, but his remark seemed to make all of his family members go quiet.

Presto hid a yawn with the back of his hand. "Now if you don't mind, I'm going to head up to bed. We have a busy day tomorrow, and I want to be well rested for it."

"Of course, Daddy." Ursula rose and kissed her father on both cheeks. "I hope you sleep well."

"I will, angel. Don't stay up too late, I have another surprise for you tomorrow and want you all to be chipper and alert." Presto addressed them all, but to Lana, he seemed to be speaking specifically to Zach. When she looked over, Lana noticed that the theater maker was pouring another glass of whisky. She had yet to refresh the others' first glasses of wine.

After the magician departed for his bedroom, Lana rose and cleared her throat. "I'm going to hit the sack, as well. I hope you have a good night."

Ursula and Harry nodded vaguely in her direction, but the rest were more interested in discussing Presto's final statements than Lana's movements.

As she exited, Lana heard Viola ask, "Kurt, are you certain he's in good health? His sudden interest in finding his roots and that comment about losing his mind are so bizarre. Not to mention going to bed so early; Grandpa is always the last one to retire for the night."

"Viola is right; Dad must be sick," Ursula announced. "He's acting too strange for it to be anything else."

Curiosity kept Lana by the open doorway. She felt slightly guilty for listening in on their private conversation, but her inquisitiveness about her guests kept her feet planted.

Kurt leaned forward, twirling his empty wine glass in his hands. Lana pushed back against the wall, hoping he hadn't seen her, when he answered, "I am embarrassed to admit that he has shut me out. I'm not certain what is happening with him right now."

"I still think we should contact a lawyer and see about having him declared mentally unfit so we can gain control of his estate. If we aren't careful, he might end up leaving everything to some Scottish genealogical society,"

Ursula declared.

Kurt shook his head vigorously. "It's a little early to deem him demented or mentally incapacitated. Presto is fully aware of his actions and consequences."

"I don't know; Ursula might have a point," Viola added softly. "And you are his medical doctor. The courts would listen to you."

"I need a drink." Kurt stood up and crossed in front of the doorway on his way to the liquor cabinet.

"Whisky?" Zach asked. Lana could hear a glass being filled, then two clinking together.

"Cheers," Kurt said.

"When I performed in Seattle a few months ago, Presto let me stay at his place for the night," Lana heard Harry say. "I swear I saw a real estate agent's brochure on his desk right after I arrived, but when I looked later, it was gone. Maybe he's planning on selling his house to help pay for hospice care or a retirement home. He didn't say anything to me about it, so he must not want any of us to know what he's thinking about doing."

"He can't sell his house! I want to open a bed-and-breakfast there, after he kicks the bucket," Ursula moaned.

"Why should you get it?" Zach demanded. "That house is worth a fortune, which means it should be sold and the profits divided equally between us siblings."

"Only the legitimate children, you mean? Or do you think the bastards deserve a cut as well?" Ursula asked, clearly baiting her brother.

"But Presto promised me I could turn his house into a private museum after he passed," Viola butted in.

"That's news to me," Ursula huffed. "Dad wouldn't put a grandchild above his daughter. You must have misunderstood his intentions. Or maybe he said that to get you off his back."

"Then why did he promise to give me all of his artwork?"

"You can have all that crap. I never did like his taste in paintings—it's all too modern and abstract for me," Zach said dismissively.

"Good, because you clearly know nothing about art if that is your opinion.

You don't deserve it anyway."

"You better watch yourself, young lady." Ursula's tone was quite threatening. "Terrance, you've been living at Presto's house for the last two months. Have you seen any real estate agents hanging about or heard whispers of a retirement home?"

"No, none. But Presto's not home often. And he tends to do his own thing when he is. We don't talk much."

"What an easy life. And Dad pays for everything, or are you paying him rent?" Ursula asked.

"I'm working on finding a job. It takes time, that's all," Terrance responded defensively.

"Not paying rent is the same as stealing from us, Terrance. It's our inheritance that he's spending to keep that gigantic house up and running. Speaking of which, why is Betty still working for him? He's wasting more of our money by keeping her on. We'll have to do something about her, as well."

Lana's shock at hearing Presto's family speak so callously about their extremely generous father and grandfather made her gasp. As she covered her mouth with her hand, her elbow caught the edge of a large vase, causing it to rock on the small table. The clinking noise must have been audible in the living room because the family went silent.

"Presto? Betty?" Ursula called out.

Maybe it was a mouse?" Kurt said as Lana mentally cursed her clumsiness.

She was beginning to tiptoe away when she heard footsteps approaching—and fast. As quickly as she could, she sprinted to the back staircase, praying she would make it out of sight in time.

13

The Rainbow Walk

August 12—Day One of the Wanderlust Tour in Edinburgh, Scotland

What a day, Lana thought, as she rinsed the toothpaste from her mouth. When she looked up from the sink, the dark bags under her eyes made her cringe. It wasn't a result of the jet lag or long walks; she was still reeling from running into her ex-husband and his new girlfriend.

Candy's youthful face flashed through her mind. It was bad enough that she was significantly younger than Lana, but the fact that Ron's new girlfriend had the same body type and flapper bob that she had sported as Ron's assistant did her head in. It felt as if Ron had traded her in for a younger model, a detail their mutual friends had failed to mention.

As Lana shook these negative thoughts away, they were immediately replaced by a wave of shame. Throughout their marriage, Ron had maintained that Presto had stolen his act, a story he'd told her hundreds of times. Yet deep down, Lana had never believed him. She lay back on her bed and closed her eyes as to better recall Ron's allegations

After studying carpentry, Ron had taken a job as set designer at a local theater, where Presto coincidently performed on a regular basis. Though Ron had always been obsessed with the world of magic and illusion, he hadn't yet worked up the confidence to actually perform on stage. Presto was already a fairly successful magician when they met. The two men hit it off immediately and became fast friends.

When Presto's act grew more popular, he hired Ron as his full-time set designer. Over time, Presto showed Ron how some of his acts worked, which prickled Ron's imagination. Soon after, her ex began experimenting with creating his own magic acts and illusions, ones reliant on technology and mechanics, instead of only sleight of hand.

After hours, he tinkered around in Presto's workshop and worked out several acts that would one day become part of his own magic show. As his list of self-created tricks grew, his dreams of one day performing as The Great Ronaldo also began taking shape.

One night, after a successful rehearsal and a few too many beers, Ron proudly told Presto that he had created a trick that was unlike anything ever seen on stage, an act that would become the finale of his own show. Curious, Presto asked him to perform it, which Ron gladly agreed to do.

Ron would always tell Lana that his proud boast was his biggest regret. He was certain that his life would have turned out much differently if he had just kept his mouth shut. After Ron performed his trick, which he called Walking on Air, Presto viciously shot down his innovative idea, calling it too complex and clunky to impress any audience. Confused and disappointed, Ron took the next day off to process his mentor's painfully blunt rejection and think about what he really wanted to do with his life.

When Ron returned to work, still uncertain whether magic was truly his calling, Presto accused him of stealing five hundred dollars from his cashbox. Ron swore up and down that he hadn't touched the money, but Presto refused to believe him. Their space hadn't been broken into, and Ron was the only other one with a key.

When Presto said he would not call the cops if Ron left quietly, her ex-husband did as asked and disappeared. With his life in tatters, he turned to the bottle. After several days of binge drinking, he finally sobered up enough to remember that he'd left all of his sketches for his magic acts in Presto's workshop. When his old boss finally returned his calls, Presto claimed that his new assistant had cleared out the workshop and thrown away everything Ron had left behind.

Presto tried to calm Ron's howls of rage by telling him that his new assistant had unwittingly done him a favor: "Mechanics and magic don't go together, son. Besides, you don't have enough charisma to become a professional magician, anyway." Those were the last words Presto had uttered to Ron before he hung up.

Heartbroken, Ron set his dreams of performing his own magic show aside and went back to work for his old theater as handyman and set designer. Three months later, he was painting a backdrop when his colleagues excitedly told him about Presto's latest show and the new act he'd performed—an incredible feat no other magician had dared try. The same act that would soon make Presto a star and household name.

Ron went into a state of shock when he realized they were describing the trick he had thought up in Presto's workshop. What Ron had dubbed Walking on Air, Presto had renamed the Rainbow Walk. Ron immediately contacted a lawyer. Yet because he didn't have his original sketches to prove he had created it, he didn't have a leg to stand on in court. Instead, Presto filed an injunction to prevent Ron from ever performing any act that resembled "his" Rainbow Walk.

Had Lana's client stolen Ron's act? As long as both men maintained that their versions of events were the truth, no one would ever know for certain.

Would the Rainbow Walk have made Ron famous—as he was convinced it would? From the few clips of Presto's acts that Lana had seen, the older magician had an almost magnetic personality and charisma that drew his audience and made them emotionally invested in his acts. Ron was a strong performer, but connecting with his public had always been a challenge for him.

Curiosity drove her back online, where she quickly found several clips of Presto's version of the Rainbow Walk on YouTube. She selected the longest one, leaned back onto her bed, and pressed play.

The curtain rose quickly, revealing a shallow, water-filled basin that covered most of the stage. Visible just underneath the water's surface was a bed of long nails that would easily pierce through the performer's organs if things went awry. On each side of the basin were five fire hoses with brass nozzles arched up and pointing towards the middle.

Presto came out on stage to loud applause and turned on all ten hoses, sending multicolored sprays of water arching out. The streams met in the middle, creating a watery rainbow that extended from one edge of the basin to the other. As the audience oohed and aahed at the water's colors and form, Presto explained the act to his audience, claiming that only through intense concentration could he walk over the rainbow to the other side of the basin. He begged his audience to remain silent while he was performing, otherwise he might fall onto the nails placed in the bath.

"A sneeze could mean my death," he stated, somberly gazing out at his captivated audience. No matter what Ron said about him, Presto was a captivating performer who sucked you into his world quite effortlessly.

Before attempting this death-defying trick, he called a male audience member up to check the water for Plexiglas or anything else that Presto could use to aid his walk. After the man agreed that it was nothing but water, Presto then asked him to visually inspect his outfit for wires or a harness that might enable him to perform this unique trick. Presto made a show of removing his jacket so that the audience member could better examine him.

After the audience member proclaimed that he could not see any wires attached to Presto or his clothes, the magician thanked him and encouraged the audience to give the man a round of applause as he returned to his seat. As they did, Presto hung up his jacket on a coat rack placed at the edge of the stage, paused a moment to pull up his pants, then slowly returned to the edge of the basin, his hands under his chin in concentration.

With his public distracted by the audience member returning to his seat, they didn't notice that when Presto hung up his jacket on the coat rack, he removed the wire array hanging off of the same hook. And when he pulled up his pants, he attached that array to a small loop at the back of his belt, which in turn was attached to a harness he was wearing underneath his clothes.

From the camera's angle, Lana couldn't see the pulley system Ron had designed, nor the multitude of thin wires holding Presto up. Her ex told her he had built a small remote control that could be attached to his thumb, allowing Ron to raise and lower himself as the pulley helped move him across the stage. The secret to this act was the array of wires; each individual wire was so thin that it was practically invisible, as long as they didn't cross. And it was thanks to Ron's specially designed array that they never did.

When Presto began his first attempt, someone in the audience gasped loudly enough to break his concentration, making him stumble on the way up and get his pants leg wet. Lana knew not having a trick work the first time was a great way of increasing tension in the audience, and Presto was a master at it. After stepping back from the rainbow and scolding his audience for making noise, he made a show of brushing the water off of his pants before again calling for complete silence as he pressed his fingertips against his temple.

When his eyelids fluttered closed, he suddenly began to rise and slowly float above the water, following the rainbow's arch, before softly landing on the other side. Even though she knew exactly how it worked, Presto was such an engaging performer, Lana was holding her breath the entire time.

As soon as Presto's feet hit the ground, his audience erupted in loud cheers and applause. With his first bow, he released the hook from his harness, then walked freely around the stage. Lana was incredibly impressed by his masterful performance and manipulation of the audience. As good as she'd thought Ron was, he simply didn't have Presto's charisma and ability to connect with the audience.

Would the Rainbow Walk have made Ron as big a success as it had Presto? Unfortunately for her ex-husband, he would never get the chance to find out.

14

Why Am I Here?

August 13—Day Two of the Wanderlust Tour in Edinburgh, Scotland

"Good morning, darling," Alex said as soon as Lana answered. His voice sounded so cheery, which made her miss him even more. "Is this is a good time to say hello?"

It was six thirty in the morning, and Lana had just stepped out of the shower, located down the hallway from her tiny bedroom. "Hello, gorgeous. Your timing is excellent; I don't have to start work for another half hour. Are you in London?"

Lana had tried calling Alex last night, but he hadn't picked up, which was quite unusual for him. As a result, she had tossed and turned, worried her boyfriend was avoiding her because she hadn't committed to living together before leaving Seattle. Only after she realized that Alex was flying over the continental United States when she rang was she able to fall into a deep slumber.

"I am. The taxi just dropped me off at my hotel, and I couldn't wait to call you back. Does that make me one of those needy boyfriends?"

Lana chuckled. "Maybe, but I like it. It makes me feel good to be needed by you."

"Darling, what's wrong? Are you alright?" Alex's voice was laced with concern. "You sound really tired."

"I'm fine physically. The jet leg has hit pretty hard this time, which isn't helping." Lana covered the receiver and sighed deeply. As much as she didn't want to do this over the phone, she knew Alex deserved to know the truth now and not later. "Hon, our tour group ran into my ex-husband yesterday. Actually, to be specific, he and my client, Presto the Amazing, got into a fight on the Royal Mile. Ron said he's in Edinburgh to ruin a dinner being held in Presto's honor, which was rather stupid because now Presto will have his security guards watching out for him."

"I'm coming up to Edinburgh."

Lana rolled her eyes at his macho response. "No, you're working in London this week. There's no reason to lose your job over this."

"Ron better leave you alone."

"He's not interested in me—only Presto."

"How can you be so sure?"

"Because he's traveling with his girlfriend, Candy."

"Oh."

Lana waited for him to continue, but her boyfriend remained silent. Did Alex not know what to say, or had his concern vanished once he realized Ron wasn't in Edinburgh to win her back?

"What about you? What's on your agenda today?" she asked, hoping to change the subject and move past this.

"There's a networking breakfast before the first workshops begin. I'll be leading sessions on team building and interoffice communication today. Which reminds me; I should change clothes before I head downstairs. Can I call you later?"

"How about I call you? That dinner honoring Presto is tonight, and I'm not certain when we're going to be back at the hotel."

"Would you call me right away if Ron bothers your group again?"

Lana pursed her lips, wondering why even the most relaxed men saw their girlfriends as territory that needed to be permanently guarded. "Sure, but I don't think he's going to be a problem. Security will keep Ron out."

"Good. I'm glad to hear your client is being proactive. I love you, Lana, and I sure wish I was there with you, instead of here with all of these computer geeks."

"The feeling is mutual. Take care, darling." Lana made a kissing noise, then hung up and returned to her tiny bedroom to dress.

When Lana entered the dining room, she was shocked to see an extensive breakfast buffet laid out on the long mahogany table. Betty hovered over the cold cuts and cheese slices, adding forks and spoons to the many dishes.

"Dotty really knows how to take care of us," she said when she noticed Lana gaping at her.

"I'm so sorry you had to do this. I thought the café was supposed to deliver breakfast at eight." Lana checked her watch, wondering whether it was set correctly.

"They were, but yesterday I asked them to bring it an hour earlier. We are all early risers and like to eat as soon as we get up."

"Of course, that makes sense." Lana was grateful for Betty's initiative, but also taken aback by the older woman's organizational skills. *Why am I really here?* Lana wondered again, realizing Betty was more than capable of organizing the entire journey. Why had Presto bothered to have Wanderlust Tours set up the trip if he had Betty at his disposal?

"Say, what is on the agenda today?" Presto's assistant asked, as if to make Lana feel useful.

"Tonight is the party, and two taxis will pick us up a few minutes before five," Lana said, as if Betty didn't already know it.

"But I didn't see anything planned for this morning," Betty pressed.

"That's true. I do have a long list of optional excursions with me. We can ask the others if they have a preference, though I'm not certain whether Presto had a last-minute addition, or if it's meant to be a free day. I was planning on asking him that once he comes down to breakfast."

Moments later, footsteps on the staircase alerted them to Terrance and Harry's arrival, shortly followed by the rest of the family, who all shuffled into the dining room and sat down around the table. Most looked groggy and hungover. They must have stayed up late drinking and bonding, she reckoned.

"I sure could use a coffee," Ursula moaned, laying her head down in her hands. Lana was starting towards the carafe when Viola grabbed it and poured her aunt a cup.

"Who else needs a shot of caffeine?" she asked, holding the canister up.

Zach raised his hand. "Black, please."

"Me, too. Please," Terrance quickly added.

"Shouldn't you be pouring coffee for us? You are the official guide on this tour," Viola chortled. Her laugh reminded Lana of a hyena. Though meant as a joke, Viola's remark echoed her thoughts. Normally the guests would have expected her to jump up and serve everyone. But this was family, not a bunch of strangers thrown together by circumstance.

Terrance laughed along with his cousin. "I guess you're right."

He sprung up and grabbed the carafe and cup out of Viola's hands, then turned to Harry. After an exaggerated bow, he asked, "And you, kind sir? Do you prefer your coffee black, or with cream and sugar?"

"Two creamers, my good man." Harry slapped his cousin on the back, playing along.

Presto entered as Terrance was pouring Harry's drink. "Excellent. I'm glad to see you're taking to your job," he said, nodding in approval.

Harry and Terrance stared at each other, then burst out laughing.

"What's so funny?"

"Nothing, Grandpa. Would you like a cup?" Terrance asked.

"Yes, black."

Lana stepped closer to her client and handed him a plate.

"Thanks, Lana." Presto immediately scooped up most of the scrambled eggs and pineapple slices.

Lana opened her mouth to ask about today's plans, when Betty said, "Presto, we noticed that there are no excursions planned for this morning or afternoon."

"That's true. I need to take care of some personal things before the dinner tonight and hoped you could entertain yourselves for a few hours. Lana can arrange a distillery or walking tour, if you don't have any other ideas." He took a sip of coffee, spilling the liquid as the cup trembled in his hand.

"Shoot!" He put the cup down and swatted the coffee off of his shirt and pants. "I guess I'll need to change before I go out."

To Lana, Presto seemed even more keyed up than he had yesterday. It made sense, though; the dinner honoring his lifetime contribution to magic and illusion was in a few hours' time. That would make anyone nervous.

"No problem, Daddy. Last night Terrance noticed the free time, and we decided to have lunch, then go shopping together."

"That's a wonderful idea. Be sure to be back here at three, instead of five. I have another surprise for you before we head out to the dinner. Okay?"

"Ooh, that sounds mysterious!" Viola squealed and clapped her hands together.

"Can you give us a hint?" Ursula asked.

"No, I'm afraid not. You'll have to wait for it," Presto said with a smile.

"Okay, I guess we have no choice." Ursula looked to the others. "So, folks, where should we head to first? I read about this shop called Great Scot that is supposed to sell the cutest souvenirs. You can even buy kilts there."

Lana filled a bowl with yogurt and fruit, then sat at the end of the table next to Betty and listened to the cousins chatting about all the shops they wanted to visit. Did they expect her to arrange for the cab or accompany them today? She felt a little awkward about tagging along, unless they specifically asked for her help. In fact, given Betty's organizational skills, she was feeling increasingly uncomfortable about being here at all. Perhaps she should discreetly ask Presto whether it wasn't better that she left and let them enjoy their family time without a stranger in their midst. After the dinner, of course; Presto was already stressed out enough.

When Lana finished her last bite of breakfast, Terrance turned to her, a smirk on his face. "I almost forgot; you can have the day off, Lana. This is a family-only shopping trip."

The dismissive tone in his voice made clear what he thought of her being here.

"Hey, that's quite rude! Presto hired her to take care of you this week. But that doesn't mean you get to treat her like a servant."

Lana's face flushed as Betty scolded the young man. "It's alright, Betty. I'm happy to have a few free hours," she said diplomatically, resolving to call Dotty and indeed ask about leaving the tour early. She only hoped her boss would still be open to her visiting Alex in London before flying back to Seattle.

Shortly after everyone finished breakfast, they all took off in different directions—Presto on his secret mission, Betty to a Harry Potter-themed walking tour of the city, and the rest to a quaint café their guidebook rated highly.

While she cleaned up the buffet, Lana briefly considered what she could do with her free time. During their walk around the city yesterday, they had seen several amazing street performers and talented musicians in town for the Fringe Festival. Presto had reserved seats for a show taking place later this week, but Lana wouldn't be surprised if it was meant to be a family-only outing. Besides, she hoped Dotty would let her leave the tour early.

Figuring it would be a shame to miss seeing a show, Lana headed back to the Royal Mile to see what struck her fancy. As she walked slowly up the long pedestrian-only stretch, she scanned the many flyers and watched several performers giving free previews out in the open, before buying a ticket to a show starting only minutes later.

Lana had to hotfoot it to a small park luckily located close by. Three circus-like tents completely covered the patch of grass. In the middle tent was the show she had a ticket to. Three up-and-coming comics performed a vaudeville-style act that kept Lana laughing pretty much the entire hour. It was fun to sit in such a small tent, on foldup bleachers, watching the three perform in the center. Lana marveled at how they kept all sides of the audience engaged and amused. When they took their final bow, the applause and cheers made the bleachers shudder. Lana stood with the rest, clapping until her hands hurt and the three comics finally exited the tent. She hoped the acts performing tonight at Presto's dinner would be as entertaining.

15

A Surprise Addition

August 13—Day Two of the Wanderlust Tour in Edinburgh, Scotland

When Lana entered the living room of their rented home at five minutes before three, she was momentarily surprised to see a younger woman with fiery red hair snuggled up in Presto's lap. His family sat around them in a half circle, and based on their expressions, they were all in shock.

Betty stood up unsteadily and gestured towards the stranger. "Lana, this is Gwendolyn. Presto's fiancée." Her voice trembled as much as her legs.

The redhead sprung out of Presto's lap, her curly hair dancing around her face as she bounced over to Lana and stuck out her hand. "Call me Gwen. It's good to meet you, Lana."

Her grip was firm. "You, too, Gwen. Presto mentioned another guest was arriving, but I didn't know it was his fiancée."

"Neither did we," Betty added softly. Lana swore she saw the older woman blink away a tear.

"Lana, please sit. I was just explaining to my family that on the last day of our trip, Gwen and I are going to get married in Saint Cuthbert's Church."

"The one we saw from Edinburgh Castle? That's wonderful. Congratulations! It does look like a beautiful place," Lana said as she settled into an armchair at the back of the room. For the first time since the trip began, Presto was visibly relaxed. *He must have been nervous about introducing his family to his fiancée*, she thought.

"No, you were telling us about the changes you are going to make to your will," Zach said. His voice was shriller than normal, and his forehead was covered with sweat. He took the last swig of his drink, then rose to refill it.

What exactly have I missed so far? Lana wondered.

"Yes, well, as I was saying," Presto continued, after pausing to kiss Gwen once she wormed her way back into his lap, "since retiring, I have finally realized what is most important to me."

"Your family?" Ursula offered.

"Helping others through my charities," Presto answered, ignoring his daughter. "You know, for so many years I have felt guilty about not being around when you kids were young. To compensate, I have given you and your children everything you desire. But now, you are all adults, and it's time for some tough love. That's why I've been so hard on you lately. You're all bright, creative people, and I know whatever you choose to do, you'll make your own way in this world—even without my help."

Ursula gasped as she held a hand to her chest. "Are you cutting us off?"

"No, not exactly," Presto said.

"Either you are or you aren't," Zach pressed.

Presto sucked in his breath and squeezed Gwen's hand. "I have created a special trust fund from which all of you will receive a monthly stipend of one thousand dollars."

"I can't pay my mortgage with that!" Ursula screamed.

"Perhaps you should sell your house and buy one you can actually afford," Presto responded curtly. "Look, the point is, when I asked Lady Gwendolyn to be my wife, I knew it meant moving to Scotland."

"And I have accepted my lord's offer," Gwen said with a smile, bowing her head as she took Presto's hand and kissed it.

"Wait—you're moving here?" Viola asked, her voice stricken. "So this whole Scottish roots thing was a lie?"

"It wasn't a lie. I'm moving to Edinburgh, which is why I became interested in our family's history."

"But why do you have to move to Scotland?" Viola asked.

"Gwen is going to host a new television show called *Scottish Bakers Got Talent*, which is why we are moving here next month."

"Unbelievable," Ursula muttered, then glared at Gwen. "You don't sound Scottish. Why did they pick you?"

"I am Scottish by birth, but I grew up in New York," she explained.

"She was just named one of the UK's most promising up-and-coming comedians. She really is the perfect choice for the show," Presto said, his voice filled with pride.

"How did you two even meet? And when? I don't like this one bit, Dad. How do you know Gwen isn't out to get your money?" Ursula said.

Presto ignored his daughter's snarky remark and kept his tone neutral. "I met Gwen on the Vegas circuit, a few months before I announced my retirement."

"I was the master of ceremony at a charity event Presto attended. He swept me off my feet, and we've been dating ever since," Gwen added.

"Is that why you were going back to Vegas so often? I thought it was to get away from Terrance!" Betty cried. Tears were welling up in her eyes, and Lana's heart went out to her. Lana could imagine how Betty's years of working with Presto could make their relationship feel more like a romance than business.

"You little gold digger!" Zach sniveled.

"Whoa there, son. How dare you talk to my fiancée like that? Besides, Gwen is not after my money. She is wealthy in her own right."

"I'm not here to take your inheritance or be your mother," Gwen soothed. "I hope we can all be friends. I would feel horrible if you didn't want to visit your dad because of me."

Presto patted her hand. "That's right. She doesn't want anything from me. In fact, she insists that any money left in my estate should be split among all of my children."

"So the illegitimates are getting a cut, too?" his daughter asked.

"You can be so nasty, Ursula. I was always too easy on you. I should have cut you off years ago," her father shot back.

"But I thought you were ill," Viola wailed.

"Why did you think that?" Presto's puzzled expression turned grim as he looked to Kurt, his friend and physician. "Because of the medical tests I had last month?"

When Viola nodded in confirmation, Presto laughed. "That's exactly why I used an outside team instead of Kurt. I didn't want you to find out about the tests and assume something was wrong."

Presto's personal physician dropped his eyes to the ground.

"I wanted to be certain that I would live a long life before I asked for Gwen's hand in marriage. I wouldn't want to burden this beauty with a sickly old man. I am thirty years older than her. But I knew if I had Kurt run the tests, I would have to tell him why I wanted them, and I didn't want you all to know about Gwen until after she had said yes."

"I'll love you no matter how old or crotchety you get." Gwen snuggled up against his neck, and Zach and Ursula looked away, clearly disgusted.

"So what did the tests tell you?" Kurt asked.

"I have a mild heart condition that is easily controllable with pills, diet, and exercise. Considering Gwen is a fitness freak, I think we'll be alright."

"Oh yes, I promise to whip you into shape." She smiled and leaned in for a kiss when Zach groaned, ruining the mood.

"That's wonderful, Grandpa. I'm happy for you," Viola enthused. "But if you are moving to Scotland, what are you going to do with your art collection?"

"Some of it will hang in our new home, but I'm going to have to sell several of the better paintings to help fund the restoration."

"The what?" Zach and Ursula looked at each other quizzically.

"We found our dream home, but it's going to need a lot of work to make it livable again," Gwen said.

"But once we're finished, our castle will be fit for a lord and lady," Presto added.

"Do you mean an actual castle?" Zach asked.

Presto laughed. "Yes, I do. Which is why I'm going to sell my home in Seattle to fund the restoration work. Between the profits from that, some of the art, and my savings, we will have enough money to ensure that the castle is perfect in every way, once we get through with it. It's going to cost quite a bit, but it will be worth it—right, Gwen?"

"I told you before, you don't have to sell your home. I have enough to cover it," she said.

"But I want to pull my own weight. And there is no reason for me to hold onto that house. Seattle's never felt like home, and there is no reason for me to stay there," Presto responded.

Terrance folded his arms over his torso and turned away angrily.

"But if you sell the house and art to fund this castle, there won't be anything left for us to inherit!" Zach screeched.

"You can't sell your paintings, Grandpa! What about your dream of opening a private museum?" Viola said. "I've worked so hard to get the artwork in tip-top shape, and you agreed that your home is the perfect place to exhibit it all."

"I agree—the art should be exhibited in a public setting. There are a few top-notch paintings in my collection, but most aren't worth what I paid for them. I talked to several friends working at different museums about your ideas. They all advised me not to create a private museum, but to donate the paintings to an existing one and have the wing or hall named after me. That way, you won't have to worry about the inheritance tax, the art will be on display for all to see, and my name will live on forever. And as much as I appreciate your enthusiasm and ideas, I would rather spend my savings on the castle than the artwork."

"Why don't you leave the art in Seattle for now until you've had more time to think this through? Maybe the Seattle Art Museum could dedicate a wing to you. I mean, you are from Seattle, not Scotland," Viola pleaded.

"That's true, but my roots are Scottish, and I was on the road far more than I was ever home. My being an absentee father attests to that. Besides, you said yourself that it would be best to restore all of the paintings before exhibiting them. And I don't want to waste any more money on it; the museums that buy them off of me can worry about all that."

Viola looked as if she was going to be sick. Presto patted her shoulder. "Don't worry; after I'm gone, you can do whatever you want with any paintings that are left."

"That's not what you promised," she sobbed and tore out of the room.

What a spoiled brat, Lana thought.

"What a drama queen," Ursula mumbled.

Lana arched an eyebrow at the actress.

"Why is she so distraught?" Zach asked.

"To be honest, I may have misled her a little. When Viola came to me with her idea of opening a museum, she was so enthusiastic; I didn't want to hurt her feelings by saying no. So I said that she could use the art as the basis for a museum bearing our family name if she documented all of the paintings and arranged for their restoration. I honestly didn't think she would do all of the work," Presto explained.

"She'll come around, Gary," Gwen said, surprising Lana with her use of the magician's real name. Even his children called him by his stage name.

"What about me? Do you expect me to move to Scotland, too?" Betty demanded.

"I'm sorry to have to say it like this, but I will no longer need your services. I'm going to hire a local to take care of the charities' administration. You can finally retire, Betty," Presto said, a grin on his face until he saw Betty's obvious despair.

"And me, old boy?" Kurt asked, concern evident in his voice.

"I'm afraid it's the same story, my friend. Our new home is fairly close to a large village with a good hospital. Besides, I couldn't ask you to move over to Scotland. Your life is in Seattle."

Kurt shook his head, his eyes downcast. "I have turned down hundreds of clients so I could be your on-call physician," he said, his normally jovial voice bitter. "Without you, I have no livelihood."

Presto turned to his wife-to-be. "I'm so sorry, Gwen, I didn't realize how selfish my friends and family were."

He glared at his physician, then the rest of his family. "Yes, me getting married and moving to Scotland will mean major changes for all of us. But why can't you accept that I deserve to be happy? I'm not stupid; I noticed how disappointed you were when you found out that I'm not seriously ill. It seems like you are all waiting for me to die so you can inherit."

"That's not true, Dad," Ursula said, albeit half-heartedly.

"Isn't it? All you've talked about since we got here is your big house, many servants, and extravagant parties. Yet you can't afford to pay for any of it without my help. When I was growing up, I didn't have two dimes to rub together. I had to make my own way in the world. But you lot seem to expect everything to be handed to you on a golden platter. None of you have done anything significant with your lives!" Presto roared.

"Honey, everyone is in shock. It's a lot for them to take in," Gwen soothed.

"I should have cut them off years ago, instead of being an open checkbook."

"Why don't we give them all a moment to digest our upcoming marriage and move before you say anything you will regret," Gwen said.

"That's a great idea. We have a lot of catching up to do." Presto picked up his wife-to-be and carried her up the staircase to their bedroom.

"Oh, great," Ursula huffed, "Presto's staying in the room next to mine and the walls are paper-thin. This week keeps getting better and better."

16

A Shot of Courage

August 13—Day Two of the Wanderlust Tour in Edinburgh, Scotland

After taking a short break from Presto's family, Lana wasn't certain what the mood would be. When she walked down to the living room at ten minutes before five, only Terrance and Harry were present, both decked out in formal suits with tails and waistcoats. Lana hoped her off-the-shoulder dress would be appropriate for this event.

"Have you seen Betty?" she asked. Both men shook their heads and continued playing their video game.

Lana walked up to Betty's room on the first floor, concerned she might not come to the dinner. Presto's news was clearly a shocker—and not in a good way. When Betty opened her door, her cheeks were puffy and her eyes red and swollen.

"I don't think I should come to the dinner. Presto doesn't need me anymore, and I'm not family. You can deal with getting them to the show on time."

"You have been with Presto for almost his entire career. If anyone deserves to be by his side tonight, it is you."

"Tell that to Gwen," Betty moaned.

"Come on, Betty, don't let this move or his engagement get you down. You knew that after he retired, he wouldn't need a full-time personal assistant anymore. If anything, try to enjoy the rest of the week with Presto. It sounds like you won't be seeing much of him after he moves to Scotland. And you've been together so long; I bet he will feel bad if you don't attend his dinner."

"Ha! He probably wouldn't even notice that I wasn't there."

"You can't mean that. You were part of his life and success. If you don't go, you'll regret it for the rest of your life," Lana counseled.

Betty sucked in a lungful of air and blew it quickly out. "You are right; I deserve to be at his table. Give me a few minutes to fix my makeup, will you?"

When she rose to wash her face, Lana crossed to the door. "No problem, I'll see you downstairs in a few minutes."

When she began walking down the main staircase, raised voices in the hallway below slowed her pace. She stopped and leaned forward, trying to hear who was fighting and what it was about.

"Are you serious, son? After how rude you were to Gwen, you expect me to help you?" Presto asked.

"I bet she lied about being well-off. Did you have her sign a prenuptial agreement?"

"You are the money-grubber, son, not Gwen. I know she's rich because she already bought the castle and I'm selling my house and art to pay her back for half of it," Presto retorted.

"How could you put this stranger ahead of your family? Without your help, I won't be able to secure a theater slot, Dad. I hope this wedding won't make you reconsider helping me out financially."

Lana shook her head at Zach's change of tactic. Presto was right—all of his kin seemed to be most concerned about how he could help them financially, and not his happiness.

Presto laughed bitterly. "The wedding has definitely not changed my mind. Even before I met Gwen, I was not planning on bailing out your terrible plays any longer. It's been ten years since one of your art-house creations made a profit. Maybe it's time for you to cut your losses and try a new line of work."

"How can you say that? You of all people know how long it can take for an artist to break through. You worked the circuit for years before you shot to stardom," Zach cried before stomping down the stairs.

Lana waited until both men's footsteps were no longer audible before descending further. *Terrible plays? Zach seemed so successful and confident about his productions and talent,* she thought. After dinner, she would have to look up his production company and see what kinds of reviews his plays received.

Eager to learn more about Presto's future wife, she'd already investigated Gwen during their downtime and discovered that the comic had toured extensively around America. A year ago, she'd landed a deal to play at one of the biggest casinos in Las Vegas five times a week. *That's right around the time that she would have met Presto,* Lana realized.

The comic's decision to leave the Strip for Scotland seemed odd to Lana, until she read that Gwen was rumored to be earning fifty thousand dollars per episode of the upcoming *Scottish Bakers Got Talent.* Given the success of similar baking programs, Lana wasn't entirely surprised. And the bits of Gwen's comedy show that she had found online were side-splittingly funny. Presto was right; her star was rising—and fast. Lana wouldn't be surprised if Gwen was soon wealthier than her magician fiancé.

When Lana entered the living room again, all of Presto's family was present. The men looked dashing in their formal suits with tails, and the women gorgeous in their ballroom-ready gowns. Lana ran her hand along her own satin dress, glad Dotty had warned her to bring fancy clothing for this dinner. Luckily Ursula and Viola were also wearing off-the-shoulder numbers, putting her at ease.

"Great, Lana is here. When is the taxi arriving?" Presto asked the moment she stepped inside.

"Any minute, sir."

"Excellent. We're all ready to go." Presto took his wife-to-be's arm and squeezed it tight.

Gwen smiled up at her fiancé, the joy on her face evident. She looked smashing in her robin's-egg-blue dress. When Presto began steering her towards the door, Lana called out, "Betty will be right down."

Presto stopped in his tracks. "Oh, right, Betty. We should wait for her."

"Are you going to announce your successor at dinner, Grandpa?" Harry asked.

Presto turned to face him. "Yes, I am."

"Finally! It's about time you made it official," Ursula said. "It will certainly help us sell out Harry's next tour faster."

Ursula's comment seemed to set Presto on edge. He released Gwen's arm and walked over to the bar. "I guess I'm getting nervous. I could use a shot of courage before my friends roast me."

Zach dashed over to the liquor cabinet. "Let me pour you one."

"Oh, thanks," Presto said, clearly taken aback by his son's offer.

"Anything for you, Dad," Zach said sweetly as he turned away from him and poured a shot of whisky.

"You know this won't change my mind about your play, right?" Presto added in a stern voice.

"Can't a son pour a drink for his father?"

Presto nodded and turned to his fiancée. "Would you like a whisky, Gwen?"

"That's okay. I'm going to wait until we are at the dinner."

"Maybe I should, too," Presto said and began walking back to his fiancée.

"Here you go." Zach had trotted after his father with two glasses, one that he pushed into the older man's hand and another that he held up. "Cheers."

Presto clinked glasses with his son as a mini-bus pulled up into the driveway. He lowered the glass without drinking from it. "Our ride is here. I guess it's showtime!"

"Cheers to you and your act, Dad," Zach shoved his whisky into Presto's face, forcing the older man to raise his own glass again.

"Cheers," Presto said, then downed his beverage. "Phew, that has a strong bite."

"It's a local blend that I picked up at a distillery yesterday. It's quite good, isn't it?" Zach said and grabbed his dad's glass.

"Well, we better get going," Presto said as he locked arms with his fiancée and strode towards the front door.

17

The Guest of Honor

August 13—Day Two of the Wanderlust Tour in Edinburgh, Scotland

As soon as Presto entered the theater, he was greeted by thunderous applause. The man of the hour preened and pranced, heartily greeting everyone he passed. Lana's group was led to a round table at the front of the hall with a makeshift throne for Presto to sit in.

Placed before each chair was a formal invitation to the party and list of guests who would be performing tonight, in Presto's honor. Lana was shocked to see several well-known comics and illusionists were on it. As she quickly skimmed the list, she noticed that Presto was listed as the finale and that he would be making a special announcement before performing his famous Rainbow Walk with his successor—whose name was listed as "To Be Announced." *That must be the surprise Betty mentioned*, she thought. She could imagine that Harry and Ursula were incredibly nervous about that moment and what it would mean for Harry's career.

After they'd all settled into their seats and received a first round of drinks from a clumsy waiter, the lights dimmed, and the master of ceremonies took to the stage. Lana recognized the portly, older man as a famous British comedian. After officially welcoming Presto and his family, he began roasting the magician while the hall full of his friends and colleagues egged the comic on. Lana didn't know Presto well enough to get all of the jokes, but she was crying tears of laughter before the MC left the stage. As she wiped her face dry, Lana could only think of how lucky she was to be here on such a special night.

After the comic wrapped up his jokes and shared several personal stories about Presto with the sizable crowd, several of the magician's good friends stopped by the table to shake his hand and ask about his surprise announcement. It seemed as if no one believed Presto was really retiring from the spotlight.

"You've got a television deal, haven't you? I bet we'll see you on the telly hosting a *Magicians Got Talent* program soon enough. Give me a call when you do; I can be one of the judges."

"That's a great idea," Presto joked, even after the fifth time a friend made the same comment. He was enjoying the attention so much that he seemed to be glowing. She could imagine he missed being onstage. Yet if he really was going to stop performing, his life was about to change dramatically. She and The Great Ronaldo had never played for large audiences like Presto had, but she knew from experience how much of an adrenaline kick performing could be, as well as how addictive it was. After she and Ron split up, that sensation was what she missed most about their life together.

As more friends stopped by, all bearing drinks as gifts, one question seemed to be asked the most frequently: "Why retire now, Presto? You're at the top of your game."

Lana wondered why, as well. From what she'd read online, Presto had earned several million dollars on each of his last three world tours. And there were plenty of internet forums that speculated his announcement was a ploy to push his next tour's profits up even higher. Was he really going to walk away from all that money? Or was it a marketing tactic? Lana assumed they would all find out tonight.

Whenever his friends asked him this, Presto gave them the same cryptic smile, saying, "You'll have to wait until my announcement at the end of the evening."

"Ah ha! I knew it! You're going to announce your comeback tonight, you old dog. You owe me fifty pounds," one friend screamed to another.

"I wouldn't cash that bet just yet," Presto yelled in response, getting laughs out of his friends.

After the master of ceremonies announced the first act, a juggler on a unicycle, he came over to their table and gave Presto a hug.

"It's good to see you, mate," he yelled over the rambunctious crowd. "I still don't believe you're retiring, but I am glad to see you've chosen a successor. And I love the idea of the handover; what a great touch. I can't wait to see your protégé in action. His reputation on the West End is quite solid. It will be intriguing to see if he can perform your signature acts as well as you do."

"Harry is pretty incredible," Ursula oozed as she wormed her way into the conversation.

"Mom, I have never played on the West End," Harry said quietly.

"Harry? I thought it was Raphael! I knew the handover was going to be exciting, but I didn't know it was family. I could have worked this into my act! I'm going to have my personal assistant's head for this," the MC raged.

"No, you heard correctly." Presto said it so quietly Lana could barely hear him over the crowd. "Raphael is taking over my act and stage name. My grandson is Harry the Magnificent. He's got talent, but he's just starting out and needs more time to work on his routines before he's ready for the bigger stages."

Harry and Ursula's mouths dropped open as the MC consulted the program. "Of course, you're one of the warmup acts. Oh, you go on after the juggler. Does that give you enough time to get ready?"

Harry gulped audibly and nodded yes.

The MC slapped his shoulder. "It's okay to be nervous, kid. It happens to the best of us."

Harry glared at the British comic. "I'm not nervous."

Lana studied his face. Harry didn't seem nervous—more like livid. Having his grandfather degrade his talents in front of his friend must have hurt.

"Sure, okay. See you backstage. Great to see you, Presto."

After the MC took his leave, Ursula turned on her father. "How can you treat your own grandson so callously? You led Harry to believe that he would be the next Presto."

"No, you convinced Harry that he would inherit my act simply because we are family, but you never actually asked me. He's too young and inexperienced to do my show justice. He needs to ripen his act first. That's nothing to be ashamed of. I worked the local circuit for twelve years before I started to break through. That's how you learn, by getting out there and trying new material until you have enough great acts to make a show out of."

"But Grandpa—"

"Harry, you're as stiff as a board, and you cackle at your own jokes. I swear, sometimes it's like watching a ventriloquist's dummy perform," Presto snapped, his voice already slurred. They had been here for less than an hour, yet the magician had five drinks in front of him, all but the first brought by friends stopping by to say hello. Only his water glass seemed to be left untouched.

Harry flushed at his grandfather's remarks. His mother laid her hand on his arm, calming him down.

"We'll see what our lawyer has to say about this," Ursula huffed. "Harry is your grandson, not Raphael."

"Exactly, which means he is your son and responsibility—not mine. And besides, I have already signed a contract with Raphael. He's going to pay me ten percent of his net profits every time he performs as Presto. That's going to be my pension."

The magician turned to his grandson and tried to pat his shoulder, but Harry pulled away. "You're just not ready to be Presto, and I'm tired of waiting to retire. It's my name and my act—I want to pass them on to a successor worthy of them both. My protégé is a true showman, which is what my acts demand. Sorry, kid, but you don't have it. At least, not yet."

"How can you share your secrets with a stranger? Your charisma and showmanship isn't what keeps them coming back, Presto, it's the acts. No living magician has figured out how you do them—that's why people pay so much to come see you! You know what, I think you're crazy. My lawyer said I could file some paperwork to have you declared incompetent. Marrying a younger woman, handing your livelihood to an outsider, and buying a castle in Scotland are all signs of dementia," Ursula said in a loud and dramatic voice.

Lana was so embarrassed for Presto. What a selfish outburst and during a dinner in his honor, no less! Worried he was going to explode in anger, Lana looked over at her guest, assuming the worst.

Yet Presto wasn't about to burst a blood vessel; he looked more amused than offended. "You know what, Ursula, you need to get a life and let me lead mine in peace. When's the last time you went out on a date?"

Ursula lunged over the table, her hands already reaching towards her father's throat. "How dare you!"

Harry pulled his mother back and held her tight, whispering to her until she calmed down.

Presto stood up, using the table to steady himself. "You should be grateful that I'm giving Harry a slot during tonight's show. There are a lot of important people here. If he's lucky, he'll find a backer for his next tour here."

"I thought you were going to back his tour!" Ursula moaned.

"Does nothing get through that thick head of yours? You are all cut off. You'll get a monthly stipend, but nothing more," Presto yelled, his face turning crimson.

Gwen pulled him in for a kiss before wiping the sweat off of his forehead. "Maybe you should lay off the booze for a while. You're getting rather worked up."

"You're right. I can't let them get to me anymore." He patted his fiancée's arm, apparently oblivious to Ursula and Harry's glares. "I guess I could use a good laugh. I can't wait to see you perform later, my dear."

"Why don't we take a walk around the room and see if you missed catching up with anyone?" Gwen suggested as she pulled her fiancé away from his kin.

"Wait, what did the MC mean by the handover, Grandpa?" Harry asked.

"During the finale, I am going to officially hand over my secrets to Raphael, making clear to the world that he is the only one who knows exactly how I perform my tricks," the magician said while pointing to a small lime-green briefcase resting in the center of the table.

"Are the secrets to your acts in that briefcase?"

"Yes, they are. And tonight, after my protégé accepts it in front of all of my friends, I will be able to retire knowing my show will continue on."

To Lana, Presto's reasoning made sense. Yet Ursula clearly did not agree. She was so mad, Lana was afraid she might strike her father. Instead she threw her napkin at him, and charged off, presumably to the bar.

"Why didn't you tell me that you'd struck a deal with Raphael, instead of letting us believe you were going to name me your successor?" Harry asked.

"Because I didn't want to have to deal with your mother whining about why I didn't choose you," Presto said as his head began to nod forward.

Lana was shocked to see how hard the alcohol was hitting him. Then again, when she noticed how many half-drunken glasses stood before his seat, she was more surprised that he was still conscious.

Harry's eyes bored into him. "You are a selfish and cruel man. I wish you were dead!"

Presto stood up straighter, almost falling over when Gwen released his arm. "Who do you think you are, saying that to me?"

The young magician ran towards the backstage entrance, ignoring his grandfather's question.

"What a bunch of ingrates," Presto huffed before plopping back down into his chair. Gwen tried to pull him up again, but he no longer seemed interested in taking a walk.

"What was that all about?" Viola asked as she set a gin and tonic down in front of her grandfather. "Here you go. I had to fight through the crowds to reach the bar. Your friends do love to drink."

"That is true." Presto laughed and held up his gin. "You're too good to me, Viola."

Gwen pulled on his arm, attempting to get him to stand up again. "Hey, I thought you were going to hold off on the booze."

"Don't be such a killjoy. It's my party."

Presto raised his glass and Viola followed suit, clicking her drink against his in midair.

When the lights dimmed minutes later, the MC introduced Harry as Presto's grandson, instead of as Harry the Magnificent. Ursula looked like she could strangle the man.

When the curtain rose, Harry performed several classic card tricks before taking a bow. He was talented enough that Lana couldn't guess how he managed to move the cards around the deck, but the tricks were simply not awe-inspiring. The fact that Harry mumbled and stumbled his way through the few jokes he had included made the performance slightly embarrassing. Lana understood Presto's decision not to hand over his famous show to his grandson; the young man definitely needed more time to improve his performance.

When Harry took his final bow, the resulting applause was light and polite. At least until the spotlight followed him back to the table his family was gathered around and Presto hugged the boy tight. "That's my grandson," he yelled into a handheld microphone, revitalizing the cheers and clapping.

Ursula sprung up and moved into the spotlight with Harry and waved to everyone, as well. "And his mother, Ursula," Presto added.

"A Hollywood actress," Ursula said, but Presto didn't repeat it into his microphone.

Presto's friends are incredibly kind was all Lana could think when they rose to give Harry a standing ovation. *It is only too bad Ursula tried to usurp her son's limelight.*

When Harry asked to sit next to his grandfather, Lana was happy to oblige. Everyone at their table had been chair-hopping since the night began. She had started off sandwiched in between Betty and Kurt. But as more friends stopped by and Presto's kin stood to chat with familiar faces, Lana found herself circling the table in order to better accommodate her guests. Unfortunately, in the frivolity, Lana kept losing track of her drink before she could finish it, and judging from the number of half-filled glasses on their table, others were having the same issue.

Their waiter came by again with his carafe of water and loitered behind the guests, as if he was unsure which glasses needed to be filled. When he leaned forward to refill Presto's, the magician laid a hand over his glass.

"That's okay, mate. I think I'm fully hydrated. However, if you can scrounge up a bottle of whisky, I won't say no."

When the waiter ducked his face away and turned to leave without acknowledging him, the magician yelled, "You're welcome! Geez, good help is hard to find these days."

"What a strange fellow," Gwen said.

Lana thought so, too. The waiters at the other tables were clearing glasses and bringing around bread baskets, but all theirs seemed to do was hover around Presto.

"He doesn't seem to understand that I'm the star of this show," the magician laughed.

Gwen frowned at the many cups and glasses filling their table, most left behind by friends who'd stopped by to chat. "Nor does he seem to know much about waiting tables. If he doesn't clear some of these glasses soon, we won't have any room for dinner."

Harry stared at the waiter's retreating figure as he sipped a cocktail. "That guy sure looks a lot like The Great Ronaldo. Funny, I don't recall him having a beard."

Presto sniggered. "Waiting tables is probably a better fit for Ron's talents."

Lana's ears perked up at Harry's comment. There was something familiar about their waiter's posture and gait. Was it her ex-husband? Lana watched the man with interest, when suddenly he looked back to their table and she could see his face. It was Ron!

"What is he doing here?" Lana mumbled to herself as she rose.

"What is there, dear?" Betty asked.

"Oh, it's nothing. I thought I saw a friend from Seattle walk by, but that is impossible, isn't it? Maybe I've had too much to drink, as well."

"You never know. Presto invited friends and colleagues from all over the world, including many from the Pacific Northwest."

"That's true. I'm going to take a look and see if it is him. Does anyone need anything from the bar?" Lana called out, but everyone was deep in conversation.

"Oh gosh, don't worry about serving anyone tonight, Lana. Thanks to all of Presto's friends, we want for nothing. Besides, they should be serving dinner soon, right after Gwen's act. We could all use a little something to eat, I think."

"Sounds good. I'll be right back."

"Take your time." Betty sipped her drink, one of several brought over by Presto's well-meaning friends.

As she rose, the MC's voice filled the room. Thanks to the free-flowing alcohol, the crowd was quite rambunctious, and it took him several tries before he could be heard over the public. "Next up is a special treat for all you magic lovers. Raphael will be performing his famous Pants on Fire trick for us. Boys, make sure you've got your fire extinguishers ready!"

The boisterous crowd went silent as the curtain rose and Raphael's booming voice filled the room. He was quite charismatic and soon had the crowd under his spell. After performing several mind-blowing illusions that left Lana stumped, he asked for silence as he prepared for his final act of the evening. After his assistant tied his hand to a rod hanging high above the stage, he closed his eyes and began breathing quite deeply. Moments later his pants burst into flames. As screams rose from the audience, he yelled for silence, then seemed to extinguish the flames using only his mind.

After the illusionist bowed for a fifth time, the MC's voice blared over the speakers. "Wasn't that incredible? Or should I say amazing?" He pointed to Presto and winked. "Raphael will be back later to perform with our guest of honor, Presto the Amazing, during the night's grand finale!"

Once the lights came back up, Lana continued stalking her ex-husband, wanting to confront him only after he had reached the other side of the room. The last thing she wanted was for her someone in her tour group to find out that she was his ex-wife.

Once they were out of Presto's sight, Lana quickened her step and called out, "Ron? What are you doing here?"

He stopped and waited for her to catch up. "I wondered if you had noticed me. I see you're still helping my nemesis."

"Are you a superhero now? Presto is not your nemesis, nor is he your archenemy. He's just someone who's had more success than you."

"Thanks for that positive message," Ron said and turned away.

Lana grabbed his arm. "How did you get inside the party?"

"No one ever looks at the waiter, do they?"

"Are you still planning on interrupting Presto's act?"

Ron stuck out his chin in defiance. "Yes, that is exactly why I am here."

"He's given the security guards photos of you. And even with that ridiculous fake beard, I recognized you. If you don't leave him alone, he is going to have you arrested. This is his night; he's not going to let you ruin it."

"Ruin *his* night?" Ron raged. "He's ruined my life. You, of all people, should know that. If I hadn't shown him my trick, it would be The Great Ronaldo that the public adored, not Presto. The man is a liar and a swindler, and I'm going to make certain the world knows it."

"But you did show him your act, and you have no one to blame for that decision but yourself!" Lana shouted back. She knew it was harsh, but she was sick of Ron wallowing in self-pity. Why couldn't he let this go and move on with his life?

"If you're smart, you'll leave him alone and let your lawyers deal with it." Lana stormed off without waiting for Ron to reply. Her ex was tenacious, and she knew he wouldn't let his feud with Presto go, not without a fight. She only hoped it didn't end with him spending the night in jail.

The noise of the crowd drowned out Ron's response. Lana didn't bother turning around to try to catch any of it. Instead, she worked her way through the throngs of chit-chatting celebrities, hoping to recover her drink from their table. She sure could use it right now. While Lana examined the unclaimed beverages, trying to recall which glass was hers, she noticed Viola standing close to Presto, who was chatting with several friends.

"Where did that waiter go?" Viola asked Lana.

"There is one over there." She pointed to a young woman serving the neighboring table.

"I meant the other one who's been serving us the whole time. Well, serving Presto anyway," Viola said.

Lana chewed on her lip, hoping Viola hadn't seen her and Ron talking.

"He's on the other side of the room," Betty said helpfully, pointing straight at Ron.

Viola smiled down at Betty. "Thanks."

Lana watched as she headed toward her ex, praying Viola wasn't about to ask about her. Before Viola reached Ron, the MC's booming voice once again filled the hall.

"Ladies and gentlemen, I hope you are ready to laugh! We have a very special treat for you tonight. The lovely Gwendolyn Campbell, Presto's fiancée and an incredibly talented comedian, is going to perform for you! Let's give this lass a special hometown welcome, shall we?"

The applause was deafening. When the crowd settled down, the curtain rose again, and Gwen stepped forward. She was such a relaxed and friendly person, Lana had trouble remembering she was also an international superstar. As soon as Gwen opened her mouth, she had the crowd under her spell. Tears of laughter streamed down Lana's face, as well as the faces of pretty much everyone in the hall. When she looked to Presto, the magician was laughing so hard he was doubled over.

After Gwen finished and took a bow, Lana's ears rang from the overwhelming response. Presto stood tall, whistling and cheering his fiancée on. As the crowd sat back down and Gwen descended from the stage, another commotion drew the public's attention back up onto it.

"Get your hands off of me!" a man screamed as the curtain moved violently.

Moments later Ron burst onto the stage and tried to run off of it, but a security guard tackled him, forcing him to the ground.

"What is going on here?" Presto yelled as Gwen rushed over to their table.

The MC ran out onto the stage. "He was tampering with your Rainbow Walk props, Presto."

"It's not his act, it's mine!" Ron screamed from his position on the ground. "I'm the one who thought up the Rainbow Walk, not Presto." A security guard pressed his knee further into Ron's back, silencing Lana's ex.

"Says you. Why can't you think up your own act and leave me be? I swear these copycats are the most obnoxious kind of fan a performer can have," Presto said dismissively.

Several of his famous friends cheered and yelled out their support. Lana wanted to slap her ex upside the head. How could Ron be so stupid as to tamper with Presto's act? If Presto or his protégé fell onto that bed of nails, it would be equivalent to murder. Lana couldn't believe her ex would be so cruel or heartless, or that his rage would push him so far.

"You haven't heard the last from me!" Ron screeched as security escorted him towards the door.

"Get this vermin out of here! I refuse to let this talentless copycat ruin my night," Presto said. When the spotlight lit Presto up, Lana noticed how flushed his face looked and that he was sweating profusely.

Gwen must have noticed, too, because she pulled Presto down into his throne and dabbed at his forehead with a napkin. "Hey, take it easy. You're covered in sweat."

"I'm just so sick of that stupid man. Why can't he accept that the Rainbow Walk is mine?" Presto said. He was getting more flushed by the second. Suddenly, Presto grabbed his head and leaned forward.

"I feel so dizzy. It must have been that last whisky. Everyone's been so generous, I haven't drunk this much in years," Presto said, his words slurred so badly Lana had trouble understanding him.

"Think of your heart. Don't let that nobody stress you out."

Presto tugged at his collar. "I think I need some fresh air." When he stood up and stumbled backwards, Gwen grabbed his arm to steady him. The rest of his family froze, as if unsure as to what they should do.

Concerned for his health, Lana grabbed his other arm. "Is he alright? Should I call a doctor? Where's Kurt, anyway?"

As if sensing something was amiss, Kurt weaved his way through the crowd to his friend and patient. "What's going on?"

"I don't know. I feel a little lightheaded."

Kurt's response was drowned out by the MC's announcement about the next act. But there was so much commotion that Lana couldn't hear who was up next. She picked up a clean napkin and turned towards Presto when a deep booming noise startled her so badly that she dropped it.

Lana whipped around to see ten pipers marching across the podium.

She stood still a moment, recovering from the shock as she watched them streaming down the stairs and into the audience, when someone behind her screamed. Lana turned to Gwen, the source of the noise, and followed the redhead's eyes down to Presto, now lying facedown on the table.

"What happened?" Zach yelled.

"When the bagpipers started playing, he clutched at his heart, then fell over," Gwen wept.

"Someone call an ambulance! This man is having a heart attack! Is there an AED here?" Kurt screamed as he gently lay Presto out on the floor. One of the waiters raced over with a portable defibrillator. Kurt used it expertly and repeatedly, but he was unable to revive his friend.

He released the paddles and shook his head, averting his gaze as he announced, "Presto is gone."

Ursula pushed Kurt aside and threw herself onto her father as sobs wrenched her body.

"What happened to Presto?" someone yelled out from the crowd as his friends gathered close.

Viola cried out, "The pipers scared him to death!"

Lana looked to the musicians, now huddled together on the podium. Death by bagpipes? Was that even possible?

18

Death by Bagpipes?

August 13—Day Two of the Wanderlust Tour in Edinburgh, Scotland

Gwen's howls of despair rang through the room. When Kurt stepped back from Presto's body, his friends surged forward, as if they had to see his corpse for themselves in order to accept that he was gone. The whole evening was so surreal that Lana was having trouble believing he was really dead, as well.

Kurt, Harry, and Zach gently lifted Presto onto the podium. Lana watched as all present crowded the stage, most sobbing as they tried to touch their friend one last time.

Only Raphael, Presto's protégé and successor, sat alone at a table, his head in his hands. Lana wondered what this meant for his future. Without knowing the secrets to Presto's signature acts, he would not be able to perform them. Lana's gaze rested on the center of their table, at the lime-green suitcase. Whoever ended up owning that would be a millionaire.

She looked to Ursula, who was now at the front of the podium, holding her dead father's hand to her forehead as she wailed in sorrow. Harry stood further behind the crowd, his head hung low. When his mother's wails increased in intensity, he returned to the table and grabbed the closest drink and downed its contents in one gulp. When he set the glass down, he noticed Lana watching him.

"I'm sorry for your loss," she said.

"If you are really sorry, perhaps you would be so kind as to get a bottle of whisky from the bar. You know what—make it three. We're all going to need a drink in a minute." He sat down heavily in a chair and stared at his granddad.

"Sure, no problem." Lana walked over to the bar to fulfill his order. Everyone dealt with grief in different ways, and apparently this family chose alcohol as their means of comfort. When she reached the front of the line, the theater doors burst open, and a team of police officers and ambulance personnel entered.

As a medical team checked Presto's body and conferred with Kurt about what had happened, the uniformed officers began ushering the rest back to their tables.

When Lana returned with three bottles of Edinburgh's finest whisky, a police officer was sitting with Presto's family around their table. The empty throne looked so forlorn without Presto in it. Lana set the bottles down in front of Harry and took a seat next to Betty.

Viola and Kurt sat next to each other. He held her close as she sobbed onto his shoulders. Ursula's tears were now dry, and she'd somehow found the time to touch up her makeup. Betty wept softly into her handkerchief, while Harry sat with his head in his hands, turned away from the rest. Lana suspected he was crying, as well. Terrance seemed completely out of place, hovering on the periphery as if he was avoiding being questioned. Gwen was by far the most emotional, and sobs continued to rack her body. A cloth now lay over Presto's corpse. Lana couldn't look at it without shivering.

When she returned to the table, the policeman stood and introduced himself as a detective before asking, "And you are?"

"Lana Hansen, their tour guide. This is our second day of a weeklong trip that Presto arranged and paid for."

"Where did those bagpipes come from?" Ursula butted in to ask. "I didn't see them listed on the program."

"I hired them as a surprise. Because he was moving to Scotland to be with me, I figured bagpipers were a fitting way to celebrate his decision." Gwen's confession brought on another round of sobs. "If I had known the pipers would scare him to death, I never would have booked them."

"Says you. I bet you hired them hoping they would kill Grandpa," Viola pushed.

"It's not exactly a smart murder weapon, is it?" the detective responded. "How could she have been certain that the bagpipes would scare him to death?"

"She was the only one who knew he had a heart problem," Viola countered.

"I didn't know his heart was so weak," Gwen sniffled. "He said his pills and exercise would keep it under control."

"It is even possible for a loud noise to kill a person?" Lana wondered aloud.

Kurt responded immediately. "A sudden noise can shock a person, which sends a jolt of epinephrine into the bloodstream. A healthy person responds normally to it and recovers quickly. However, in someone suffering from severe heart disease, the body's ability to respond to epinephrine is drastically reduced. The jolt can cause the heart to fail to beat effectively or stop altogether. Which means the person would not suffer an actual heart attack due to blockage or oxygen deprivation, but the effect is the same. And Presto had quite a few drinks in quick succession, which would also have affected his heart's ability to function normally."

"So Gwen's surprise killed my father?" Ursula eyed the comedian warily.

"Technically, yes. At least, that's what appears to be the case," Kurt responded.

"Can we sue her for wrongful death?" Ursula asked.

The policeman stared at Ursula. "Whoa, lassie, let's all take a step back, shall we? Presto's heart condition may have played a role in his demise, but until our medical team has had a chance to examine him further and see how advanced his heart disease was, I cannot tell you anything more," he responded diplomatically.

It was an unusual situation, to say the least. Both Presto and his fiancée were wealthy celebrities who were in the process of moving to this officer's jurisdiction. Lana could imagine he didn't want to implicate anyone in Presto's death until he had all of the facts.

"Maybe she poisoned him first," Viola suggested. "To further weaken his heart."

"Why would I kill the man I love?" Gwen cried.

"For money?" Terrance offered.

"Then waiting until after the wedding would have been smarter, don't you think?" the officer reasoned.

"Maybe that crazy waiter put something in his drink. He only seemed interested in topping up Grandpa's water glass and couldn't bother to fill mine once. He was hanging around the table all night but clearly wasn't interested in cleaning up," Viola said as she gestured towards the table, still full of glasses. "And then he tried to sabotage Grandpa's final act. The security guards took him into custody a few minutes before the bagpipes started to play."

"You mean The Great Ronaldo?" Harry asked.

"Isn't that the magician who threatened Dad when we were on the Royal Mile?" Zach asked.

Lana ducked her head automatically, almost afraid someone might figure out they were once husband and wife. She turned her head so as to keep an eye on Ron without seeming to be interested. Police were questioning him on the other side of the hall, yet his protests of innocence were audible to all. When an officer pulled something out of Ron's jacket pocket, he began to scream, "That's not mine!"

She couldn't hear the officer's response, but she did see him pull out handcuffs. Ron head-butted the policeman and tried to make a break for it, when another officer tackled him to the ground.

"See, he must be guilty. He's resisting arrest," Ursula said in an emotionless voice.

Lana was afraid to speak, worried her voice would crack.

"He was caught messing with Presto's props backstage. If he had cut even one of the wires, Presto or his protégé would have fallen to their deaths," Gwen stated matter-of-factly as she watched the officers take Ron away.

"I can't believe Ron would have gone so far as to kill him," Lana said. The words tumbled out before she realized she was saying them aloud.

Ursula turned on her. "How do you know The Great Ronaldo?"

"He performed at a theater I used to work at in Seattle," Lana stammered. "It was several years ago, but he never seemed like a killer to me." She hadn't lied to her group, but she hadn't told the whole truth, either.

"If he did put something in Presto's drink, maybe Ron was hoping it would make him sick, so he couldn't perform his act?" she rushed to add, not wanting to make Ron look suspicious.

Another policeman approached the detective seated at their table and held out a ziplock bag containing a small, transparent vial. Through the plastic, Lana could see a handful of pills were inside of the bottle.

The policemen whispered to each other, then the lead officer turned to Kurt. "You were his medical doctor; do you recognize these pills?"

Kurt held the vial up to the light and squinted through the plastic. "They appear to be digoxin. It's a heart medication."

"Do you know if Presto had a large supply with him?"

Kurt shook his head and looked down to the table. "I don't know about his condition."

"What? You were his personal physician." The detective seemed quite confused.

"Not anymore. I'm here on this trip as a friend, not his doctor."

"Interesting, thank you." The officer rose, as if to leave.

"Wait, where did you find those pills?" Ursula asked.

"In that waiter's jacket pocket."

"If someone added those pills to Presto's drinks, it would account for his dizziness and the flushing of his face," Kurt said. "If they put enough in, Presto would not have survived the meal—bagpipes or not. The sudden noise would have just sped up the process."

Lana felt the blood draining from her face. How was that possible? Ron seemed convinced he was going to win the lawsuit—why would he kill Presto instead?

19

Murderous Intentions

August 13—Day Two of the Wanderlust Tour in Edinburgh, Scotland

Silence descended over the hall when the coroner placed Presto's corpse into a body bag and zipped it closed. When he was wheeled away, the joy and laughter filling the hall earlier was replaced by tears and cries as Presto's friends said goodbye to their friend, mentor, and inspiration.

After the police finished questioning them, Gwen rode with Presto to the morgue. Hearing her ask whether she could hold his hand on the way just about broke Lana's heart. She wished she could do something to alleviate Gwen's pain, yet knew there was nothing she could do or say to make it better.

After getting the rest of the group back to the rented house, Lana excused herself and took a long walk through the neighborhood. During her aimless wanderings, she barely noticed the imposing architecture, the laughing festival-goers filling the streets, or the dark night sky slowly lighting up with a plethora of stars. All she could think about was Ron and Presto.

Could Ron really be a cold-blooded murderer? Lana wondered. *Why was he hanging around our table all night? Did he know about the suitcase and was he trying to find a moment to steal it? Or was he so mad that he decided to give Presto an extra dose of his own medicine, regardless of the implications or possible results?*

Lana shook her head, doubting herself. *How would Ron have gotten Presto's bottle of pills, anyway? And why would he poison Presto? Tampering with the magic act would have been a surer way to kill the magician.* None of this made sense.

It was after midnight by the time Lana returned to their rented home. Uncertain whether her group was awake, she took off her shoes on the porch and opened the door as quietly as she could. The living room lights spilled into the hallway. Someone was either awake or had drunk themselves into a stupor. With this family, either was possible. She was tiptoeing past the door when she heard furtive voices speaking softly on the other side. Curiosity made her stop and listen.

"It's not inside, Mom. Where else could Granddad have kept it? He said he was going to give it to Raphael at the end of the night. Or did he steal it before we could grab the case?"

It was Ursula and Harry, and from the sounds of it, Harry was quite upset.

"I wouldn't put it past Raphael. He did usurp your right to become Presto. I simply cannot believe Dad chose a stranger as his successor, instead of family," Ursula said. "Was there even going to be a handover, or was it one of his stupid pranks? All that work, for nothing. We have to—"

Lana leaned in to hear better when she felt a strange vibration in her pocket. Seconds later, her phone began to ring. She fumbled to answer it, dropping a shoe in the process.

As she picked it up and answered her phone, Ursula threw open the door. "What you are doing?"

"I just got home. My phone rang and I dropped a shoe. Sorry to disturb you," Lana replied, then put her phone to her mouth. "Give me a minute," she said to the caller, whose number she didn't recognize.

Ursula eyed her warily, as if she was trying to discern whether Lana was lying, then nodded and closed the door.

Lana breathed a sigh of relief and rushed down to her room. When she was safely inside, she put her phone back up to her ear. "Sorry about that. This is Lana Hansen."

"Ronnie didn't do this!" a woman's voice cried. She was difficult to understand through all her sniffling.

Ronnie? Lana felt a deep-seated rush of anger rise to the surface. Ron had hated being called by any nickname when they were married. "Is this Candy?"

"Yes," the woman said.

"How dare you call me? Ron and I are divorced—he's your problem now."

"Please, Lana, I'm begging you to help us. Ron didn't kill Presto."

Lana stared at the line. Was her replacement actually asking her to help clear her ex-husband's name? She didn't think this night could get any more surreal. "How did you get my phone number?"

"Ron gave it to me when we first started touring. If we ever got into trouble during the tour, I was supposed to call you."

Lana crumpled onto the bed.

"Ron's already hired a lawyer and is suing Presto for intellectual property theft and damages. He's going to win that lawsuit, which means he had no reason to kill him. I swear Ron wanted to humiliate Presto, not murder him!"

"Then why did he crash Presto's party instead of letting his lawyer deal with it?"

"Ron figured Presto would try to settle out of court so he could hush this whole mess up. But humiliating him was worth more to Ron than any financial compensation. When Presto announced his retirement, Ron was crushed, thinking he'd missed his chance to get him back. And then he found out about this dinner and decided that this was the perfect opportunity to expose Presto as a liar and thief."

"If he didn't want to harm Presto, then why was he tampering with his props?"

"He was going to remove the wire array from the pulley system so he could go up on stage and show the audience his invention, along with a copy of the sketches he had made. He was certain this would convince the magicians in the audience that he was the designer and not Presto. But it never happened, so the police probably won't believe him."

"I don't know if I believe you either. Maybe Ron saw his chance to off

Presto and took it."

"There is no way Ron would do that to me or his unborn child."

Lana couldn't believe her ears. Candy was pregnant? "Does Ron want it?" she whispered.

"Of course he does. It was his idea to try now, before he got to be too old to be a father."

Lana burst into tears as Candy's words cut her soul to shreds. She had also wanted to start a family soon after they married, but Ron wanted to get his act off the ground first. He was convinced that with enough dedication to his craft, he would be tapped for a permanent show in Reno. However, nine years and twelve tours later, they were still crisscrossing the country to survive. Lana's baby wishes were always pushed to the background.

After all those years of telling her to wait, that he wasn't ready to be a father, he'd told Candy to hurry up. Lana had never felt so betrayed or rejected in all of her life.

"You're with Presto's family day and night. Ron didn't do this, so it must have been one of them. Who else wanted Presto dead? You have to find out. That's the only way I can clear Ron's name."

"Don't you ever call me again!" Lana shouted into the line before hanging up.

20

Dotty Asks a Favor

August 13—Day Two of the Wanderlust Tour in Edinburgh, Scotland

It took Lana quite a while to get her emotions in check. How could Ron do that to her? She'd sacrificed so much to help him succeed. And he'd replaced her not only with a younger model, but also one with whom he did want to start a family. Only after she'd settled down enough to speak clearly did Lana call Dotty. It was imperative for her boss to understand her request.

As soon as the older lady picked up the phone, Lana blurted, "I need to leave the tour."

"What's going on? Are you okay?"

"No, I'm not," Lana cried before relaying the horrible events of the night, starting with Presto's death and ending with Ron's arrest. By the time she'd finished, Dotty was also in tears.

"He was such a good man," she wailed. "I didn't know he was ill."

"Apparently no one did, well except for his fiancée."

"His what? I didn't know he was getting married again. That poor woman. I hope she's holding up."

"She is pretty upset right now. Though honestly I haven't seen her since the police took Presto's body away."

Dotty's wails poured through the line.

When they subsided, Lana said, "To make things even stranger, Ron's new girlfriend just called me and begged me to help her free Ron. And she's pregnant, Dotty, and it was Ron's idea! I just can't take it. I need to leave."

"Hon, I know you're hurting and confused, but I really need you to stay on a little longer," Dotty pleaded.

"I doubt anyone will want to finish the tour."

"We may need your help getting everyone home," her boss said calmly.

"Betty, Presto's personal assistant, is extremely well organized," Lana insisted. "I'm certain she can rearrange their flights, if they can't do it themselves."

"Presto paid a pretty penny to ensure he and his family were well cared for, and I'm not going to renege on my promise to him," Dotty sniffled.

"I don't know…"

"Please at least ask them if they want to stay or go. Then we can decide what to do, okay?"

"Alright," Lana agreed, albeit reluctantly. "I'll talk to them first thing in the morning. We could all use a good night's sleep to process tonight's events, I think."

21

Condo For One

August 14—Day Three of the Wanderlust Tour in Edinburgh, Scotland

A restless night's sleep left Lana feeling drained. As soon as the clock struck seven, she crept up to Betty's room and knocked softly on her door.

"Who is it?" Presto's assistant called out.

"It's Lana, the tour guide," she whispered.

"Come in—it's open," Betty said.

When Lana opened the door, Betty was sitting in an old rocking chair, weeping softly into a cloth handkerchief. Her bed was made, and her suitcase was open. It looked as if she had already packed up most of her belongings.

Lana put a comforting arm around the older woman's shoulder. "It is such a horrible shock, losing a loved one and especially watching him die."

"You are the only one who seems to understand that. No one else has even bothered to check on me. Presto's family never really did consider me one of them; they see me more as Presto's check distribution center." Betty blew her nose loudly, then laid her head on Lana's shoulder. "I don't know how to go on."

"What about your sister in Florida?" Lana felt a little awkward having a virtual stranger crying on her shoulder, but she figured Betty needed this emotional release.

"I don't want to go to Florida!" she wailed. "I only said that to make Presto

117

jealous. I thought if he thought that I was leaving him for good, he would finally realize that we were meant to be together. But he didn't think of me as a potential romantic partner, not in the slightest. He had been flying to Vegas to see Gwen all that time."

"So you really didn't know about their relationship?"

"No! Trust me, if I had, I would have quit the moment he told me. He was no picnic to be around after he retired."

That must be why he kept Gwen a secret, Lana thought. He probably knew Betty was in love with him and used it to his advantage. "I'm so sorry."

"Don't you feel sorry for me." Betty sucked up her tears. "I have suffered far worse humiliations and survived. This is not the first time Presto unexpectedly came home with a new wife, and it probably wouldn't have been the last."

Lana felt her brow furrowing. "What do you mean? They seemed so happy."

Betty wiped her cheeks dry. "Frankly, I doubt his marriage to Gwen would have lasted long. Presto thrived on attention and being the life of the party. He would have gotten bored living in a big castle in the middle of nowhere. And she would have gotten sick of his eccentricities, unrealistic expectations, and, eventually, his age."

"Why did Presto retire this year? Because of his heart?" Lana asked.

"Lord, no, that man was as fit as a fiddle. He said his heart wasn't in it anymore and he wanted to retire at his peak. I don't blame him. Performing pretty much the same act for the last twenty years would get tiresome for anyone, at some point. And he was rich enough that he didn't have to work."

"That's a nice position to be in." Lana thought of her own savings account and how she would need to lead a lot more tours before she could even consider retirement.

"So why did you come by? To check in on me or is there something else?"

"To check on you, but also to let you know that I would prefer to fly back to Seattle. Before I do, I want to ask everyone if they want to stay or go home."

"You can't leave. Presto is dead, so my work here is done. I have no desire to take care of his spoiled family. You were hired in to do just that."

Wow, that's pretty harsh, Lana thought. "Is that why Presto hired a stranger to be here? It's been pretty uncomfortable being around them; I feel like I'm intruding on a family reunion."

"He hadn't seen most of them in a year or longer and didn't know what to expect. He figured they would all be looking for a handout, so his backup plan was to send them out on daytrips with you, if they got too intense. But they were better behaved than Presto expected."

"Aha. That makes so much more sense now. But Terrance is here; he can take over."

"No way! To be honest, Terrance is pretty useless. That boy can't tie his own shoe without me hovering over him, and I'm done mothering him. Presto knew it, too, but he didn't want him to turn into a do-nothing who expected handouts, like Ursula and Zach. That's why he was pushing Terrance to do something with his life."

"I thought Zach and Ursula were successful!" Lana exclaimed.

Betty laughed manically. "They do know how to spin a good tale, don't they? I have got to get away from this family, especially if Gwen plans on hanging around. I really do need you to stay and take care of them, as you were hired to do."

As much as Lana wanted to bail, she couldn't shove her duties onto Betty's shoulders. The poor woman had dealt with enough over the years. She was clearly still reeling from Presto's death as much as the existence of his latest fiancée.

"You're right; Presto did pay for everything in advance. Of course I'll stay. I'll go talk to the rest and see what they want to do."

"Great. Now I'm going to finish packing up. Could you change my flight back? I would like to leave as soon as possible."

"Of course. Let me talk to the others and see if anyone else wants to go home right away. Then I'll arrange a new flight for you."

"Thank you, Lana." Betty wrapped her up in a bear hug. "Good luck with that lot. You're going to need it."

22

The Lawyer Calls

August 14—Day Three of the Wanderlust Tour in Edinburgh, Scotland

Lana poked her head into the dining room and noticed their breakfast buffet had already been delivered but not yet unpacked. She spread out the many dishes, then set the table before she entered the living room.

Presto's family were already present. Only Betty, Kurt, and Gwen were still in their rooms.

"Breakfast is ready, in case anyone is hungry," Lana announced.

"I can't stand the thought of food right now," Viola said.

"Me, either. Poor Daddy. I can't get that image of him facedown on the table out of my mind," Ursula said.

"I was wondering what you all want to do—stay on and complete the tour, or fly home?" Lana felt awkward for asking so directly, but didn't know how else to broach the subject.

"That's rather morbid. Granddad hasn't even been dead for twenty-four hours!" Viola cried.

"It's her job to ask, Viola. Why don't you give her a break?" Terrance growled.

Lana was shocked that he had come to her defense.

"If we want to leave, she can change our tickets for us." Terrance turned to Lana. "I would like to fly back to Seattle. Today, if possible."

"And where do you think you're going to live? In Presto's house?" Ursula demanded.

Terrance shrugged. "I guess. I mean, he was letting me stay with him."

"Until you found a job," Ursula said, wagging a finger at Terrance. "I'm on to you. Don't get too comfortable. I'm certain he's left his house to me, which means you'll be moving out as soon as I have the deed in my hand. Unless you want to work at my bed-and-breakfast."

"How can you be so sure you're going to get it? Grandpa agreed with me that his house would make a perfect museum, once he passed. I bet he left it to me, along with his art collection."

"And Presto promised the house and his memorabilia to me so I could open a magic-themed hotel in it," Ursula stated resolutely, as if it was a fact.

Why would Presto promise his home to both his daughter and granddaughter? Lana wondered. Especially if it was worth a fortune, as Zach claimed.

Before Viola could retort, Zach's phone rang. "What did you say?" he yelled into the receiver as he shoved a finger into his free ear.

"Oh, hello. Yes, Ursula, Harry, Viola, Terrance, and I are here. Let me put you on speaker."

"Thanks, Zach. I'm sorry for your loss," Presto's lawyer said after introducing himself. "I don't want to appear callous by calling you so soon, but I understand you are all still in Edinburgh. Is this correct?"

"We are," Zach confirmed.

"Excellent. Because you are spread out around the world, it would be easier for me to fly over and read Presto's last will and testament to you all before you leave Scotland."

"Are we required to be present at the reading?" Viola asked.

"No, you are not," came the faint response via the loudspeaker. "However, Presto left most of you plots of land in the Highlands. Since you are already there, you may wish to see it before you leave Scotland. Presto had already added a visit to the property onto your itinerary, I believe at the end of your trip. The land meant quite a bit to him."

"Did you say Dad left each of us property?" Zach asked, his face flushed from excitement.

"Yes, I did."

"We will be here," Zach and Ursula said simultaneously.

"Could you also let his doctor, personal assistant, and fiancée know that I'll be flying over? They are also mentioned in the will."

"How did you know about Gwen?" Zach demanded.

"Because Presto changed his will to include her, a week before he flew to Scotland."

"And she swore she wasn't mentioned in it! Some nerve. I knew she was a gold digger," Zach mumbled.

"Until the official reading, I cannot confirm who benefits from Presto's will, only let you know who is mentioned in it. The tour was supposed to last another five days, so I assume everyone can stay at least two more. I can book a flight that will put me in Edinburgh tomorrow morning."

"We'll make certain the others know you're flying over," Zach answered for the group.

"Excellent. Until then, you have my deepest sympathies."

"Sure, right, thank you," Zach said before hanging up. He turned to Ursula and clapped his hands wildly. "I can't believe Dad left us all property!" He danced around the room. "Thank you, Presto papa!"

"Do you think I'm included in his will, as well?" Terrance asked, daring for the first time to speak up.

"I don't know. You did only reappear a few months ago," Viola said without looking at him. From her tone, it was clear that she did not expect him to inherit anything.

"But that lawyer said Presto recently changed it," Terrance pressed.

"I wonder if Presto left me any of his magic acts," Harry mused aloud.

"If the man had any sense, he would have. I simply cannot believe Dad chose a stranger as his successor, instead of family."

Ursula's remark about strangers made Lana think of Gwen. How would she be holding up this morning? Lana rose and walked out of the room without a word. No one seemed to notice her departure.

She could hear the sound of soft weeping before she reached Presto's room. Lana was slightly surprised that Gwen had chosen to sleep here last night, considering how badly Presto's family had treated her yesterday.

After Lana knocked on the door, Gwen answered; her face was puffy, and the tears were still streaming down her cheeks. Lana pulled her in for a spontaneous hug. The comic squeezed her tight.

"Are you doing alright?" Lana asked.

"No, I'm far from alright. This is not how I expected this week to go. Please, come in."

When Lana entered, she was surprised to see Presto's clothes strewn everywhere, as if he was in the middle of getting dressed. Lana wondered whether she should offer to clean them up or whether having reminders of Presto spread around was a comfort for Gwen.

"I'm sorry to disturb you. I thought you should know that Presto's lawyer just called. He is flying over tomorrow to read Presto's will and hoped you could stay until he gets here."

Gwen's lip began to tremble.

Poor woman, widowed a week before her wedding day, Lana thought. "Is there anyone I can call for you, Gwen?"

"No, but thank you. You're the first person in this house to offer me their condolences. Presto's kids don't like me."

"They don't know you. This is a pretty horrible way to meet your future family."

"They are going to hate me even more after Presto's will is read." Gwen brushed a tear from her eye. "Let me wash my face."

Gwen stood up, and Lana bit her tongue. As much as she wanted to ask her why the family would be upset, she knew it was not her place. Besides, she would hear the contents of Presto's last will and testament herself soon enough.

23

Sneakers or Flats?

August 14—Day Three of the Wanderlust Tour in Edinburgh, Scotland

"Terrance, when is the taxi arriving for Arthur's Seat?" Viola asked.

The young man didn't look up from his phone. "I dunno."

"Shouldn't you?" she pushed.

"You know, dear boy, you remind me of a guide I once had in South Africa. The poor fellow couldn't find the exit to the safari park, and we rode around for hours before another guide led us to safety," Zach said.

"Thanks for your support, uncle." Terrance spat the words out yet didn't put his phone down.

"It's a good thing Dad sent over a real guide to take care of us. Lana, what time does the taxi arrive?"

"In ten minutes."

After the lawyer's call, Presto's family had decided unanimously to stay on and finish the tour their father, grandfather, and friend had planned—at least until the will had been read. A hike up the hills outside of the city center, with a picnic at the top, was on this morning's agenda. Lana was hoping that Terrance would help her carry the food and beverages, as a lead guide should do, but she doubted he would offer.

"Shoot, I didn't bring any hiking boots. I wish Granddad had told us to bring outdoor wear," Viola grumbled.

"It's a park in the middle of Edinburgh; it can't be too difficult a hike," Zach said, waving his hand in exasperation.

Viola held up two shoes for Lana to examine. One was a tennis shoe and the other a dressy flat. "What do you think? Which ones should I wear?"

"I think the sneakers will be better. It is a steep hike up to the top, but the phenomenal views should make it worthwhile," Lana said with confidence. The guidebook Dotty provided specifically mentioned that hiking boots or a sturdy pair of sneakers were highly recommended. Considering she had never been to Edinburgh before, Lana had to rely on her books for information.

Viola frowned at the sneaker. "Alright. They aren't fashionable, but I have little choice."

Betty came downstairs with a suitcase in hand. "Okay, I'm off to check in to my hotel, then have lunch at the Elephant House Café. Lana, can you call me after my flight has been rebooked?"

"Where do you think you're going?" Zach demanded.

"Away from all of you."

Zach's features and tone softened. "Betty, just because Dad is dead does not mean you are no longer needed."

"You mean to pick up your garbage, call you a cab, or buy your booze? I am not your servant, Zach. Gwen and Lana are here; they can deal with your crap from now on."

From her chair positioned well away from Presto's family, Gwen began violently shaking her head. "I don't think so. I meant what I said—I'm nobody's mother. You're all adults and can take care of yourselves. Presto agreed with me on that."

"Well then, if you need anything, Lana is at your disposal until Tuesday. After that, you're all on your own. Good luck!"

A horn beeped outside.

"That's my taxi. Lana, you have my number. Let me know when my ticket has been rebooked, will you?" Betty walked out and let the door fall shut with a loud bang.

"Geez, I knew she was holding a candle for Presto, but I didn't expect her to drop us all so quickly. He's not even in the ground yet," Ursula exclaimed.

Harry walked into the room, a half-eaten apple in his hand. "When are we leaving for that hike?"

"The taxi should be here any minute," Viola responded.

Harry plopped down on the couch next to his cousin and scanned the room. "Where's Betty?"

"She left us," Ursula responded.

"That's too bad. She had taken a couple of my shirts in for dry-cleaning yesterday. I wonder which shop she took them to. How rude of her not to let me know. I suppose I have no choice but to call her."

Poor Betty, Lana thought, *no wonder she wanted to get out of here.*

24

Hiking up to Arthur's Seat

August 14—Day Three of the Wanderlust Tour in Edinburgh, Scotland

Lana stared out at the vast city center as a strong wind whipped through her hair. It was a short yet strenuous hike up to Arthur's Seat, but the incredibly dramatic panoramic views of the city and surrounding countryside were indeed worth the walk.

Arthur's Seat, the highest viewpoint in Holyrood Park, was a grass-covered hill and remnant of an extinct volcano that erupted 350 million years earlier. Some claimed it was the location of King Arthur's Camelot, but Lana could find no definitive proof in her books or online.

On her right was the Firth of Forth, a large body of water that connected to the North Sea. To her left, all of Edinburgh was spread out before her. Standing on the edge of this hillside, she felt so small and insignificant. It was breathtaking to be so high up and surrounded by green, yet in the middle of one of the world's largest metropolises.

She took a step closer to the edge, letting her eyes get lost in the landscape. The distant sea was as tumultuous as her emotions. Had Ron killed Presto? And if so, why had he done it now? His unborn child and hopes of finally humiliating Presto in court were strong reasons not to.

More importantly, Lana knew Ron was a pretty smart guy. If he had put pills in Presto's drink, he would have known that he wouldn't be able to get out of the theater after the magician keeled over. So why had he risked tampering with Presto's gear if he had already poisoned him—instead of fleeing the scene while he still could?

When Zach and Ursula crested the summit, Lana snapped open a large picnic bag-like backpack. After leading them up from Holyrood Palace to the Arthur's Seat trailhead, she had sprinted to the top, in the hopes of having a few moments alone. The last stretch of trail was far steeper than the rest, and she was in better shape than all of her clients. She'd had plenty of time alone with her thoughts.

Lana spread a red-and-white checkered picnic blanket onto the ground moments before Zach plopped down next to her feet.

"Do you have any more bottled water, Lana?" he panted as he wiped off his forehead with an already damp rag.

Before she could retrieve a bottle from the basket, Ursula sat down next to her brother and pulled a flask out of her purse. "Here's something stronger."

Zach's eyes lit up. "You thought ahead." He took a long swig and wiped his mouth off with his coat sleeve. "That's the stuff."

Lana held out the water, but Zach waved it away. "I'm good, thanks."

"Anyone else?" she asked and held the bottle up high. Her group was slowly making their way over.

"Yes, please," Viola said as she sat down next to Ursula and held out her hand.

Lana had to bend over the blanket to reach her. *No wonder Betty wanted to get away from them*, she thought. Presto's kin were nice enough, yet they seemed incapable of doing—or unwilling to do—anything for themselves. No wonder the magician was encouraging them to stand on their own two feet, instead of relying on him to bail them out time and time again.

When Kurt rambled up to them, with Harry and Terrance in tow, Lana placed plates and the leftovers from this morning's extensive breakfast out onto the blanket.

Before Lana could grab the silverware, Zach had a plate in his hand and was adding slices of meat and cheese to it. "Don't mind if I do."

"If anyone is hungry, there is plenty." Lana stepped back to give her clients room.

After everyone filled their plates, she scooped up a few cheese blocks and apple slices, then took a seat on the grass. Once Presto's family was sated, they all turned to the sea and took in the views.

"Being up here reminds me of filming *Treasure from the Sea*," Ursula said. "The cliffs we filmed on were so windy! It was a nightmare for hair and makeup. Daniel Day-Lewis was so believable as that whaling captain, he made it easy to play his wife, yearning for his return from sea."

She posed momentarily, pulling her scarf around her head and looking longingly out at the water. Lana watched her carefully, amazed by how quickly she could transform her features. When Ursula whipped around to face her, Lana automatically leaned back, startled.

"Have you heard of *Treasure from the Sea*? None of my family could be bothered to watch it."

Harry looked to the ground as his mother scolded the rest.

"I'm afraid the title doesn't ring a bell," Lana said with a shrug.

"That's alright," Ursula replied, but it was clear that it was not. "That reminds me. I'll have to ask Daniel to be a guest at my new B&B. He's sure to have famous friends who'll want to tag along."

"Aunt Ursula, why do you want to open a bed-and-breakfast? I thought acting was your passion," Viola asked.

"That's why I'm doing it, darling!"

When Viola stared at Ursula blankly, the older lady continued, "It's a way to get a television deal. So many celebrity reality shows are based in a hotel or resort these days, it will be easy enough to interest a producer in our concept once we get everything up and running. And the bigger the names we can book as guests, the better our chances. I know a lot of famous actors through my work, and my best friend is a realtor for the stars; her contact book is full of celebrities we can call on."

"But there are so many reality shows these days. How is yours going to be different? Dad's house isn't located in a pretty bay or on a tropical island—it's in a residential neighborhood in Seattle," Zach said.

"Yes, but Dad is Presto the Amazing. That's why setting up the B&B in his house is so important to me. I'm going to make magic our theme and fill the walls with Presto's old posters and photos of him performing, as well as build a small podium in the garden where magicians and illusionists can perform. If Harry inherits the secrets to Presto's tricks, then he can perform them there, as well. It gives us a niche angle that will make it even more appealing to a reality show producer."

"If you inherit Dad's house, that is," Zach added, causing Ursula's smile to turn upside down. "I don't see why he promised it to you or Viola. He should have ordered it sold so we can all share in the profits. The proceeds from that sale would mean total artistic freedom for my production company. I'm going to ask the lawyer if giving the house to one child is even legal."

"Of course it's legal. Dad can do whatever he wants with his possessions," Ursula snapped.

"Exactly, so I hope you two don't get upset if he leaves it to me," Viola pushed.

"You're only a grandchild; his children should be the ones to inherit the bulk of his possessions. I'm going to talk to the lawyer about that, as well," Zach responded.

"The inheritance has already been decided. Go ahead and tell the lawyer whatever you want, but you can't cheat Ursula or Viola out of their fair shares," Kurt said.

"What's it to you? You're not even family, just a friend who loves to tag along for free trips abroad. Dad didn't even trust you to be his physician anymore. I doubt you'll receive more than a pittance."

"The lawyer did ask me to stay, so it must be more than that," Kurt retorted.

"Hey, come on, you two. Knock it off. We'll see who inherits what tomorrow, won't we?" Harry reasoned.

"You know what I can't wait to find out—who did Presto leave his house to and why?" Ursula pondered aloud.

"And who gets his art," Viola added.

"And his magic acts," Harry asked.

"At least we aren't too late. Presto died before he married Gwen and sold off all of his possessions to pay for that stupid castle. Cheers to his early demise," Zach said before taking a hefty swig of Ursula's flask. "We really should thank whoever did it."

"You mean we should thank The Great Ronaldo," Viola said.

Zach tittered. "Yes, that's what I meant."

Lana sat stock still, unable to believe what she was hearing. She had figured the family would spend the day reminiscing about their wonderful father and grandfather, but no one had a kind word over for Presto. None of them cared that he was gone—they were relieved that he had passed on before selling off "their" inheritance in order to finance his dream home.

As Lana listened to them bicker about who should get what and why, a single thought kept repeating in her head—maybe Ron hadn't killed Presto, after all.

25

Whose Side Are You On?

August 14—Day Two of the Wanderlust Tour in Edinburgh, Scotland

After getting her group back to the Holyrood Palace and then to their rented home, Lana sped off to her basement-floor room. During their walk, it had become clear that all of her guests had a more pressing motive to harm Presto than her ex-husband did.

It was time to learn more about her group. She had about three hours to herself before she had to get ready for the last excursion of the day. While her laptop was warming up, her phone began beeping. It was another text message from Alex. "Racing to next session. Miss you!! Talk tonight? Sending a thousand kisses."

Lana's heart melted at his words as she replied with kissing emojis. Seeing his sweet message made her feel as if she was somehow betraying him for wanting to help Ron. Why did she care what happened to her ex-husband? He was Candy's responsibility now.

She started to close down her laptop when her phone rang. Lana figured Alex had found a few free minutes to talk after all. She was wrong.

"How are things going, Lana? What do your guests want to do—leave or stay?" It was her boss.

"Gosh, I'm so sorry for not calling you back straight away. Presto's lawyer called yesterday and asked them all to stay until he can come over. Only

Betty, Presto's assistant, wants to fly back early."

"That's easy enough to arrange. But wait—do you mean Presto's lawyer is flying to Scotland just to read the will? That's pretty unusual."

"Apparently Presto left them all property in the Scottish Highlands, and they want to see it before they leave."

"That was so generous of him. Do the police know more about how he died? Did those bagpipes really scare him to death, or was it something else?"

"I haven't heard anything more from the detective so I guess Ron's still in custody for poisoning. They did find a vial of Presto's heart pills in his jacket."

"Poor Candy."

"Excuse me?" Lana's voice rose an octave. "Whose side are you on?"

Dotty's sigh traveled through the international line. "Yours, Lana. But I don't envy Candy having to raise that baby alone."

"At least Ron wanted to have a child with her. He didn't want to have one with me, and it really hurts." Lana spat the words out as angry tears coursed down her cheeks.

"I'm sure it does…"

"And Candy should have known better than to get involved with him, anyway. She knew Ron was married when she took the job."

"True, she should have. But maybe it was for the best. You're writing again and have made peace with your mom. Your job takes you around the world, and you have a wonderful boyfriend who encourages you to pursue your passions. What more could you want? Do you really miss Ron and his magic act? I can't recall you ever saying that you missed touring, only performing. As a tour guide, you get to perform all you want, in a manner of speaking, and you are home more often than you were before."

"It's not the same, Dotty, and you know it."

"Do you really think Ron killed Presto?" her boss asked.

"I honestly don't know. He was caught tampering with Presto's props and had pills in his pocket. But, if Candy is to be believed, he had no reason to do so. In fact, it would have been better for Ron if Presto had lived."

Her boss was so quiet that Lana thought they'd been disconnected. "Dotty? Are you still there?"

"Lana, Presto was more than a client to me; he was a friend. If he was murdered, his killer needs to be brought to justice. If you really believe Ron caused Presto's death, then I am glad the police have him in custody. But if you think one of his family members poisoned him on purpose, you need to alert the authorities. Presto didn't deserve to die so soon. There was so much more life left in him." Dotty began weeping softly into the phone. "And if someone he loved did this to him in order to inherit more money, then they don't deserve a penny! It would be an insult to his memory."

"Oh Dotty, I'm hugging you through the phone right now."

"You promise you'll keep your eyes and ears open?"

"I do." Lana said the words, knowing she was now committed. A promise to Dotty was the same as swearing under oath.

"Don't do it for Ron or his unborn child, but for Presto. If anyone in your group harmed him intentionally, I know you'll figure out who did it."

After Dotty hung up, Lana stared at the phone, trying to sort out her feelings for Ron. By investigating Presto's death, she would be helping to set her ex-husband free. How far was she willing to go to help the man who had broken her heart?

If she told Dotty that she thought he did it, then her boss would believe her, and that would be the end of the matter. Yet as much as she hated *how* he had left her, she still didn't hate Ron. After nine wonderful years together, how could she? Their break was so sudden, she never had a chance to despise him. His deceit had burned away many good memories, but not all of them.

Could she let Ron rot in jail for something he probably didn't do?

No, Lana realized reluctantly. It was time to investigate her clients' backgrounds and see who had the most to gain from Presto's untimely death.

26

Investigation Time

August 14—Day Three of the Wanderlust Tour in Edinburgh, Scotland

Lana spent her free time behind her laptop. The more she learned about Presto's family, the more she realized that none were as successful as they claimed to be.

In Lana's mind, the biggest shocker was discovering that Ursula was lying about her illustrious acting career. Despite her claims of starring in several films after being nominated for an Emmy, it appeared that Ursula had only had a handful of small parts during the past decade. Her claims of acting alongside Daniel Day-Lewis were also false, unless Extra #5 appeared in the background of a scene he was in. According to several gossip columns, her on-set temper tantrums and tendency to insult her directors were why her roles had dried up.

Why was Ursula lying about her success? What did she have to gain from convincing her family that she was still acting? She and her brother, Zach, did seem to be one-upping each other with their stories about American and British celebrities. Perhaps it was simply pride that made her so boastful.

Though Lana couldn't find any recent photographs of Ursula online, she did come across many taken in the late '80s when she was starring in *Weatherly Lane*. The many snaps of Ursula's house parties were a "who's who" of Hollywood, and in most photos she was hanging off the arms of her famous guests.

Lana wondered how Ursula could still afford to live in her mansion with its walled garden and swimming pool, if her starring roles had dried up years earlier. She didn't seem to be the type to save money. However, if Ursula was still in touch with any of her celebrity friends, her dreams of starring in a reality show about a bed-and-breakfast might not be pure fantasy, after all. Yet, if Ursula had such great connections in Hollywood—as she'd repeatedly claimed during this trip—surely they could have arranged a few acting roles for her.

Curiosity had Lana looking up Presto's home address in Seattle's Madison Park neighborhood. She was amazed by what she saw. His mansion was even larger and grander than Ursula's, and it was built in the middle of a private garden the size of a city park. No wonder his kin were fighting over who had the right to either use or sell it—it must be worth a fortune.

Would a daughter have more right to inherit the house than a granddaughter? Lana was no legal expert, but she had a feeling the bloodline didn't really matter, only what Presto wrote in his will.

Regardless, Presto's home would indeed make a wonderful art museum or bed-and-breakfast, though Lana chuckled at the idea of Ursula serving anyone. The actress was clearly used to being waited on, not being the hostess. And even if she did inherit the house and open her magic-themed B&B, would any television producer really want to film a reality series there? Zach was right; the house itself was beautiful, but the location was rather pedestrian for a television show.

Ursula was quite keen on getting her B&B off the ground, and she may have seen her father's death as the only obstacle. Yet she could not have been certain she would inherit it, especially if he had told Viola it would be left to her.

Was Ursula ruthless enough to kill her dad? Lana still wasn't entirely certain, but she put the former actress on her list of suspects, nonetheless.

Lana's next target was Ursula's son, Harry. He was indeed a magician performing as Harry the Magnificent. Yet his West Coast tour did not sell out all thirty dates, as Ursula claimed. Several were canceled due to a lack of interest, and ultimately only nineteen shows took place.

Ouch, Lana thought. An occasional cancellation happened, but so many in one tour would have crushed Ron. And if Ursula had invested money in Harry's tour, she probably didn't recoup it all.

Harry was convinced he would be named Presto's successor and inherit the secrets to his grandfather's signature acts. Without obtaining Presto's notes, sketches, and detailed lists of props, he would never be able to safely reproduce them. Yet his grandfather had chosen another to carry on his namesake—Presto the Amazing—without even telling him. Ursula was just as upset by Presto's rejection, in part because she was counting on the announcement to help sell tickets for Harry's next tour.

Lana thought back to the snippet of Harry and Ursula's conversation she'd overheard the night of Presto's death. It sounded like they were talking about the briefcase containing his book of secrets. Yet Harry was upset because it wasn't inside. Had his protégé, Raphael, removed Presto's book of magic before the police arrived, as Ursula and Harry suspected?

After Presto died, that lime-green briefcase was still on the table. Where was it now—in police custody or had Harry stolen it? Lana jotted down "briefcase's location?" on her notepad.

Presto was about to announce that Raphael was his successor, but died before he could do so. Did that mean Harry still had a shot at inheriting Presto's secrets and name? Ursula's pit bull lawyer was up for anything, it seemed. Lana imagined that Ursula already had him working on it. And Presto's acts were worth millions; if Harry and Ursula were willing to kill him to obtain them, then that was exactly the right moment to do so. Lana wrote down "Rights to Presto's acts?—ask lawyer" and moved on to the next name.

Betty was thankfully exactly who she said she was. She had been Presto's full-time personal assistant for thirty-one years and often toured with him. Lana even found a reference to her sister in Florida and the condo complex Betty had mentioned. So why would she want Presto dead? In almost every off-stage photo taken of the magician, Betty was visible in the background. She had literally been by his side for three decades and had forgone any relationship to do so. Yet Presto was clearly not interested in her romantically. Could Gwen's unexpected appearance and Presto's decision to let Betty go have driven her to murder? Lana hoped not.

Why was Betty so keen on leaving Scotland immediately? Was she trying to get out of the country before the police found evidence against her? Or did she simply hate Presto's family and want to get away from them? As much as she liked the older woman, she couldn't cross Betty's name off of her list of suspects.

Next up was Presto's mystery grandson. When she ticked Terrance's name in, she thought she'd entered it incorrectly. It was as if Terrance Craighead didn't exist. Lana did find a few references to his father, George, Presto's oldest son. And his obituary did mention leaving a wife, Arabella Sanders, and a fifteen-year-old son named Terrance, behind in Reno.

Apparently neither mother nor son had done anything significant enough to be posted about online. Yet after she checked several popular social media sites, she began to wonder whether something else was going on. Lana could find no profiles for Terrance Craighead, which was extremely odd. The boy spent most of his time staring at his smartphone; she assumed he would have several active social media accounts. On a whim, she ticked in "Terrance Sanders" and quickly found her fellow guide. Lana stared at his photos and posts, most of them about his punk rock band and video games he'd purchased. This was definitely her Terrance. So why was he lying about his last name?

Betty said he had shown Presto a copy of his birth certificate and that George was listed as the father. Terrance also had several photos in his possession that he could only have gotten from George. So how did he know Presto's oldest son and why was he lying about being a Craighead? Money was the obvious reason, but perhaps there was more to it. Lana added "Find out who Terrance really is" to her to-do list.

With trepidation, Lana typed Zach's name in, curious to see whether he was really as successful as he claimed. Sure enough, he was also lying about his current endeavors. It had been a year since one of his productions played on the West End. According to several gossip columns, most of

Zach's financial backers had pulled their support after his wife left him for a more successful producer. It must have been an amicable parting because they were photographed together at several charity events held after their divorce. Yet without her by his side, his production company had been going downhill fast and was now on the verge of bankruptcy.

The play his family saw in London, before flying up to Edinburgh, wasn't a West End production as he had told her, but a tryout performance meant to round up more interest and funding. From what Lana could find online, it didn't work. The reviews were quite harsh, and she could not find any mention of the play being scheduled in any theaters. She would have to try to casually ask Zach about that, if the opportunity presented itself.

Kurt was more of an enigma. According to several magazine articles, he had been the owner of a successful medical practice in Seattle until he sold it ten years ago to become Presto's full-time physician.

The news that Presto had hired a personal physician to travel with him shocked many newspaper reporters and gossip society columnists alike. In a lengthy interview about Presto in *People* magazine, Kurt explained how he prescribed massage therapy, exercise, meditation, and dietary supplements to help Presto keep his stamina up during the long-running tours he favored. His physically demanding performances drained him significantly, and Kurt's regimen kept the magician limber and his injuries to a minimum. A few months after the article's publication, the magazine ran a follow-up about how an increasing number of celebrities were hiring physicians to tour with them.

As complimentary as it must have been to be asked, Lana thought it was odd that Kurt had sold a successful medical practice to become a nutritionist and massage therapist. It seemed like a huge step backwards, though he did get to travel the world and was presumably well-paid for the work he did. Her suspicions about his salary were confirmed by a more recent article about Kurt's messy divorce and the financial repercussions. Three years earlier, his wife had divorced him and taken half of his earnings—rumored to be eleven million dollars. A nondisclosure agreement kept his ex from confirming the actual amount. Yet according to a nasty gossip column in a

Seattle newspaper dated six months ago, a series of bad investments led to Kurt's car being repossessed. Whatever Kurt was doing with his money, he was obviously not investing or spending it wisely. And if Presto had lived and moved to Edinburgh, Kurt would have been out of a job and salary.

But why would he want to harm Presto? That wouldn't get him his job back. Would Kurt would also receive a portion of Presto's inheritance, if only out of guilt? Lana doubted it would be enough to kill for.

Although he was a doctor with the medical knowledge and pills to murder, Lana still didn't see why he would want Presto dead. She put a question mark next to his name and moved on to the last suspect, Viola.

The twenty-seven-year-old was an assistant curator of fine arts at the privately owned Tylers Museum, located in a gorgeous art-deco building in downtown Seattle. A search of her name brought up several articles she'd written for museum journals and art-oriented magazines, as well as references to presentations she'd given at some of the most prestigious arts conferences in the United States.

Viola was also responsible for organizing several exhibitions during her tenure. The latest, entitled *Modernizing the Masters*, was more experimental than the rest. Ten Pacific Northwest artists "updated" famous works of art to match their contemporary world. In Georges Seurat's *A Sunday Afternoon on the Island of La Grande Jatte*, kids riding skateboards and playing Frisbee were interspersed among the park's visitors. Another was an copy of Pierre-Auguste Renoir's *Luncheon of the Boating Party*, but in this version all of the passengers had mobile phones and cameras in their hands.

As Lana skimmed the Tylers Museum website, she noticed that Viola only worked at the museum two days a week. That would explain why she had so much time free to document Presto's art collection, but it didn't explain how she could afford the expensive clothes she favored, let alone the jewelry.

So where was she getting the extra money to pay for it all? Did she have a rich boyfriend? Lana tapped her chin, trying to recall whether Viola had ever mentioned being romantically involved with anyone. She couldn't recall the younger woman mentioning the name of a specific boyfriend or partner, but so much had happened in the past twenty-four hours, she couldn't clearly remember much of anything.

Although Kurt seemed to be infatuated with the younger woman, Viola kept him at a distance. And even if they were dating, Kurt couldn't afford to buy her anything fancy, not if the gossip columns were correct.

Was Presto paying Viola to document and restore his artwork? Viola hadn't mentioned that she was getting paid to do so. Lana would have to ask her about the work she did for Presto, as well as her relationship with Kurt, when and if she got the chance. Considering how uppity and distant Viola was, Lana doubted the opportunity would ever present itself.

Whatever Viola expected to inherit, Presto made it clear that he no longer believed in her vision of creating a private museum. In fact, he intended to sell several of the better paintings to finance his castle. That obviously made Viola angry, but was she angry enough to kill him?

What would she gain by doing so? Did she assume that she could regain control of the entire collection, if she killed Presto before he could ship it abroad or sell it off? Was that even possible? To know for certain, Lana would have to ask Presto's lawyer, but she doubted she would get the chance to do so. Either way, Viola did seem to think the artwork was worth quite a bit of money and that it was worth fighting for.

She added "Viola and the paintings' value" to her list. Viola had also mentioned the name of the restoration studio she'd used to restore the paintings and write up the taxation reports. They might be willing to tell her more about the artwork's worth. Lana wrote "Call Henry & Sons" on her notepad.

Lana reviewed her list of suspects—a fake grandson, bankrupt physician, greedy art lover, wannabe reality star, disgruntled magician, and scorned assistant.

The more she learned about Presto's family, the more she realized that all of them had a strong motive for wanting Presto dead. At least, a more pressing reason than Ron did.

All of them stood to inherit a portion of Presto's estate, and all needed the cash fairly badly if they wanted to maintain their current lifestyles. However, if Presto had lived long enough to marry Gwen and sell his properties and possessions—as he said he would—they would not have received more than a pittance, at least in their eyes.

As Lana looked over her notes, the knot in her stomach grew tighter.

Anyone in her tour group could be a cold-blooded killer.

27

Checking Off Her To-Do List

August 14—Day Three of the Wanderlust Tour in Edinburgh, Scotland

When Lana went upstairs, the late afternoon sun was spilling into the hallway through the stained-glass windows above the front door.

"Hello?" she called out. She cocked her head, straining to hear anything, but it was mouse-still inside the house. Lana checked the living room, in case someone had fallen asleep. Viola was lying on the couch with a magazine in her hand. She lowered it when Lana entered, saw who it was, and raised it back up again without saying a word.

"Hi, Viola. Do you know where everyone is?"

The younger woman sat up and laid her magazine aside. "Kurt, Harry, Ursula, and Terrance went to a whisky distillery with Zach. Some friends of his told him it was the best one in Scotland."

"Why didn't you go with them?"

"I don't like whisky."

"That makes sense. Do you know if they want to go to the museum later?" The last planned excursion of the day was an after-hours tour of the Scottish National Gallery, led by an old friend of Presto's who was also the museum's senior curator.

"No, those heathens can't be bothered."

"And Gwen?"

143

Viola's eyes narrowed to slits. "I have no idea. If she's smart, she'll leave this family alone. I still cannot believe Grandpa didn't tell us he was getting married!"

Lana stifled a snort; she completely understood why Presto didn't tell them. He must have known that his family would do anything they could think of to discredit Gwen, out of fear of losing their inheritance.

"Alright, I'll check Presto's room in a minute and see if she's in."

"Suit yourself. What time do we leave, anyway?"

"In about an hour."

Viola looked at her diamond-studded watch. "I better get changed." The young woman stood up and began walking out of the room, her gorgeous dress made of several layers of chiffon billowing out behind her.

"Is that Chanel?" Lana ventured a guess at the designer's name.

"No, Vera Wang. She designed it specifically for me."

"It does fit you perfectly. Did your boyfriend pay for it?"

"I'm not seeing anyone. You aren't wearing that to the museum, are you?" Viola wrinkled her nose at Lana's comfortable clothes and floated towards the door.

"Oh, I heard you tell Presto that your secret admirer bought you that diamond watch," Lana pressed.

When Viola turned toward her, her expression had grown dark and brooding. "Are you accusing me of lying?"

"I'm just curious as to why you changed your story. I don't understand how a part-time curator can afford such nice things." Lana knew she was pushing the envelope, but she was tired of all the lies. No one in the family was who they seemed to be.

Viola flushed red. "My private life is none of your business. But if you must know, Nancy Drew, my mother left me a trust fund. That's how I'm able to afford designer clothes on a curator's salary."

Lana watched Viola stalk out of the room, wondering why she'd reacted so strongly. Did the arrogant young woman simply think Lana was out of line for asking such personal questions? Or was she lying and upset that she'd been caught?

As she followed Viola out of the room, Lana caught a glimpse of her outfit in the mirror. Her black jeans and silk blouse were far from designer, but did fit her body and budget. Considering her company on tonight's tour, though, it probably was better to change into a dress before they left for the museum.

First, she wanted to check on Gwen. Lana skipped up to Presto's room on the second floor then walked down the short corridor, listening for any sounds of human activity. She heard none.

"Gwen? Are you in?" Lana called out as she knocked.

No one answered, and she didn't hear any movement. Uncertain whether she should call Gwen's phone to let her know about the tour or leave her be, Lana stood still a moment, contemplating.

It is best to leave Gwen alone, she decided and turned on her heel, just as another thought struck. She and Viola were the only two people home right now. If she was going to find out more about this family's motives for wishing Presto harm, this was the perfect moment to begin. And finding out whether Harry had taken Presto's suitcase was a great way to start. If he had, stealing the secrets to Presto's million-dollar acts could have been his motive for poisoning his grandpa.

She stepped softly over to Harry's door and turned the handle. It was unlocked. Lana opened it enough to squeeze inside, hoping the squeaking hinges didn't attract Viola's attention.

She left the door open a crack in order to better hear if someone returned early. Lana felt so strange sneaking around in her client's room that her hands trembled terribly. Harry's room was typical for a single man in his early twenties. His clothes were strewn everyone, several glasses were stacked up on the dresser, alongside a half-eaten sandwich, and the room even smelled of dirty socks.

Maybe a hotel with a daily cleaning service was a better fit for the Wanderlust tour groups, Lana thought, instead of a rented home.

Lana carefully opened the dresser drawers and checked his closet, but found no hidden briefcases. Using her phone as a flashlight, Lana bent down and shined the lamp under Harry's bed. Pushed back against the headboard was the suitcase!

She crawled under his bed to retrieve it, but she was shorter than Harry and couldn't quite reach it. Lana squished further underneath, stretching to reach the case. When she finally wrapped two fingers around the handle and shook it, something rattled around inside. *Jackpot!*

Lana began pulling the suitcase out from its hiding place when she heard the front door open. *Shoot!* Panic replaced euphoria as she released the handle and pushed herself back out from under the bed. Lana eased out of Harry's room and bounced loudly down the steps just as Gwen was coming up them.

Gwen's brow creased when spotted Lana. "What are you doing up here?"

"Looking for you," she said with a smile. "Do you want to join me and Viola for the art museum tour? The taxi will be here in about forty minutes."

"I wouldn't miss it; Roger is a close friend of Presto's and mine. Or was…" Her voice trailed off.

"I'll come get you when the taxi is here. Can I make you a cup of tea before we go?"

Gwen's features softened. "That's kind of you to offer, but no. I'm going to rest until the taxi gets here."

She continued up to her room while Lana retreated to hers, grateful she hadn't been caught.

28

Fake Or Genuine?

August 14—Day Three of the Wanderlust Tour in Edinburgh, Scotland

After the taxi arrived, Lana skipped up to the second floor to retrieve Gwen. As she approached her door, Lana heard a man's voice pleading with someone in the neighboring room.

These walls are paper-thin, Lana thought as she tiptoed closer, curious to see what this problem was all about.

"I'm begging you for one more week, then I'll have the deposit to you," Zach pleaded. "If you don't put me on your schedule now, we'll miss the entire season, my investors will demand their money back, and my company will go bankrupt! We've been friends for so long; isn't there anything you can do?"

Zach was silent as his conversational partner responded.

"How can I be so sure? Because Dad promised me an eighth of his estate. Even after the inheritance tax, it'll be several million dollars."

He was quiet a moment, then barked, "Dollars—not pounds. But what does it matter? It's still more than I need and means I can finally produce the plays I want!"

Silence again.

Lana held her breath, wondering what the man would say.

"Thank you," Zach cried.

Before Lana could move, Gwen's door opened. "There you are. I thought I heard the taxi honking. Let me get my jacket."

"Great, I'll go get Viola."

Before she reached the stairs, she could hear someone descending them.

"Is the taxi here?" Viola asked when Lana came into view.

"It is," she responded cheerily, turning quickly so that her dress twirled around her knees. "Are you ready to go?"

"Yes." Viola walked past her without seeming to notice her change of clothes.

"Great," Lana mumbled, wondering whether the younger woman would ever remove the stick stuck firmly up her backside.

Their short journey brought them outside the city and past Dean Village. The Scottish National Gallery of Modern Art was housed in an impressive neoclassical building surrounded by forests and stately homes. A unique land art installation, consisting of steps of grass leading down to petal-shaped ponds, covered most of the field in front of the museum.

As soon as they arrived, the museum's senior curator first shook hands with Viola and Lana before turning to Gwen. The short, older man kissed the comic's cheeks, then grasped her hands. "This isn't how I hoped to welcome you today."

Gwen bent her head forward, using her curly hair to hide her face as she squeezed his hand. "Thank you, Roger."

"Are you certain you want to go through with this?"

"Definitely. I want to see where Presto's paintings will soon hang."

"You mean, my paintings," Viola grumbled as she jutted her chin out. "Any deals Presto was planning on making are as dead as he is."

Lana cringed at her crassness. Did Viola—or any of his kin, for that matter—even like Presto? They didn't seem to care that he was dead, only that they would get his possessions.

"About that," Roger responded to Gwen, ignoring Viola. "You know how incredibly grateful we are to Presto for wanting to enrich our collection."

"Yes?" Gwen nodded, encouraging him to continue.

"Well, we have some doubts about a few of the paintings' authenticity."

"What do you mean?"

"We won't know for certain until we have seen the art, but some of the pieces seem off, at least in the photographs. It could be the lighting, or it could be that Presto bought a few fakes over the years and they weren't detected during earlier taxations."

"Really? Gosh, I had no idea. Presto did say he bought what he liked and never bothered to have them authenticated, so it is highly likely that he got fooled a few times over the years."

"I feel horrible for putting you through this, especially considering none of the paintings are worth more than fifty thousand apiece. But we can't accept them into our collection if they aren't genuine. It costs too much to care for them on a long-term basis. But don't worry; we've recently purchased new equipment with which we can perform several noninvasive tests on the paint, canvas, and frames. They should tell us if Presto's paintings are genuine or forgeries."

"Oh, okay, I trust your experts' judgment," Gwen said.

Viola grew whiter by the second as she listened to the two chat. Lana was slightly worried that she might faint.

"I'm sorry, Gwen. I know Presto wanted to get this deal done as soon as possible so he could pay you back, but I can't cut you a check until I know for certain that they are genuine."

"Don't worry. I understand completely. To be honest, now that he's gone, I'm not entirely certain what I'm going to do with the castle. It was going to be our project, you know, something we could fix up together. I might put it back on the market. However, he had already promised you these pieces. And you two already signed an agreement, correct?"

"Yes, we did. All twenty paintings are named in the contract."

"Twenty paintings?" Viola shrieked. "That's a quarter of his collection! I want to see that list. All of the restored paintings should go to me—I did all of the work documenting them already and specifically chose those as the basis of my, I mean, Presto's museum."

"And Presto made clear to me that his art was always meant to be an investment. He didn't like to contradict you to your face, but trust me, your grandfather was not as keen on this private museum idea as you seem to think he was. He and Roger already agreed he would sell these twenty to the museum at a discount, and that they would hang in a hall renamed after him."

"Speaking of which, I have some mockups of the lettering we are planning on using. If you want, I can show them to you after this tour," Roger said.

"How would you know what Granddad really wanted?" Viola raged, refusing to let the other two shut her out. "You barely knew him. We worked on this project for months! He was fully committed to opening a museum in his Seattle home until you came along."

"Oh, you're Presto's granddaughter," Roger said as he turned to Viola, addressing her directly for the first time since they'd arrived. "Are you the one responsible for ordering the restoration work and tax reports?"

"Yes, I am," Viola stammered, as if she was caught off guard by his question.

"I had some questions for you that Presto couldn't answer. The two paintings my experts suspect of being forgeries were recently cleaned and restored by Henry & Sons. A quality restorer should have noticed that they were fakes—if they indeed are. I don't know them personally, but my staff informs me that they are one of the best art restoration firms on the West Coast of America. That is the reason why my curators didn't immediately reject those paintings after examining the photographs."

"You have some nerve accusing a reputable company such as Henry & Sons erof forging artwork, especially since your opinion is based on a few photographs," Viola said.

"It is the close-ups of the brushstrokes that make my curators nervous. They don't match with the artists' typical style."

"Oh! I didn't realize you could tell so much from a close-up. Now I understand why you requested them," Gwen said.

"We'll need to analyze the original paint and canvas to know for certain, but it is odd, to say the least."

"Presto had not taken good care of his collection before I came along," Viola said. "Those two paintings had been left hanging in the sunlight for several years and were badly cracked, and in some places, the paint had chipped off.

Sure, Henry & Sons' restorers may have repainted a few missing sections, but that's normal in a restoration workshop. Thanks to their excellent work, both look practically new and are worth a lot more because of it."

Roger held up his hands in defense. "I apologize. We will reserve our judgment until we have had a chance to examine them."

"If you ever get that chance," Viola growled at Roger. "I'm certain Grandpa left the art to me. Once Presto's will is read, you are in for a nasty surprise."

Gwen laughed. "Sweetie, I think you are the one who is going to be shocked, not Roger."

Viola started to react, but Roger appeared tired of their squabbling.

"Ladies, shall we try to forget this unpleasantness? We have forty-five minutes before security kicks us out. Gwen, where would you like to start?"

29

Good News for Betty

August 14—Day Three of the Wanderlust Tour in Edinburgh, Scotland

On the ride back to their rented home, Dotty called with good news for Betty. Her tickets had been rebooked, and she could fly out the next afternoon. Lana called Presto's personal assistant to let her know as soon as she was back in her basement-floor room.

"Hello, Betty. Your tickets have been changed. Where can I email them?"

"That's great news, Lana, thanks," Betty said, before reading off her email address.

"Are you certain you don't want to stop by in the morning so you can hear the will being read?"

"No way. That would mean having to sit in the same room with his ungrateful kids again. Whatever he has left me, the lawyer can send to my home in Seattle."

"What are you going to do?"

"Sell my apartment and travel the world for a while, I think. When I was touring with Presto, we were always too busy with the show to actually see the sights. I'm not ready to retire to a condo on the beach just yet. In fact, I'm going to try talking my sister into joining me for part of the journey. It'll be good for her to get out and live a little," Betty said, her tone resolute.

Her comments made Lana think of how her own life could have ended up, if she and Ron had stayed together. As much as she had enjoyed performing on stage, she didn't miss the kind of travel Betty was referring to—driving or flying into a new city, frantically trying to find the theater they were performing in, unloading all of Ron's gear and setting it up, only to dismantle and repack it five hours later, before speeding off to the next town and doing it all again.

Even when she and Ron had been home in Seattle, he had always been in his workshop practicing and perfecting his shows or creating new acts. They had spent very little time together doing fun, non-work-related things.

In contrast, Alex loved doing non-work-related things with her. Since they'd started dating, Lana had discovered more new restaurants and fun hidden hotspots than she had in the previous ten years of living in the city. And they got along so well that she felt as if she'd known him for years.

A sudden realization made her drop onto the bed. Then why was she resisting moving in with him? Was it only because she was worried he would move her to second place once they shared the same address? Or was the risk of getting hurt again preventing her from committing fully to Alex?

30

Tough Love

August 15—Day Four of the Wanderlust Tour in Edinburgh, Scotland

When Presto's lawyer arrived at ten in the morning, Presto's family was already gathered in the living room. Their bravado about who would inherit what had melted, it seemed. Based on the jittering porcelain cups and Zach's second whisky, they were nervous about what the lawyer had to say.

Gwen greeted Presto's lawyer and led him into the living room. He introduced himself as Johnathan before asking for a coffee. Lana poured him one and set it on the largest table in the room, while the lawyer opened his briefcase and pulled out three sheets of paper.

He made a show of sipping his beverage and straightening up his paperwork before beginning the official reading of the will. Presto's family watched his every move with bated breath.

"My condolences to you all. I appreciate you waiting for me to arrive, especially during this difficult time. I know Presto was looking forward to showing you the land he has left you in the Highlands, which is why I asked you to stay. The project meant quite a bit to him."

"Where is it exactly?" Zach asked.

"He gifted each of you a one-thousand-acre souvenir plot located close to Loch Linnhe. I have an information packet for each of you that explains more about the plots and the reserve," the lawyer said as he removed several thick envelopes from his briefcase and passed one to each of Presto's children and grandchildren.

"One thousand acres," Zach exclaimed. "That's wonderful!"

"I didn't realize he bought all of you souvenir plots. Could I have a look at one of those certificates?" Gwen asked. She reached her hand out to Ursula.

"So you can steal our right to it, as well? I don't think so!" Ursula stated and turned away.

"Gwen, he left you his plot." The lawyer handed her a packet, as well. She grabbed it from his hand and immediately pulled out the certificate of ownership, her smile growing in intensity as she read through the terms.

The lawyer cleared his throat, garnering their attention once again. Presto's family set aside their packets and gave him their undivided attention.

"One week before he left for Scotland, Presto changed his last will and testament. These plots are part of your inheritance," he explained. "Let me highlight the most important modifications, then I'll give you each a copy of it."

He held up the first sheet of paper and read from it. "Kurt, his personal physician, will receive a one-time payment of ten thousand dollars for services rendered above and beyond the call of duty."

"I'm touched. I really didn't expect to get anything." Lana looked to Kurt, who seemed to be having trouble controlling his emotions. Despite his words, he looked to be livid. And why wouldn't he be? He'd lost his only client and source of income. Considering his financial woes, ten grand wasn't a large enough sum to get him back on his feet.

"Betty, Presto's personal assistant, will receive a one-time payment of fifty thousand dollars. Presto wrote: 'You were my rock for twenty-nine years and three marriages. I couldn't have done it without you.'"

Ursula snorted. "What a waste. She wasn't even one of us."

"And what about the art? Who gets his collection?" Viola asked.

"Viola, you will receive a one-time payment of twenty thousand dollars for helping to document and restore Presto's collection. He had already signed contracts to sell twenty paintings to a museum in Scotland and another ten to the Seattle Art Museum. He's set aside five for you, but the rest are to be sold and the profits donated to several cultural charities."

"That's not what he promised me!" she wailed.

"And his home? Who gets that?" Ursula asked.

"He bequeathed his Seattle home to Gwen, so that she could sell it and recoup the money she loaned him to purchase their home in Scotland."

"That's not fair," Ursula cried. "Before she came along, we all inherited equally. Now she's walking away with the lion's share of Dad's estate."

"And his magic acts? Who gets those?" Harry asked.

"He already sold the rights to his show and stage name to a magician named Raphael."

Harry stood up. "When?"

"Two months ago."

"That bastard!" Ursula yelled.

"So his book of secrets wasn't in that suitcase, after all. It was just a prop," Harry mumbled as he fell back onto the couch.

"What suitcase?" the lawyer asked.

"Never mind," Harry said and looked away.

"And what about his savings account? How is that going to be divided up?" Zach asked.

"I'm afraid there won't be much left, after the funeral costs are paid."

"What? He earned millions! Where did it all go?"

"Presto spent hundreds of thousands of dollars a year on travel, food, and clothing. He also contributed twenty percent of his net profits to charity. But it was settling several long-outstanding lawsuits last year that drained his accounts."

"What lawsuits?" Zach asked.

"If he didn't tell you about them, then I'm not at liberty to say. It was part of the nondisclosure agreement reached with the plaintiffs. From the money remaining, he set up a trust fund that will pay all eight of his children one thousand dollars a month, until the fund is depleted. The rest will be distributed via his charity organization to a long list of cultural organizations he was fond of."

"Unbelievable! So all he left us are plots of land?" Ursula yelled.

"And one thousand dollars a month," the lawyer responded.

Zach cackled. "Dad led us to believe we would be inheriting millions. And now this—a monthly check and plot of land in the middle of nowhere? His promises to us were just like his shows—all smoke and mirrors."

31

This Is An Outrage!

August 15—Day Four of the Wanderlust Tour in Edinburgh, Scotland

"This is an outrage!" Ursula screamed as she whipped around to point a finger at Gwen. "Zach's right. Dad must have been insane to make such rash decisions. My lawyer is going to fight you on this."

"How?" Presto's lawyer asked, his calm tone momentarily breaking Ursula's stride. "It is incredibly difficult to prove that a parent didn't have full mental or testamentary capacity when they changed their will. And I can attest to the fact that Presto was of sound mind and body when he made these alterations. To be honest, I hadn't seen him so happy or determined in months."

"But Gwen must have been a bad influence on him. Otherwise, why were these changes so drastic? Isn't there a way to prove she forced him to alter his will in her favor?" Ursula glared at Presto's fiancée, clearly trying to intimidate her, but the woman didn't flinch.

"In order to prove that Presto was under Gwen's influence, you would also have to show that she had taken complete control over his assets and day-to-day decisions. Gwen didn't live in Seattle, nor did she pay his bills or do any of the things that would prove she was controlling him and his estate," the lawyer stated calmly.

"And Presto didn't actually favor her in his will. He bequeathed his home to her, in case it hadn't sold before he passed on. But he was planning on using the profits from the house to pay Gwen back for half of the purchase price of their new home in Scotland."

"But Dad promised me his house!" Ursula cried.

"No, he promised me his home—and all of his art," Viola insisted.

"A daughter's claim should be stronger than that of a granddaughter."

"Well, he must have been mentally incompetent if he promised both of them the same house. It should go to all of us," Zach said.

"I am afraid you cannot contest a will because the parent verbally stated something different than what is recorded in it. His last will and testament is what stands."

"Whose side are you on, anyway?" Zach yelled.

Lana looked over to Gwen, expecting her to be raging mad. Instead she was hiding a grin behind her hand. Given how horribly Presto's kids had been treating her, Lana could see why she'd find their reactions amusing.

"You little hussy! You poisoned Dad's mind. He never mentioned wanting to live in a castle before you came along. You said you didn't want to be named in his will, and yet you are getting the bulk of his estate," Ursula raged.

Gwen slowly shook her head. "Now I understand why Presto was cutting you all off. You really were just waiting for him to die! And so you know, Ursula, it was Presto's idea to buy that castle and turn it into a space for artistic retreats and workshops. It was definitely not my choice—I would have preferred to live in the city."

"Then why don't you sell your castle and give us back Dad's house?" Zach pushed. "That way you won't need the money from the sale to cover your costs."

"That is the only way you would get his home back, if Gwen does rescind her claim on it," the lawyer broke in to clarify.

"What if the person who stood to inherit the most was implicated in his death?" Viola asked as her eyes locked with Gwen.

"Anyone implicated in Presto's death would not inherit any of his assets. Why are you asking?"

"Because the bagpipes killed him and Gwen was the one who hired them."

Gwen's eyes began to bulge. "How can you think that, let alone say it? I loved Presto with all of my heart. I would never have hurt him."

"It was premeditated murder!" Ursula exclaimed, ignoring Gwen's impassioned response. "She was the only one who knew about his heart condition."

As the accusations between family and fiancée began to fly, the lawyer stood up and yelled, "Please, everyone calm down! Viola, I don't think that's how a judge would interpret it. Gwen didn't actually murder him, even if she did arrange for the pipers to play."

"Did Gwen pay you? Because you sure don't seem to be looking out for our best interests," Ursula accused.

The lawyer shook his head. "I am only here to inform you of Presto's wishes and to see that they are fulfilled."

"I want a second opinion—I'm calling my lawyer. Be ready for his call, Gwen," Ursula stated.

"Grow up, Ursula," was Gwen's response.

"How dare you! You and Dad weren't even married! If you had any decency, you would give us back his home and get out of our lives."

"Your dad wanted to help talented individuals whose families couldn't afford a cultural education, as well as rising stars whose talents needed nurturing. That's why he wanted to buy that castle. And I'm going to make sure his wishes are fulfilled," Gwen said, her tone resolute.

"But he promised to help us! Why should our inheritance go to strangers?"

"Because he was tired of you spending his money to maintain your extravagant lifestyles, instead of using it as the basis for creating your own futures. Ursula, he said your acting career dried up years ago, yet you refuse to accept it and move on. Why didn't you use the money he gave you to invest in that bed-and-breakfast idea you keep rambling on about? Instead you continued making payments on a house you can't afford and lounging around your pool moaning about how the world is against you."

"You horrible person!" Ursula cried, then fled the room.

"Zach, without Presto's support, your last five plays wouldn't have made it into any theater, and the reviews were absolutely dreadful. Your work clearly isn't resonating with a wider audience, and it doesn't sound like you've found a network of financial backers who share your artistic vision. Maybe it's time to try something else?" Gwen offered.

"You have a lot of nerve saying that to me," Zach growled.

"This is what Presto told me about you. He loved you all, but he was concerned you were stuck in old patterns and couldn't get out of them. And he admitted he wasn't helping by giving you money anytime you whined for it. That's why he was pushing you all so hard these past few months. He wanted you to find another way to achieve success and fulfill your dreams— one that wasn't reliant on his money."

Zach stood up and looked around the room. "Maybe Dad did leave us another way. Where's the tour guide?"

Lana raised her hand. She'd been sitting at the back, trying to be as still as possible during this family feud.

"There you are. Dad organized a trip to our property. I want to see it. Can we leave tomorrow?"

Lana blew out her cheeks. Moving reservations for a minivan, castle visit, eight hotel rooms, and a guided tour up two days was going to be a challenge. But then again, that's what she was paid to do. "I'll do my best."

32

A Visit From The Police

August 15—Day Four of the Wanderlust Tour in Edinburgh, Scotland

It had taken several phone calls to move their planned Highlands excursion forward. As soon as the hotelier, landowners association representative, tour bus company, and castle's receptionist learned the reason for the change, all were incredibly accommodating.

Lana went upstairs to find the family and let them know they would be leaving the next morning at six. Before she could reach the living room, there was a hard knock on the front door.

Wondering who it could be, Lana looked through the peephole and saw the detective who had interviewed them at the theater after Presto passed away.

"Hello, officer. How can we help you?" Lana asked, as soon as the policeman and his partner stepped inside.

"Good day. We are here to search Presto's room and belongings. The suspect we have in custody has made several claims that we may be able to confirm by doing so."

Lana reeled at his mention of "their suspect," knowing he meant her ex-husband, Ron.

"Presto's fiancée is upstairs in their room. Let me lead the way."

"Who's there, Lana?" Zach called out as he entered the hallway. He stopped suddenly when he spotted the police. "What's going on? Have you figured out how Dad died? Or if that magician poisoned him?"

"Our medical examiner can confirm that Presto ingested an overdose of his heart medication shortly before his death. We are still not certain if the suspect we have in custody did poison his drink, though he did have Presto's personal vial of heart medication in his possession. Until we know for certain how Presto ingested the overdose, we will keep our suspect in custody."

"What do you mean you haven't figured out how the pills were administered? Why are you keeping him in custody if you aren't even certain he did it?" Lana said.

The detective looked at her strangely before answering. "We found the vial in the suspect's pocket and assume he stole it from Presto's jacket sometime during the dinner."

"So did the noise from the bagpipes killed Dad, or the pills?" Ursula pressed.

"The overdose, in combination with the alcohol and sudden noise, stopped his heart from functioning properly," the officer stated as he cast his eyes downward in respect, unaware of the joy he was bringing to the family.

"Good enough for me—I'm calling my lawyer," Ursula said in a sing-song voice as she scampered off to her room.

Poor Ron, Lana thought. He had the opportunity, means, and motive. The fact that the police still had him in custody meant things were looking pretty grim for him. As much as she wanted to tell the police about her guests' possible motives, she knew it would be pointless—and even stupid—to do so. If she did, the police would want to know why she was getting involved with their investigation. And as far as she was aware, they didn't know about their marriage or divorce. For now, Lana had little choice but to remain silent and continue watching her guests for clues as to their wrongdoings.

"Can you take me to Presto's room now?" the detective asked.

"Certainly." Lana led him up the staircase then stepped aside so he could knock on Gwen's door.

The comedian opened it immediately. "Yes?"

"Good afternoon." The detective bowed deferentially. "I would like to check Presto's possessions, if you do not mind. We are specifically looking for paperwork that concerns a lawsuit recently filed by The Great Ronaldo against Presto."

"Oh, I haven't seen anything referencing that, but you are free to search his belongings. I haven't moved any of his things."

Gwen stepped out into the hallway to give the officers more space.

"Are you leaving town?" the detective asked as he nodded towards the partially packed suitcase on her bed.

"We are all going to the Highlands tomorrow. Presto had purchased property there, and his family wants to see it before they fly back to the States in a few days."

"It is a lovely part of the world," he answered without looking up from the stack of paperwork in his hand. Folders and notebooks were strewn across the only desk in the room, many bearing the names of home restoration companies and interior design firms. "Was he interested in buying property here?"

"We purchased a home in the Highlands a month ago and were trying to decide how best to remodel and renovate it so that it's livable again."

"Property is always a good investment," he said noncommittally and returned his attention to the desk. Once he and his colleague had gone through the contents of the desk, bathroom, and closets, they thanked Gwen for her time and began walking down to the front door.

"Wait—is that it? What happens next?" Gwen asked.

"I hoped to learn more about the relationship between Presto and our suspect, as well as the lawsuit he claims has been filed. Unfortunately, I don't see any mention of The Great Ronaldo or the lawsuit in Presto's paperwork. But we aren't giving up. Until we know for certain how the overdose was administered and by whom, we will keep searching for clues."

Gwen's brow crinkled. "But you have a suspect in custody, and he was seen repeatedly filling Presto's glass with water throughout the evening."

"Yes, we do have several witnesses who confirm our suspect repeatedly poured water into Presto's glass. However, we have had all of the carafes used by the waitstaff tested, and none contained traces of the medication."

"And the glasses on our table?"

The detective sighed deeply. "We could not find any residue of digoxin in any of those glasses. We are now checking all of the glasses and cups used that evening, but it's going to take quite a while to test them all."

"Are you going to continue to hold Ron in custody while you run your tests?"

"Yes, we are. You are Lana Hansen, correct?" the detective asked.

"Yes?" Lana's rising voice morphed her statement into a question.

"Can we speak to you, in private?"

Lana glanced over at Gwen, who looked as perplexed as she felt. "Okay, sure. Why don't we talk in the dining room."

Their descending footsteps brought Presto's kin out into the hallway. After the policemen waved Lana into the dining room and closed the door, she could hear the family's footsteps coming closer. The detective raised one finger, as if to silence his partner and Lana, then quickly opened the door.

Indeed, Presto's family was leaned forward, straining to listen. Without shame, they stepped back and looked around at the furnishings, as if they were simply examining the hallway when the officer happened to come into view.

"There is one more thing I wish to ask. Can anyone recall seeing a lime-green suitcase on Presto's table after his death?

When the family remained silent, the investigator added, "Several patrons mentioned seeing it on Presto's table before his death, yet after we interviewed and released all of the theater-goers, we discovered it was missing."

"Oh, no!" Ursula threw her hands against her cheeks as her mouth formed a tiny O. "Did someone steal it?"

Lana looked to Harry, but he was staring down at the ground. "I saw it right after Presto died, but I don't know if it was still there when we left the theater."

The officer made a notation in his notebook, then looked to the rest. "Anyone else?"

"No, I don't recall seeing it, but all I could think of was poor Dad," Zach said.

"What was inside of it?" Harry asked.

"Apparently Presto placed a gift for his successor, Raphael, inside. We've already questioned him, but he's not certain what it was," the investigator explained.

Harry shook his head slowly. "I don't know what happened to it. The night was a blur after Grandpa died."

"Alright. I have a few questions for your guide, then I will be off. You will all be in Scotland a few days longer, correct? In case I have further questions?"

The family seemed stricken by the idea that he might be getting back in touch and began shuffling back into the living room, giving the officers space.

He smiled and ushered Lana back into the dining room. Once the door was closed, he said, "Where were we? Oh, yes, The Great Ronaldo claims that you two were once married. Is this true?"

"Yes, it is. But our divorce became final in December." Lana's voice caught in her throat.

"That is a strange coincidence, you being here on this tour with Presto, the same man your husband claims to have filed a lawsuit against."

"Ex-husband. And I had no idea Ron and his new girlfriend, Candy, would be in Edinburgh, or that he would go so far as to crash Presto's party. I knew they had problems in the past, but I didn't know about this new lawsuit until our group ran into Ron on the Royal Mile," Lana said, emphasizing Candy's presence in the hopes the officer would believe their relationship was well and truly over.

Thinking of Candy brought another thought into her head. "Say, did Ron have a sketch of a wire array in his possession?"

The officer's eyes narrowed. "Yes, he claims it was his design. How did you know about it?"

"His girlfriend, Candy, told me that he was trying to remove the wire array for the pulley system so he could prove to the audience that he'd designed it."

"That is what he told us, as well. That's why we are here, looking through Presto's things for proof of that connection."

The detective nodded to his fellow officer, signaling the end of their interview. When he put his hand on the door handle, he turned back to Lana. "Does Presto's family know you were once married?"

She jutted out her chin. "No, should they?"

The policeman looked at her for quite a long time, as if he was weighing the pros and cons of her coming clean. "I guess not. I'll leave it up to you."

"Thanks." Lana breathed a sigh of relief. There was no way on God's green earth that she was going to volunteer that information to Presto's family.

33

The Secret To His Success

August 15—Day Four of the Wanderlust Tour in Edinburgh, Scotland

After the police left, Lana stood alone in the dining room, waiting for her heart rate to return to normal. She had expected the interrogation to be harsher, but Candy's presence in Edinburgh was evidently enough for the police to take Lana off their list of suspects.

When there was a knock on the door, Lana figured the detective had another question for her. She turned to instead see Harry enter, then close the door tight. He leaned against it and eyed her warily.

"I know your secret, Lana Hansen. I watched a few videos of The Great Ronaldo's performances last night. Your hair was shorter, but there's no denying you used to be his assistant."

"You're right," she answered, wiping the smug expression off his face. "And the police know it, too. That's what the officer wanted to talk to me about."

"Why didn't you tell us?"

"Because it isn't relevant. Ron and I are divorced, and he's seeing someone new."

"Not relevant? Your ex killed my grandpa!"

"Did he? What about Presto's briefcase, Harry? It was there on the table when Presto died, and now it's missing."

Harry's bravado melted. "I don't know anything about that."

"Really? I found it under your bed yesterday."

"Why were you in my room?"

"I heard you and Ursula talking about the suitcase and wanted to know if you'd really taken it. Ron may be my ex, but it doesn't mean I want him to pay for a crime he didn't commit," Lana said, fibbing a little. She felt funny telling Harry the truth—that she'd promised Dotty she would investigate the family to ensure Presto's killer didn't profit from their dastardly deeds.

"Unfortunately, Gwen came home before I could check its contents. If you don't tell me what's inside it, I'm going to tell the police that you stole it. Considering you just lied and told them you didn't know what happened to the case, they'll probably take you in for questioning."

Harry's head hung low. "His lucky rabbit's foot and an old book with an inscription to Raphael on the inside cover. He wrote, 'My gift to you—here's where I learned all I know about magic.' All that talk about it containing the secrets to performing his acts was a lie."

"What's the title of the book?"

"*The Conjurer Unmasked* by Henri Decremps."

Lana had to bite her tongue to keep her expression neutral. *So that's what Presto meant*, she thought. He'd claimed the secrets to his acts were inside that case, and in a way they were—but not in the way that Harry expected.

The young magician's disappointment was so evident that she doubted he was lying about what was inside. "Why did you take it?"

"It was Mom's idea. She thought if we had the notes to Presto's acts in our possession, her lawyer would have a better chance of proving that I had the right to perform them, and not Raphael. She snuck it out by wrapping it up in her shawl. Everything was so chaotic, no one noticed. But we didn't kill Presto for it—stealing the case was a spur-of-the-moment decision. And it was all for nothing, anyway. It was just a prop."

"But why steal the case if Raphael already had the rights to his name and act?"

Harry's calm cracked as he growled, "We didn't know that Presto had already signed a deal with Raphael. He'd been leading us on for months. Mom was convinced I would be named his successor after he retired, and

Grandpa never corrected her assumption. Why couldn't he have told the truth, instead of letting us believe that I would be the new Presto?"

"I'm so sorry, Harry."

"All I wanted was for him to acknowledge that I could be a successful magician, too, one day. I didn't expect him to take me under his wing, but he could have shown a bit of interest in my show. Did you know that he didn't even come to see my show when I played in Seattle? He said he had another engagement, but when I asked him about it later, he said he stayed in and watched reruns all night."

Harry was clearly heartbroken by his grandfather's repeated rejections. As much as Lana wanted to suspect Harry of murder, she couldn't see this young man harming another soul. Still, she needed to hear him say it.

"Did you put anything in his drink or food, Harry?" Lana gazed up at the younger man with the sternest expression she could muster.

Harry threw up his hands as if he was warding off her question. "No way! Grandpa was my hero. All I ever wanted to be was a magician, like him. Sure, I was upset, but I never would have hurt him, nor would I have let my mom do anything to harm him. We didn't have a hand in his death, I swear!"

Harry's plea was made even more passionate by the zealousness of youth. The boy probably wasn't a killer, but Lana still believed that his mother might be. Ursula was convinced that if Harry obtained the rights to Presto's name and act, his own shows were guaranteed to be a financial success. She was also lying about her acting roles and was apparently having trouble paying her mortgage. And Ursula hadn't known about Presto's deal with Raphael until they were at Presto's dinner.

What if Ursula had chosen that moment to poison Presto, so as to prevent him from publicly naming Raphael as his successor? She had a pressing motive and opportunity, and would have had as much access to Presto's heart pills as Ron did. On Lana's mental list of suspects, Ursula shot up to number one.

34

Ursula Comes Clean

August 15—Day Four of the Wanderlust Tour in Edinburgh, Scotland

At lunch, Ursula and Zach continued their game of "who knows who." The alcohol was definitely fueling their one-upmanship. *How long will they keep up the charade?* Lana wondered. Presto was gone; there was no one left to impress but each other.

At least they had taken a break from obsessing over his will. The family had spent most of the morning discussing different ways they could contest Gwen's right to inherit anything Presto had owned, before Ursula had called her lawyer. After their long conversation, she proclaimed that everyone could expect to hear great news regarding Presto's house quite soon. Based on her conversation with her legal representative, she was now convinced that Gwen had no claim on it because they weren't married. Lana wondered whether that was true, especially considering that Presto's lawyer was quite adamant that the magician's will stipulated that Gwen was now the legal owner.

After telling her family and neighboring tables about her recent lunch with Quentin Tarantino, she stood up suddenly and announced that she had to powder her nose.

When Lana saw Ursula stumble across the dining area towards the bathroom, only to end up in a broom closet, she set off to help her inebriated client. After Ursula relieved herself, she leaned close to the mirror and began touching up her makeup. Lana figured this was as good a time as any to find out the truth about her acting career. If anything, her drunken state would make her less able to quickly fib her way out.

"I watched a few clips of *Treasures of the Sea* last night," Lana said.

Busy with her mascara, Ursula froze midswipe. "Oh, what did you think of it?"

"Daniel Day-Lewis was incredible, as always, but funny enough, another actress was playing the lead. Why did you lie about being in it?"

Ursula threw her mascara against the glass and pinched her nose. "No one in my family could be bothered to watch any of my work—even after I got nominated for that Emmy. What do you want—money?"

"No. Only to know why you lied."

Ursula's chin momentarily shot up in the air, before her shoulders slumped. "I guess it doesn't matter now. Because Dad was going to loan me enough money to save my house, but only if I had enough work to be able to pay him back."

"Were you even in the film?"

"I was an extra during the Cliffs of Devon sequence, but they cut that scene from the movie. Work as an extra didn't pay enough to satisfy Dad's requirements, so I fibbed a little."

Lana's eyes widened. "How could you be so sure he wouldn't watch it, especially if you were asking for a loan based on having that role?"

Ursula's laugh sent chills up her spine.

"I told Presto about it twice, and he expressed absolutely no interest in viewing it. Heck, he couldn't be bothered to watch even one episode of my Emmy-nominated series."

"Why didn't you sell your house instead of asking for a loan? I looked up your address; that house must be worth a fortune."

"Looks can be deceiving, young lady. If you must know, I had to double-mortgage it to help Harry pay for his tour."

Which lost money, Lana added in her mind.

"You're right. If there is no other way, I can put my house up for sale. My realtor friend is dying to sell it. She's certain it'll go in a heartbeat because of the location. But it holds such sentimental value to me, I'm trying everything I can think of to save it. It was thanks to *Weatherly Lane* that I could afford it, and being there reminds me of better times."

"Presto is dead. You can stop pretending and tell your family the truth about your house and acting career."

"I can't come clean now; Zach would never let me live it down."

"I don't know about that," Lana mumbled, thinking of his own lies, adding, "Did you harm Presto?"

"No! I was mad at Dad for lying again, but I would never have hurt him."

"What do you mean, lying again?"

"He was always making promises he didn't keep. I was counting on that loan and my inheritance. If he wanted to cut us off, he should have been more upfront about it." Ursula stopped and looked Lana up and down. "Why do you care who killed him? You aren't inheriting anything, are you?"

"No, of course not."

"Phew, for a second I thought you might be another mystery cousin looking for a handout. Harry told me that you used to be The Great Ronaldo's assistant. You're still infatuated with him, aren't you? Is that why you're doing this, so you can get him out of prison?"

Lana blushed. "No, Ron is not my concern anymore. He and I are divorced, and we are both in new relationships."

"Huh, I don't see his girlfriend hanging around asking questions."

Before Lana could respond, Viola burst through the bathroom door.

"There you are! I thought you'd fallen into the toilet, Aunt Ursula. Are you coming back to lunch? They are about to serve dessert."

35

Did Ron Do It?

August 15—Day Four of the Wanderlust Tour in Edinburgh, Scotland

Drat! Lana thought as she pounded her fists against her temples. Dotty had asked her to investigate Presto's murder, but it felt as if she was doing this for Ron.

Had her ex done it? Candy certainly didn't think so, and his unborn child was a great reason not to. The man she knew was not capable of harming another person. But then again, she had once thought he took their marriage vows seriously. There was only one way to find out for certain—it was time to visit Ron.

Now that the police knew about their previous relationship, she didn't have to lie about why she was there to speak to him. When they escorted Ron into the visiting room, Lana was shocked by the sallowness of his skin.

"Lana, what are you doing here?"

"My boss wants Presto's killer brought to justice, and I need to know if you did it."

"I swear I didn't harm him! It's not what it seems."

"It never is with you illusionists. Why were you tampering with his props?"

"I wasn't! I was trying to remove the wire array from the pulley system so I could show all of his friends that it was identical to my sketch. I thought if I could embarrass Presto into admitting he stole Rainbow Walk from me, it would make it easier for my lawyer to prove it in court."

"Are you kidding me? You actually thought Presto would freely admit that he'd stolen your idea to a hall full of people there to honor his career?"

"A career founded on my act! Rainbow Walk is what propelled him to stardom. It should have been me—not him—up on that stage."

"Ron, you sound delusional. Anyone in their right mind would think you saw your chance to get your revenge and you took it."

"My revenge?" Ron's eyes bulged out of their sockets. "I wanted to take him to the cleaners, not the morgue. Now that he's dead, it's going to be even more difficult to sue his estate for intellectual property theft. You've got to believe me, Lana. I did not do this."

Lana spoke her thoughts aloud. "It'll be tougher than you think; Presto sold the rights to his act before he died."

"He what? Oh, great." Ron threw his hands up in the air. "My lawyer's fees just went way up."

"If you were only there for the wire array, why were you hanging around our table so much?"

"I hoped Presto would say something incriminating about me or the lawsuit. I recorded the entire evening on a portable recorder and even gave it to the police. Unfortunately, there was nothing useful on it."

Lana thought on Presto's family and their motives for wishing the famous magician harm. Their reasons were much stronger and more pressing than Ron's. If Presto had married Gwen and sold his possessions—as he said he was going to do—then his family would have received a fraction of what he had promised to leave them before Gwen came into his life. Unfortunately for Presto's killer, the magician had already changed his will. Yet the family still stood a chance at getting the house back, if they could convince Gwen they had more right to it than she did.

Which one of them was desperate enough to harm their own flesh and blood? If she was going to honor Dotty's wishes and help the police unmask Presto's killer, then she should be focusing her inquiries on Presto's family instead of Ron.

She had nothing more to ask her ex about Presto, but there was one more thing she had to know before she left. With the plate of glass between them, it was easier to ask the question that had haunted her since she had received his text message telling her their marriage was over.

"Why do you love Candy more than me? We had nine great years together. Wasn't I enough for you?"

Ron hid his face in his hands. "I love you with all of my heart and still do to this day. But something happened when Candy and I were on tour together; there was a sort of chemistry that I couldn't deny."

His words tore at her heart. "Why couldn't you have fought your feelings for her? It's not like I wasn't ever attracted to other men after we married—but I never acted on it. You made a choice when you stood before God and your family and said 'I do' to me."

"What we had together was special, Lana, but my attraction to Candy goes even deeper. It's as if I've met my soulmate. I never wanted to hurt you, but you deserve to be with someone who loves you most of all."

"Luckily, I've found someone who does." Anger forced Lana out of her chair. She began to walk away from Ron, when another thought made her turn back. "Candy called me. She told me she's pregnant and it was your idea."

Ron's face went white as he began to stammer. "I never meant for you to find out. You'd been after me to have kids, but it never felt like the right time. After we split up, I realized how close I was getting to fifty and if I was going to have children, I'd better not wait much longer. Candy wants to have a large family and..."

"Just like I did." Lana felt the sting of tears. "Goodbye, Ron."

"Lana?"

She'd rushed over to the door, but his tone made her stop.

"I am sorry about how things ended up. When I said yes to you, I meant it to be forever. But it didn't work out that way."

"That's life, isn't it? Things don't always work out the way we expect them to." Lana walked out of the visiting room and jailhouse as fast as she dared. When she was back outside, she found a nearby park bench and bawled her eyes out.

After their separation, Lana had gone crazy trying to figure out what had happened to make him stop loving her. When he'd left to go on tour, he had still been her loving husband. Yet a month later, he had left her for another. As much as his words hurt her, she felt as if a chapter of her life was now closed and she could finally move on.

When she stood up, Lana felt lighter than she had in years. As she signaled for a taxi, her thoughts shifted to Alex and his asking her to move in together. Being with him felt so right. So what was she waiting for?

36

Family Ties

August 16—Day Five of the Wanderlust Tour in Edinburgh, Scotland

When Gwen came downstairs to breakfast, Lana wondered whether the comic would join them on their trip to the Highlands. She had reserved a place for Presto's fiancée, but she wouldn't blame the woman for not wanting to be stuck in a car with his family for two days straight.

"Hi, Lana," Gwen said as Presto's kin stared at her, as if they were daring her to sit at the table with them. "When is the bus leaving?"

"In about an hour." Lana handed Gwen a plate.

Ursula gasped. "You aren't coming with us, are you?"

"It was a special place to Presto, and he left me his plot. I have as much right to be there as you do, and I want to see it again, which means I'm coming with you. Besides, I can't wait to see what you think of the land."

Gwen's voice was sweet and innocent, but Lana felt a sinister undertone in her last remark.

Kurt trotted down the stairs and set his suitcase by the door. As he entered the dining room, Terrance came down with a backpack swung over one shoulder.

"Why are you packed?" Kurt asked.

"Because Grandpa left me land, too."

"I don't know how you fooled Presto or his lawyer, but you shouldn't have inherited a thing. I bet you aren't even related to Presto. He should have ordered a DNA test before he wrote you into his will."

Terrance moved in closer, glaring at the older man. "Will you stop it already? I'm George's son. It's not my fault he and Presto had a falling-out before I was born."

"I don't know how you got those family photos, but I would bet money that your birth certificate is a fake."

"Look, I didn't expect to be named in the will, but I'm grateful to Presto for leaving me anything," Terrance said. "Why are you coming? You didn't inherit any land."

"It was important to Presto, so I want to see it. He booked a ticket for me, too. Right, Lana?"

"Yes, that's correct," she confirmed, keeping her voice as neutral as possible. She didn't want to interrupt the flow of their argument. It sounded like there was more going on between them than either was admitting to, and she hoped they'd accidentally reveal more.

"I don't know why you get to come—you took enough from him when he was alive. More than you deserved," Terrance said.

"Watch yourself, son," Kurt growled.

To Lana's surprise, Terrance grinned at him, but backed down, choosing that moment to make a show of dropping his backpack by the front door. When he re-entered the dining room, Kurt clanked his plate onto the table and scowled up at him.

Terrance laughed as he grabbed an apple and a croissant. "I'm going to eat these up in my room. See you when the taxi gets here."

"Good," Kurt muttered, loud enough for all to hear.

As casually as she could, Lana slipped away from the dining room and followed Terrance upstairs.

"Can we talk?" she asked as she slipped into his room and closed the door.

"What do you want?"

"Why are you Terrance Sanders on social media, and not Terrance Craighead?"

The young man stared at her, his mouth agape, before he recovered enough to sit down on the bed. "You're the first one to even look at my social media. Presto was only interested in watching clips on YouTube. Harry, too."

"Are you really George Craighead's son?"

"Sort of," he mumbled.

"You either are, or you're not."

"It's complicated. He's not my birth father, but he was in the process of adopting me when he died. The paperwork didn't go through until after he passed, which is why I never bothered to officially change my last name."

Lana sat down next to him. "Oh, okay, that explains a lot. So what happened?"

"George and my mom had been together for almost ten years when he found out he had inoperable prostate cancer. They got married so she could gain access to his pension funds after he passed. He started the official adoption process, but the cancer took him faster than anyone expected. Technically, though, I am Presto's grandson. At least, on paper."

"Why didn't you tell Presto the truth?"

"I doubt he would have done a thing for me if he'd known I wasn't George's biological son. But Presto felt so guilty about how it ended up with George that he bought my whole story without checking a thing. Those old photos really did the trick. I'm pretty sure Kurt wanted him to hire a private investigator and force me to get a DNA test, but Presto couldn't bear asking me."

Lana nodded, taking in Terrance's story. "Okay, that explains how you got ahold of the family photos and knew about George's history with Presto. But what about that birth certificate?"

"It's real easy to buy fake documents on the Strip in Vegas."

Kurt was right, Lana thought.

"Why did you get in touch with Presto?"

"If I had any other choice, I would have steered clear of him. George always said his dad was a controlling jerk. But after Mom died, I didn't have anyone left, so I figured I had nothing to lose by contacting him. I called up to Seattle and explained who I was. The next thing I know, he's flying me up to meet him."

"That was really kind of him," Lana said.

"I thought so, too, at first. But George was right; Presto didn't care about anyone but himself. He wasn't at all interested in getting to know me. He just felt guilty about how things ended up with George and thought helping me get on my feet would somehow make things right. When I resisted, he came up with this tour guide ultimatum so he could kick me out and not feel bad about it."

"That's pretty harsh."

Terrance snorted. "You didn't know him. I'm glad Presto's dead, and so are the rest of them."

"Did you poison Presto?"

"No! I didn't have any reason to. I really didn't know he'd already added me into his will. I mean, I showed up on his doorstep two months ago. And a plot of land is great, but if I could have convinced him to finance a new album, he would have been worth a lot more to me alive than dead."

Lana examined his facial expression as he spoke, trying to determine whether he was lying. *Terrance isn't motivated enough to be a tour guide, let alone a murderer*, she thought. She was looking for someone more devious, and right now, Ursula or Zach fit the bill far better than Terrance did.

"If you really think one of them killed Presto, I would start with Kurt," Terrance added when Lana remained silent.

"Kurt? Why would he hurt Presto? It's clear you two have some sort of feud going on, but I don't understand why he would harm his boss."

"He's a doctor, so he's got access to medicine and knows how much it would take to kill a man. And..." Terrance looked away to hide the smile growing on his face. "If Presto was dead, he wouldn't have to pay me blackmail."

Lana's forehead creased. "What are you talking about?"

"I caught him stealing two Rolex watches from Presto's closet right after I moved in. He's been paying me to keep my mouth shut ever since."

"So if he killed Presto, he wouldn't have to pay your blackmail anymore."

"Exactly," the young man said, his expression and tone smug.

"Well, Terrance, you're full of surprises. I didn't think you had it in you."

The young man shrugged, but Lana could see he was proud of his ingenuity. *He fits in perfectly with Presto's family*, she thought.

When she turned to leave, he laid his hand on her arm. "You aren't going to say anything to the others about me being George's adopted son, are you? If you tell the family, they'll take the land away from me."

Lana thought of Presto's children, locked in battle over everything their father possessed. None of them seemed to care that he was dead; they were only worried about how they could swindle the others out of their share. She had no interest in stepping into the middle of that wasp's nest.

"Your secret is safe with me."

37

Suspects Abound

August 16—Day Five of the Wanderlust Tour in Edinburgh, Scotland

"Hey, Lana, are you okay? I haven't heard from you for a while."

Alex sounded so tired. It was not yet seven in the morning, meaning he must have had a long night of networking parties, Lana realized.

"Oh, Alex! It's so nice to hear your voice. It's been so hectic here; I'm sorry for not calling you after the dinner, like I promised."

"What's going on? Did Ron try anything funny?"

"Will you stop with Ron? No, he did not. In fact, he's been arrested for Presto's murder."

"What happened? Are you okay?"

"I'm fine. Presto dropped dead during that dinner. The police don't know if he had a heart attack or was poisoned. But they found Presto's bottle of heart medicine in Ron's jacket, so they took him into custody."

"Did he do it?"

"I don't think so, but the police don't have any other suspects. That's why Dotty's asked me to help them by keeping my ears and eyes open."

"I hope you didn't interpret that to mean you should also actively investigate his family."

"It's important to know who I'm dealing with."

"That's true. But, honey, are you sure it's safe to be around them if you suspect one of them is a murderer? I can be up there by dinnertime. Just say the word."

"That's really sweet of you to offer, but we're leaving for the Highlands in a few hours. And I don't think I have to worry about being bumped off. Each of them had a great reason for wanting Presto dead before he married again; it's not like they have a problem with the tour or excursions."

"So do you have any suspects? Who do you think did it?"

"His son and daughter have the strongest motives, though his doctor may have been desperate enough to murder him. And I can't forget about his grandkids—they had their own reasons for wanting Presto to vanish permanently. All of it relates to money and who gets his millions. Yet, I can't see any of them being ruthless enough to actually kill him."

"Yikes! It sounds like you have more than enough suspects for one vacation," Alex laughed. "So why are you so certain Ron did not do it?"

"Because Presto's death actually inhibits his chance of winning the lawsuit he was bringing against the magician. Besides, he swears he didn't do it, and I believe him."

"Wait—did you visit him in jail?"

"I needed to talk to him first, before I crossed him off of my list of suspects."

"Honey, are you investigating Presto's death for your boss or to help free your ex-husband?"

"Trust me, Alex, I'm not going to risk my life to save my ex."

His voice broke as he whispered into the phone, "Are you still in love with him?"

"No! Ron is my past. You are my future, Alex Wright."

"Why can't his new girlfriend do the investigating?" he pressed.

His mentioning Candy brought tears to her eyes. As much as she wanted to share everything with Alex right now, it was too painful to tell him about Candy being pregnant. "I'm with them day and night, and Candy is not."

Alex was silent a moment. When he continued, his tone was far more somber. "I have to be honest with you; it scares me that you're going with them on this Highlands trip. I know you said they aren't after you, but what if someone poisons the wrong drink or meal this time?"

"Sweetheart, I meant what I said. I would never put myself in harm's way to save Ron."

"Will you keep in touch? I don't know what I would do if anything happened to you."

"Oh, Alex, I can't imagine my life without—"

Her passionate cry was interrupted by a loud speaker in the background.

"They are playing my song, Lana. My next session is about to start. I'm sorry for cutting this short. Please take care of yourself, my love."

"I will. Talk to you soon. Love you."

38

Hunting Unicorns

August 16—Day Five of the Wanderlust Tour in Edinburgh, Scotland

The ride through Edinburgh was hampered by heavy traffic, meaning they were later getting out of the city than planned.

Gwen sat close to the driver and Lana, while the rest of the family was clustered at the back. Lana figured they would ignore Presto's fiancée, but soon after they were underway, Ursula, Zach, and Viola each tried to get a moment alone with Gwen. Apparently they refused to give up on Presto's home or art collection.

Unsurprisingly, Gwen blew them off, leaning her head against the window and closing her eyes. Lana couldn't help but wonder why Gwen was torturing herself by tagging along. If she had truly wanted to see the land Presto left her, she could have arranged for a private car and driver to take her there.

When it became clear that Gwen refused to engage with them, the whispers at the back of the bus shifted into high gear. Lana wondered which tactic the family would employ next to try to regain the rights to Presto's possessions.

During their hour-long ride up the M9 freeway, Lana gazed unseeing out the window, letting her thoughts run wild. Only the bus's revving engine broke her meditative trance. They were in Stirling, she realized, and the steep hill made it difficult for the large vehicle to accelerate. The town's castle was perched on the top of a long, thin crag rising out of the valley floor that was surrounded by cliffs on three sides. Lana understood why this dramatic location had been chosen for a fortified castle.

After their driver dropped them off close to the front entrance, Lana and her group walked up a long pathway leading them towards a gate made of gray stone. Two raised paths, wide enough to accommodate several horses and riders, rose on either side of their walkway, each leading to other sections of the massive compound that was Stirling Castle.

When they were in view of the entrance, a woman with a name badge rushed over. "You must be the Wanderlust Tours group?" she said, gesturing towards Lana's badge.

"Yes, we are. I apologize for our delay; traffic coming out of Edinburgh was horrendous."

"Why don't we nip inside and get started with our tour?" she asked as she walked towards the entrance.

Before them stood several buildings sporting towers with notched roofs, delicate spires, massive chimneys, and tiny windows looking onto the cobblestoned courtyards. Lana recognized the architecture as Renaissance with late Gothic influences.

As soon as they were inside, their guide began her rehearsed speech. "Stirling Castle is the most strategically placed fortification in Scotland, which is why the Scots and English fought so hard for control of it. Within a span of fifty years, it changed hands eight times. It overlooks two important Scottish battlefields—that of Stirling Bridge and Bannockburn. Movie fans may have heard about William Wallace thanks to the film *Braveheart*. The Battle of Stirling Bridge is where he and his men enjoyed their first major victory over the English, during the First War of Scottish Independence in 1297. The Scots were able to retake the castle thanks to this triumph."

As they walked through the complex, their guide shared much about the castle's extensive history and royal inhabitants.

"Stirling Castle was home to several of the Stewart monarchs. It was here in our Chapel Royal that James V was crowned king of Scotland in 1513 when he was seventeen months old. His daughter, Mary, Queen of

Scots, was crowned in the same chapel thirty years later, when she was nine months old. Both her eldest son, King James VI, and one of her grandsons were baptized here, as well."

Their guide pointed out the Great Hall as they passed. Its yellow-gold stone glowed in comparison to the dark stone buildings surrounding it. When they reached the Royal Palace, located on the far end of the castle grounds, Lana's group was awed into silence by the intricate tapestries, richly woven draperies, and delicate paintings covering pretty much every surface of its interior. She now understood why their guide claimed it was one of the best-preserved Renaissance buildings in the United Kingdom. Simply walking around these lavishly decorated spaces was akin to being transported back in time. The many museum attendants—all dressed in full Renaissance regalia—reinforced the idea.

As they walked along the Queen's Inner Hall, Viola suddenly darted towards a particularly vibrant tapestry that was taller than she was. "I can't believe they are here! I always thought the Unicorn Tapestries were in New York. Are these the originals or replicas?"

"You know your wall hangings," their guide said as she doubled back to Viola. "These are the Stirling Tapestries. They are indeed quite similar in style, theme, and composition to the *Hunt of the Unicorn* series, which were woven in Brussels in the early 1500s and are now on display in the Cloisters Museum in New York."

She turned to the tapestries behind her, gazing lovingly up at the elaborate scenes they portrayed. "Only the very wealthy could afford tapestries, and King James V had a large collection, including two sets featuring unicorns. These mythical beasts are considered to be a symbol of purity and power. They were believed to be real when King Robert adopted them as the national animal of Scotland in the late 1300s. They still feature prominently in the royal coat of arms of Scotland and of the United Kingdom."

Lana was intrigued by the wall hangings' intricate designs. She moved closer to better examine the many tiny details woven into the busy and chaotic scene. When she did, Lana could better see the story that was being told. In the foreground of one tapestry, several noblemen seemed to be stabbing at a unicorn. The hanging was so well-executed she could see real fear in the beast's eyes. In the next scene, men were forcing the same unicorn into a round fence. *What were they doing with that poor beast?* she wondered. Regardless of the slightly disturbing designs, they were true works of art.

Viola leaned so close to the tapestries, Lana was surprised she wasn't actually touching it. "An artist I worked with last year during an exhibition created a copy of one of the *Hunt of the Unicorn* series that was almost indistinguishable from the original."

Lana knew which one she meant. One of the pieces in Viola's *Modernizing the Masters* exhibition was indeed a tapestry, but in that version the hunters used Tasers to tame the unicorn, not spears.

"The Stirling Tapestries you see here are newly woven, yet were faithfully re-created from the original designs. It cost two million pounds and thirteen years to hand-weave them."

"They are magnificent," Viola whispered as she walked slowly around the room, absorbing their rich colors and detailed designs. She and their guide spent several minutes examining and discussing all seven, as well as the difficulties the weavers encountered when re-creating them. Viola was obviously in her element, yet the rest of the group was clearly less enamored with them.

Kurt stood forlornly by, watching Viola with puppy-dog eyes. Lana couldn't take it anymore. What was his relationship with Viola? And would Presto really have cared if they were dating? Lana wished Betty hadn't already left for home; she had so many questions about Presto's family.

Lana walked casually over to Kurt. "Could I talk to you for a moment?"

"Sure, what can I do for you? Are you injured in any way?"

Lana smiled and leaned in closer. "No, nothing like that. There has been a lot of suggestive remarks made about you and Viola during this trip. And I can't help but notice how you stare at her. Are you two romantically involved?"

Kurt's eyes widened as he grabbed her arm and pulled her away from the rest of their group. Once they were out of earshot, he turned to her and whispered, "No, we were definitely not dating! I admit, I do have a crush on her, but she doesn't see me as anything but her grandpa's friend."

"Then why did you get so upset when Ursula and Zach threatened to tell Presto that you were dating?"

"Because those two can spin any story to make it seem true; it's second nature to them. The last thing I wanted was for Presto to think I was chasing after his granddaughter. I need my salary and didn't want to risk losing my job over a silly rumor. He'd already started shutting me out of his life. I figured big changes were on the horizon, and I hoped he would keep me on, regardless. But I didn't know he was planning on getting remarried or moving abroad."

"Why are you paying Terrance blackmail?"

Kurt grabbed her blouse and pulled her face up to his. "What did that little turd tell you?"

Lana was shocked by his sudden change in attitude. He looked as if he wanted to strangle Terrance with his bare hands and was practicing on her. She swatted at his arms until he let go, then took a step back and eyed Kurt warily.

"That'd you'd been stealing from Presto and were paying him to keep his mouth shut." She brushed off her blouse and wagged a finger at the much larger man. "Don't you ever touch me again."

He held up his palms. "I'm sorry. Terrance has made my life even more of a living hell than it already was."

Lana's tone softened. "What do you mean?"

Kurt diverted his eyes. "I'd made a few bad investments last year and got behind on several payments. I needed a cash injection to get me through the next few months. I didn't dare ask Presto for a loan because I didn't want him to know about my financial trouble. So I started taking cufflinks, rings, and watches that he had probably forgotten he owned. I hocked them in different shops around the city so nobody got suspicious. Everything was going great until Terrance caught me in the act."

"Weren't you worried that Presto might realize they were missing?"

Kurt shrugged. "He's got a whole closet full of stuff that he rarely wears, so the risk was low. Besides, he owed me. I gave up everything to go on the road with him, but he treated me like a servant. I'm a respected medical professional, not a massage therapist."

"So why did you pay the blackmail?"

"I didn't need Terrance bringing my thefts to Presto's attention, now, did I?"

"With Presto dead, you don't have to pay the blackmail anymore. That sounds like a good reason to bump off your boss, especially when you suspected he was cutting you out of his life."

Kurt snorted and folded his arms over his chest. "I am a doctor; I could have killed him at any time. Why would I do it now?"

"Because he was firing you."

"What would I have to gain from that? At least with him alive, I had a salary. If he'd survived, I could have guilted him into paying me for a few more months. But with him dead, I have no paycheck or access to his jewelry, thus no source of income."

Lana's eyes narrowed as she considered his words. As much as she hoped Kurt had done it, given the facts, she had to admit that the chance was small.

39

Taking in the Views

August 16—Day Five of the Wanderlust Tour in Edinburgh, Scotland

Viola and their guide discussed the tapestries for so long, their allotted time ended before she could finish their guided tour. After apologizing profusely, the castle guide rushed off to meet her next group.

As soon as she bid them farewell, Zach turned to Lana. "I hear the views across the valley are pretty spectacular, but our guide didn't bother to take us along any of the viewpoints. Do we have time to walk around before our taxi leaves for Loch Linnhe?"

She checked her watch. "We can take a forty-five-minute break before we head out again. Why don't we meet by the entrance in forty?"

After her group dispersed, Lana checked the map and decided to skip the Chapel Royal in favor of the Ladies Lookout. The views from this open terrace, situated high above the valley floor, were indeed phenomenal. From the fan-shaped balcony, she could see far across the valley. She took in the umbrella-like trees, tiny towns, and patchwork of fields that stretched for as far as her eyes could see.

After snapping several photographs, she took out a pad and jotted down notes about the location. Stirling Castle would make a perfect feature for her Travel Time blog. Her articles about the places their groups visited brought in an increasing number of website views, as well as a growing stream of income.

Though she had been recently cleared of committing libel and her reputation as a reporter had been restored, Lana had decided that investigative journalism was no longer her calling in life. Her travel-oriented blog gave her a creative outlet and the artistic freedom to write about what she wanted to, without having to worry about her words instigating legal action.

Focused on her notetaking, Lana hadn't noticed that Gwen was walking rapidly towards the other side of the lookout and that Zach was scurrying close behind. When Gwen reached the low stone wall surrounding the overlook, she turned on him. Lana couldn't hear their words, but based on their facial expressions, their conversation was not a pleasant one.

Lana scooted as nonchalantly as she could along the balcony wall, moving close enough that the strong wind carried their conversation to her.

"Dad promised to help fund this production! He knew if he didn't, my company would go bankrupt. This is my last shot at success, and I'm not going to let you take it away from me, as well. That's not what Dad would have wanted."

Gwen's laugh was bitter. "You're lying, Zach. It's exactly what your father wanted. He was sick of you relying on him for financial support. He was not going to help you out again—he was quite adamant about that. If your friends and business associates refuse to support your projects, why do you expect me to?"

"I can't ask them; Dad understood that. It's not fair that you get everything and my future suffers for it."

"Life isn't always fair, Zach. If it was, I would be getting married to your father later this week instead of being here with you insufferable crybabies. Did you even love your father? It seems like you only loved his checkbook."

"No, it wasn't like that. Whenever he was in London, we would get together. Dad and I didn't always see eye to eye, but he was there for me when I needed him."

"And when was the last time you flew over to see him? Or called to say hi, even when you didn't need anything from him?"

Zach intently studied his shoes.

"That's what Presto said—none of you did. You only picked up the phone when you were short on cash. Speaking of which…"

Lana and Zach both followed Gwen's gaze towards Ursula, striding out onto the balcony, a determined frown on her face. It softened to a sort of smile as she grew closer and realized her target was watching her approach.

"Gwen, darling. Do you have a moment? Alone?" Ursula glared at her brother.

"Good luck," he mumbled as he scampered off.

"What is it, Ursula?" From her tone, it was clear that Gwen already knew what Presto's daughter wanted.

"I don't know if Dad told you before he—you know." She slumped her head forward as her tongue lolled out of her mouth, miming a death. "But he promised to loan me ten thousand dollars to help tide me over. Work has been slow lately, and I'm already two months late on my mortgage payments. And I can't pay for Harry's next tour because my credit cards are maxed out. Either a check or wire transfer would be fine; whatever is easiest for you. Do you need my bank account number?"

"Gosh, what would be easiest for me?" Gwen tapped her chin. "I know— not to not give you any money."

Ursula's brow creased. "I don't understand."

"Your father made it quite clear to me that he was done helping you and your brother out of every financial problem you came up against. He wanted you both to learn to live within your means. He said he had been warning you for months that he was going to stop helping you, yet the first thing both of you did after you arrived was hit him up for more money."

Ursula looked at her and began to laugh. "You knew my father for what—a year? We were his children; you were about to become wife number four. And I doubt your marriage would have lasted long."

"How dare you talk to me like that!"

"I'll talk to you however I please. I don't care what you did to twist my father around your finger, but I am not standing for it. My current lawyer may not think we have a leg to stand on, but I want you to know that I'm on to you. I'm going to find one who specializes in contesting wills and see what he thinks. You can't just waltz into my father's life and take his possessions away from us. We put up with his crap for our entire lives and deserve to be compensated for it."

"Wow. I cannot believe what I am hearing."

"If you hadn't talked Dad into buying that silly castle, he wouldn't have had to worry about his pension and would have certainly have made Harry his successor, not Raphael. Presto's act should have stayed in the family!"

Gwen laughed manically. "You think I influenced Presto? Ha! That man was as stubborn as a mule. Buying the castle was his idea, as was turning it into a cultural center. He wanted to use his money to help talented individuals who didn't have the means to pursue their dreams."

"And his family, then?"

"He thought he was helping you by pushing you to provide for yourselves, instead of relying on him to take care of you. He knew he wasn't going to be around forever. That trust fund he set up for you and your family was to ensure that you never went without."

"A thousand dollars a month is nothing!"

"To most people, a thousand dollars a month is quite a bit of money. And he chose to sell his acts and stage name to Raphael because he is a talented magician worthy of them. If your son was a better performer, then Presto would have chosen him. Unfortunately, he's not. At least, not yet."

"That's it! We have put up with your presence for far too long. As far as I'm concerned, you are no longer welcome on this tour. I'm going to talk to Zach and see what he thinks." Ursula stormed off before Gwen could respond.

"What a horrible family!" Gwen screamed into the abyss before her. Lana started to walk towards her, figuring she could use a friend, when Viola entered her view. She, too, headed towards the comedian.

"Gwen, do you have a minute?" Viola's snooty tone and arrogant manners were grating on Lana's nerves.

"No, I am not going to give you any money!" Gwen yelled before Viola could continue.

She frowned but didn't retreat. "I don't want your money or Granddad's.

I only want what he promised me—his entire art collection."

"That's impossible. He'd already signed contracts with both the Scottish National Gallery and Seattle Art Museum before he died. All that remained was to arrange the paintings' transportation."

Viola grew ashen. "I don't care what he promised any museum director—we had a verbal agreement, and I upheld my end of the bargain. I spent hundreds of hours documenting all of the paintings' histories, researching the artists, and creating a classification system based on their genre, material, and period. All that was left to do was work out where each would hang. And I did all that without asking for a single dime, mind you."

"Yes, and he did leave you a large sum of money as thanks."

"You have got to be joking. That's nothing compared to what I would have earned as the museum's director. I did all of that work because it was supposed to be mine—all of it. If you hadn't come along, he never would have sold any of his paintings."

Gwen threw her hands up in the air and tried to push past, but the younger woman blocked her way.

"Viola, he didn't tell you that he was selling any of his artwork because he knew you wouldn't understand why he was doing it. His friends explained to him why his collection was too much of a jumble to draw in a crowd. But several of the paintings are high-quality examples of the artists' oeuvres, and the two museums were happy to pay good money for them. Presto wanted to see his name immortalized on a wall, and the artwork was nothing more than an investment to him. I'm sorry if he misled you to believe you could have the house and artwork, but you should have known that your aunt and uncle would have never have let that happen."

"Ursula and Zach are my problem—not yours. I still don't understand why Presto lied to me, but frankly, I don't care. And I don't believe your supposed friends acted in Presto's best interest. They just wanted the art for their own collections! I'm going to tell Aunt Ursula's lawyer about this."

"Send her pit bulls over. When she loses, she can pay my lawyer's fees," Gwen said, then walked off, unwittingly towards Lana.

Lana watched Gwen break down in tears as soon as Viola stormed off. She walked closer, unsure whether she should leave the comic alone, when Gwen's head turned sharply towards her. Her expression softened significantly when she noticed who it was.

"Are you doing okay?" Lana asked.

Gwen leaned down to rest her arms on the low stone wall and stared out into the distance. "No, not really."

"Presto's family is quite something, aren't they?"

Gwen gazed up at her in confusion, until she realized that Lana was being sarcastic. "They are pretty horrible. I can't believe he put up with their begging for so long."

"From what I have gathered from their conversations, he was rarely in Seattle when they were growing up. Perhaps giving his children money to help them with their problems was his way of compensating for not being around."

Gwen considered her words. "That's more or less what Presto hinted at, though he never said it aloud. He wasn't proud of being an absent father, but he loved performing, and the attraction of the stage was too strong to resist. I guess he figured their mothers could handle raising them without his help."

"Why did you come on this trip, knowing the family hates you?"

Gwen's expression grew sad again. "Presto took me out to the nature reserve last month, after we bought the castle. It's a gorgeous place, and I have beautiful memories of our trip. He loved hiking the land and rowing on the lake. I hope being there will remind me of our time together. Besides, I cannot wait to see his greedy family's faces when they find out what Presto really left them."

"What do you mean?" Lana asked.

Gwen smiled wickedly. "You'll see soon enough. But trust me, those leeches deserve what's coming to them."

40

A Little Time Alone

August 16—Day Five of the Wanderlust Tour in Edinburgh, Scotland

Gwen squeezed Lana's hand. "Thanks for listening. If you don't mind, I would like a little time alone before we have to get back on the bus."

"Of course, I understand completely." Lana left Gwen at the lookout and walked towards the center of the castle compound.

Since she had a few more minutes before they were to meet back at the front entrance, Lana decided to photograph the sleek, black cannons lining the Grand Battery. There were relatively few tourists here, at least in comparison to Edinburgh Castle. It was refreshing to take photos that didn't include a multitude of strangers.

When she walked back to the entrance, she was glad to see most of her group was already present. Only Gwen was missing. Since they were all early, Lana didn't think much about it, at first. But when five minutes turned into fifteen and the comic still hadn't returned, she set off to find a security guard and see whether it was possible to page her missing guest. When he shook his head, Lana had no choice but to look for Gwen herself.

"What is with this group? How hard is it to keep an eye on your watch?" Lana grumbled as she speed-walked through the many pathways winding around the exterior, on the lookout for Gwen's curly red hair. Unfortunately for Lana, many women in Scotland had curly red hair, which slowed down her search considerably.

When she circled back to the Queen Anne Gardens at the front of the castle compound, Lana checked her map, making certain she hadn't missed an overlook or passageway. The grounds were extensive enough that Gwen could have been moving in the opposite direction and Lana simply hadn't seen her. She turned to walk back to the entrance, hoping Gwen had already reappeared, when screams drew her back to the Ladies Lookout.

A woman pointed over the low wall, hysterically yelling for an ambulance as other visitors leaned over to better see what was upsetting her so. Lana followed their gaze until she spotted a body halfway down the cliff. Through the thin tree line, Lana could see curly red hair spread out over the rocks and a pool of blood slowly painting the cliff face crimson.

41

Corpse On The Cliffs

August 16—Day Five of the Wanderlust Tour in Edinburgh, Scotland

The castle's security ushered the many visitors out into Queen Anne Gardens as soon as they were aware of the corpse on the cliffs. After the police arrived and confirmed it was Gwen, everyone present was questioned. Lana's group was first up because the deceased was one of her guests.

Unfortunately, none of them admitted to seeing anything useful or suspicious, meaning the police were reliant on the other witnesses and the castle's security guards for further clues. Given the size of the complex and the low number of visitors milling about, there was a chance that no one had seen the incident.

Based on her guests' statements, none were anywhere near the Ladies Lookout when Gwen fell. Yet they also claimed not to have spoken to the dead comic since the guided tour ended. *Why would they lie?* Lana wondered. She'd seen at least three of them talking to Gwen shortly thereafter. Were they not willing to say something for fear of being wrongfully implicated in her death? Or was it because they didn't want to get caught?

She had been so focused on taking pictures for her blog, she hadn't paid attention to the visitors around her. Before she could get up the nerve to contradict her guests in front of the police, Ursula offered up a theory.

"Do you really think someone pushed her over the edge? Maybe she fell,"

Ursula said. "I mean, she was fairly petite, and it is quite windy."

Lana's irritation with her group spilled over. "I'm sorry, but that's a load of bull-honkey. Gwen wasn't a napkin; she didn't just blow over the side. Someone must have pushed her!"

"But who?" the officer asked, his pen and paper at the ready.

Lana bit her lip, unable to accuse any of her guests without knowing for certain that they were guilty. "I don't know."

"It is possible that another tourist accidentally bumped into her, she fell over, and the person who did it is too scared to admit the truth," the officer reasoned. "Luckily, there are security cameras on that side of the castle. We should know soon enough if Gwen's fall was captured on film."

Lana noticed the policeman's comments visibly affected her group, causing most of them to tense up.

"But, Officer, we have to leave right away. We have an appointment in Loch Linnhe and can't be late," Viola insisted.

"We are asking everyone to remain here until we have reviewed all of the security footage. Based on what we see, we may have further questions. Please have a cup of tea or coffee while you wait." He said it in a friendly way, but it was clear that staying was not voluntary.

As they waited for the officer to return, Lana's nerves were jangling. Was it an accident, or was someone in her tour group a cold-blooded killer? And if Gwen's fall was not captured on camera, would they get away with murder—again?

When the police officer returned and let them know that Gwen's fall had not been filmed, her group released a collective sigh of relief. Lana, on the other hand, couldn't stop trembling. Maybe coming along on this trip was not such a hot idea, after all.

If one of them had poisoned Presto and pushed Gwen off that overlook, what else would they do to prevent the others from inheriting? And did Lana want to risk getting accidentally caught in their crosshairs?

42

Levels of Deviousness

August 16—Day Five of the Wanderlust Tour in Edinburgh, Scotland

The narrow road they were traveling upon split the hillside in two. Long ago it must have been a riverbed, Lana figured, and a deep one at that. Now it was a winding path leading them through the desolate and starkly beautiful Scottish Highlands.

The rolling hills on both sides towered over their taxi. Clouds passed overhead, their shadows racing across the scraggly greens and yellows of the hillside. Everything seemed bigger somehow in this vast, open space—the roads, hills, and even the sky. Lana had never felt so small and alone. There were very few trees, as if the wind had swept them all away, and they traveled long stretches without seeing other cars. She truly hoped their minivan didn't break down.

As the taxi drove on, Lana stared out the window unseeingly. All she could think about was who stood to inherit the most from Presto and Gwen's deaths. Whoever had killed them was not only ruthless, but also unafraid of taking chances. There were enough visitors taking pictures and shooting videos around the Stirling Castle complex that there was still a chance Gwen's murder had been recorded on film. But would the person show their footage to the police before her group left Scotland?

Lana wouldn't be surprised if the one responsible for both deaths would try to leave the country as soon as possible. But, on the other hand, she wouldn't be shocked if all of her guests wanted to leave after they'd seen their property. From what Presto and Gwen had said, it didn't sound like they could do much more than hike around it at the moment.

She contemplated sneaking off and letting her guests fend for themselves, but she knew Dotty would fire her for doing so. Not that her boss would want her to risk her life. But was she really in danger? Without her help, Lana doubted any of them could find their way back to Edinburgh, let alone their plots of land. The more she thought it, the more she'd come to realize the murders couldn't have been premeditated, but had been spur-of-the-moment decisions. If she kept her guard up and made certain no one tampered with her food or drink, she should be alright, she reckoned.

Besides, if she left now, she would never truly know whether one of her group had harmed Presto or Gwen, and Ron would remain in custody for a murder he most likely did not commit.

As their taxi drove on to Loch Linnhe, Lana realized she had no choice but to figure out who was behind both murders, before another victim fell or her group wanted to fly home.

When Zach approached the front of the bus, Lana saw her chance to continue her investigations.

"Hi, Lana, do you know when we will be arriving at Loch Linnhe?"

"In about two hours."

"Okay, thanks."

When he turned to leave, Lana patted the chair opposite her. "Have a seat. I need to ask you something, Zach."

He startled at the use of his name, but did as he was told. "What can I do for you?"

"How about telling me the truth. I know you lied about your play's recent success. Your romance isn't playing on the West End; it was a tryout. I also know that you lied to the police about when you talked to Gwen last; I saw you two fighting on the Ladies Lookout after the tour ended. Did you go back later and push her over?"

"No!" he shrieked and then lowered his head and voice so his family couldn't hear their conversation. "I did not hurt Gwen. Why would I? Killing her isn't going to get us Dad's house back. You were there when Presto's will was read; the only way we could have done that was to wear her down. Now her relatives will probably inherit it."

"But Ursula's lawyer—"

Zach finished her sentence. "Doesn't stand a chance. Now that Gwen is gone, we can kiss Dad's house goodbye. Viola will probably get any paintings that he hadn't already sold, but that's it. And I'm sure Ursula will fight her claim on them now that the house seems to be unattainable. That's for my sister to duke out; I honestly don't care what happens with the rest of Dad's things."

"But why did you insist Presto drink that whisky before his dinner? Did you put something in it?"

"Heavens, no! Why would I have killed him?"

"For the money. I heard you talking on the phone. You were telling someone that you were about to inherit millions."

"I was bluffing in the hopes that he wouldn't cancel my dates. Even if we had inherited the house—as I expected we would—it would have taken months, perhaps years, to sell it and split up the profits. I wouldn't be surprised if Dad had double-mortgaged it and didn't tell us. He was that kind of guy. No, I forced that drink on him because I just wanted to loosen him up before I asked him for another loan."

Lana's eyebrows shot up. "You were going to hit him up for money during the dinner honoring him?"

"Yes, well, I only had a few days left to reserve my spot. The theater has given my dates to another production company now that there is no inheritance to speak of. Don't you see? Presto was worth more to me alive than dead. He said we'd only get an allowance, but if he had moved to Edinburgh, I could have talked him into giving me more."

Lana was shocked by his resoluteness and calmness. *That's real love*, she thought sarcastically. "But you needed the money to fund your play. Your dad's loan was your only chance at securing the dates, right?"

"No, I wanted Dad to loan me the money so I wouldn't have to go crawling back to my ex-wife. But she found out about my investors abandoning me and Dad cutting me out of his will. She feels so bad about it that she's arranged a two-week run at a theater close to the West End. She's even put word out among her friends and associates that my plays are worth investing in. With a little luck, we'll find a few new backers and be back on our feet in no time."

"But why all the begging if it was so easy for you to get help?"

"I'd always told Dad that it was my talent that got our productions into West End theaters, but it was really my ex-wife and her connections. After we divorced last year, I wanted to prove to her that I could do it on my own. But I couldn't and felt ashamed. That's why I refused to ask her for help."

Lana leaned back and studied Zach with new eyes. "That actually makes sense." She was so surprised by his admission that she didn't know what to ask next. Despite all of his begging, he really didn't need to kill Presto to achieve his goals.

Zach looked at her questioningly. "Can I go now?"

"Yes, of course, thanks for your time," Lana said as he hurried back to his family. *I guess I can cross him off my list of suspects*, she thought.

43

Lord Zachery

August 16—Day Five of the Wanderlust Tour in Edinburgh, Scotland

After Zach returned to his seat, Lana noticed that Ursula was talking on the phone. "You have to get that will invalidated. Presto's things shouldn't go to Gwen; they weren't even married!"

It must be her lawyer again, Lana thought. She hoped he was getting paid well to deal with Ursula's constant calls and numerous demands.

When Ursula hung up, her phone immediately began beeping, signaling she had a new text message. After she read it, she turned to her family and announced, "Good news and bad news, folks. My lawyer still thinks we have a teeny-tiny shot at getting Dad's house back. A lot of it depends on who Gwen left her possessions to, and whether or not Presto signed any documents stating he owed her for half of that castle. If he didn't, and Gwen didn't specifically mention the property in her will, then we have a fighting chance. He's now going to get in touch with Gwen's lawyers and try to find out more about who she named as beneficiary. That's the bad news."

"And the good news?" Harry asked when his mother paused to heighten the tension.

"My realtor friend said one-thousand-acre plots are worth at least a half-million, maybe more."

Zach clapped his hands as the rest cheered.

"No way!" Terrance exclaimed. "Now I can get my band back together and pay for a great producer."

"And I'll be able to use the profits of my plot to pay for my next tour," Harry said happily.

"Now my bed-and-breakfast idea can finally happen! I already told her to be on the lookout for a cute hotel for sale, preferably on the ocean. More celebrities will come if they know they can sunbathe and surf on a private beach," Ursula said.

Viola's brows furrowed together as she gazed at her aunt. "But Aunt Ursula, why don't you open a B&B in your home? It's certainly spacious enough, and you shouldn't have trouble getting ahold of Presto's old movie posters and props to use as decoration, now that Gwen is gone."

Ursula sucked up a lungful of air. "If you must know, my acting roles have been a bit more sporadic lately than I may have let on. I've gotten behind on the upkeep, and it would need extensive renovation work before it would be glamorous enough to attract jetsetters."

Zach's eyebrows arched as a smile played on his lips. Ursula pushed on before her brother could get in a jab. "Besides, a new idea deserves a new space. It will be inspiring to start afresh." She turned to Zach. "What about you, little brother?"

"If I sell the whole plot, I won't have to worry about finding investors anytime soon."

"What about you, Viola?" Kurt asked. "What are you going to do with your land?"

"That's a great question. I'm a city girl so I can't imagine wanting to live out here. Maybe I'll hang on to it for a while and let it appreciate in value before I sell it."

Viola held up the thick envelope of information that Presto's lawyer had given her and the rest of her family, concerning their plots of land. "Have any of you read this? I wonder where our land is located exactly."

"Gosh, after everything that happened since the lawyer gave them to us, I forgot to look through it!" Ursula tore hers open and let the brochures and documents fall into her lap.

"Oh, my. There's so much information here: a welcome letter, membership card, landowners' handbook, and a certificate of ownership…ooh!" Ursula squealed as she held up a notepad with a Scottish coat of arms on it. "Would you look at that—it's got our emblem on it! Aren't they cute?"

"We can call ourselves Laird, Lord, or Lady of Linnhe," Viola said, reading another piece of paperwork aloud.

"Really? That will make a huge difference in London. They are so obsessed with titles. It'll probably be even easier to find more backers now," Zach said.

"What's this DVD?" Harry asked, holding up a disc. *Highland Park: The Story So Far*. What's that supposed to mean?"

"It looks like Dad was contributing to a nature reserve in the area," his mother replied. "Harry, do you have a postcard in your packet?"

He held his up for his mother to see.

"That's odd; it's the same postcard I received. It says that the photo is of our property, but that's not possible. Dad didn't leave us all the same piece of land, so this must be of that nature reserve."

Zach's face started to pale. "There's one way to check. The GPS coordinates of our plots are on the certificate of ownership. Are they the same?"

He ticked the coordinates of his land into his phone as Ursula did the same with hers. After they'd confirmed where each other's plots were, Zach said, "They appeared to be next to each other, but are definitely not the same location."

"Phew, for a second there, I thought Presto was pulling another one of his tricks and had gifted us all the same plot of land," Viola said.

"Lord Zachery." The theater maker's voice took on a lilting tone. "Wouldn't that be the life? I could sell half of my plot and build my own castle and live like a real lord." He picked up the landowner's handbook and began flipping through it.

Ursula stared outside, seeming to take in the dramatic landscape for the first time. "We could scrap the ocean idea and build a hunting lodge on one of our plots, instead. It would be a great angle for a show—celebrities abroad always do well with the ratings."

"Would you really want to live out here, Mom?" Harry asked, his voice filled with disdain as he gazed out at the windswept hills and lonely stretch of road. "It's so boring."

"Nonsense—it's beautiful, in a dramatic way. We could first see how much we could get for the land before deciding, but I think it's got potential. We could hire a caretaker or hotel manager to run things, if we don't want to live out here permanently. Presto did say you could hike and sail in that nature reserve. That would draw people to our lodge."

"Wait a second, sis." Zach held up the landowner's handbook. "It says here that hunting and fishing are forbidden."

Ursula shook her head resolutely. "That can't be; you must be reading it incorrectly. What else is there to do out here? I'm certain that will be the big draw for my lodge's clientele. We could buy a few boats and arrange tours and fishing trips. We might want to work together, little brother," she said. "It would make a wonderful retreat for artists and theater makers, as well."

Ursula turned to her niece. "Viola, if you want to rent me the rights to your land, I could add a camping ground next to my hunting lodge."

"No matter what the land is like, I'm just glad that Grandpa thought to leave us all property," Harry said.

"After all those threats about cutting us off, he really was taking care of us, wasn't he?" Ursula agreed.

"Do you remember when Granddad cancelled one of his tour dates so he could perform at my tenth birthday party, Mom? He freaked out my friends with his illusions. Billy even peed in his pants!"

Ursula laughed along with her son. "That was hilarious. Poor little Billy. Dad could be so generous, when he wanted to be. That reminds me of the time that he…"

For the first time since Presto's death, his family shared stories about their father and grandfather, laughing together about his silly jokes and kind-hearted actions. Lana was glad to hear them talk about Presto in a positive light; it was only too bad that he had to leave them something significant before they remembered the good in him.

44

Highland Park Nature Reserve

August 16—Day Five of the Wanderlust Tour in Edinburgh, Scotland

When they stepped out of the taxi, Presto's family gasped simultaneously, overcome by the beauty surrounding them. The visitor center was located in a deep valley surrounded by tall, sloping hills covered in young trees and saplings. In the distance was a lake; the sunshine sparkling off of its surface seemed to beckon to them.

"I can see why Dad bought us property out here. It's gorgeous," Ursula whispered, as if she was afraid to disturb the natural perfection.

"Although an airport closer by would help attract more customers. I'll have to see how we can spin that long ride over. It would have been better if he'd bought us land closer to a city center," she added as she wandered over to a cluster of saplings. "Why are these trees so young? The way Dad went on and on about this place, I expected to see old-growth forests."

And we're back, Lana thought, wondering whether anyone in Presto's family was capable of appreciating his generosity.

"Welcome to Highland Park Nature Reserve!" a voice exclaimed in a thick Scottish burl. Lana turned to find an older woman dressed in hiking gear standing behind them. A name badge that read "VOLUNTEER" was pinned to her chest. "Those trees are so young because this land was heavily logged and practically barren when we purchased it, which made it a perfect

210

location for our restoration project."

The older woman glanced over the group, apparently not noticing that most were appropriately dressed for a ballroom gala, not a hike in the woods. "Did you already reserve a tour of your property? I hope you did; there are so many sponsors who want to see their plots, we're booked up for the next three days."

"Sponsors?" Zach asked, a frown creasing his forehead.

Lana stepped forward and handed the woman a sheet of paper. "Here is our reservation. It was originally made in the name of Gary Craighead, but I am afraid he can't be with us today," she said, unable to tell the volunteer the full truth. There was no reason for her to know that he was dead.

"That's too bad Gary can't join us; we always enjoyed it when he visited. Why don't we head over to the golf carts? I am afraid we can't delay the tour any longer, otherwise we won't have time to see all of your plots in the time we have together."

"How many other investors are part of this development project?" Zach asked.

The woman laughed. "Investors? You must live in the city. We have thousands of 'investors,'" she explained, using her fingers to emphasize the last word spoken, "but most live overseas and have not yet visited their souvenir plots. Still, we do have about fifty visitors a day."

"There's that phrase again, 'souvenir plot.' What does that mean exactly?" Zach asked.

"Who cares, little brother, as long as our names are on the titles." Ursula brushed his question off as she lowered her sunglasses and took in their surroundings. "The scenery is definitely dramatic enough for television. Do they have reality shows in Scotland?"

Their guide, however, did not ignore Zach. "There is a loophole in Scottish law that allows us to sell souvenir plots in exchange for your financial support. The owner is not allowed to live or build upon the land, but they do have the right to use the title laird, lord, or lady. That's how we were able to restore this area so quickly. When we started fifteen years ago, there was not a single tree left, and the lake was nothing more than a mud pool.

Thanks to our conservation work and your generosity, future generations will only see a wild forest they can hike through and a clean lake they can swim in."

Ursula bowed to her son. "Lord Harry, I presume? Or do you fancy laird?"

"I don't think my friends could spell the second one. Though a title will be great for marketing: Lord Harry the Magnificent," he said with a laugh as his mother offered him a smile in return.

Zach stopped and put his hands on his hips. "Will you two stop it? Lady, what exactly are you saying? You keep talking about support and conservation. We were led to believe that we were one of a few participating in this project, not one of thousands. How many neighbors are we going to have to put up with?"

Ursula laid a hand on the volunteer's arm. "Have any of them already built a hunting lodge?"

The woman's eyes widened to saucers. "Heavens, no. Hunting and fishing are strictly forbidden in this nature preserve. We are doing all we can to restore the natural balance, not create hunting grounds for the rich."

She started to walk towards a row of parked golf carts, when she added, "And as I said, no one is allowed to build here. We are considering creating a basic campground outside of the property's boundaries, but are concerned it will upset our current sponsors. They are paying to create a natural reserve, not a tourist facility. We're sending out a survey with our next newsletter."

"Wait—what? That makes no sense. Why did our father leave us property that we can't build on? What kind of place is this?" Ursula demanded.

"A natural sanctuary," the volunteer responded, a puzzled frown on her face. "Did you not get the welcome packet? Everything is explained in detail. We even included a video for those who don't want to read the fine print. By purchasing a souvenir plot, you are donating to the restoration of this land in exchange for the use of the title Lord, Laird, or Lady of Linnhe."

"A sanctuary—as in a park? Dad bought us plots inside of a national park?" Zach screamed, as the truth finally sank in.

"Yes," the woman answered, unaware of the reaction that single word would bring.

Ursula raised her fists to the heavens and began screaming obscenities at her deceased father while Zach squatted down and sobbed quietly into his hands. Kurt tried to comfort Viola, but she brushed off his attention and strode away from the group, her gaze focused on the lake beyond. Harry and Terrance walked off to the side and sat on a log while they watched their elders.

Lana silently watched the family break down, their hopes and dreams having been dashed by this nature-loving volunteer.

"Would you like to see your plots or to take a tour of the park?" the Scottish woman asked.

When the family didn't react, Lana said, "I don't think they do, but thank you for your time."

The volunteer moved in close to Lana and softly asked, "Lassie, why are they reacting so strangely? It's as if they thought they had purchased large plots of land—not a souvenir title."

"I'm afraid that's what they were led to believe."

The volunteer's mouth dropped open. "That's horrible. But I don't understand how it could have happened; everything is spelled out quite clearly on the website and in the information packet."

"Their recently deceased father left them all a souvenir plot. They got caught up in the excitement of inheriting land and didn't look through the information they'd received about it. I don't think their dad even considered that none of them would read the documents you provided."

Lana really didn't think Presto was trying to trick his family. This trip was part of the tour he had arranged. If he had lived, he would have shown them that their plots were part of a nature conservation, not a place to build a castle or hunting lodge.

The volunteer tsked as she looked at Presto's family, spread out around the small clearing, each dealing with this news in their own way. "If there is anything we can do to ease their pain, please let me know. I can always take them on a tour later, if they wish."

"I really don't think they are really interested in seeing the land anymore."

The woman nodded. "I'd better get ready for my next group. Good luck."

"How much can we sell it for?" Zach called out when the woman started to walk away.

She slowly turned towards him. "You can gift your plots to someone else, but you cannot sell them. Besides, they only cost a few hundred dollars; it's not an investment that grows in time."

"A few hundred dollars? That's all Presto could fork out for us?" Ursula yelled. The volunteer backed slowly away from the family, before quickly turning and sprinting towards the visitor center.

45

It Was All For Nothing!

August 16—Day Five of the Wanderlust Tour in Edinburgh, Scotland

For the first time during this trip, Lana actually felt bad for this family. They may have been spoiled and arrogant, but none of them deserved this nasty surprise.

Curiosity drove Lana to walk away from the others and look up the Highland Park website. From what she could see, it was not a scam, but a reputable conservation project. Thanks to Scottish law, anyone who donated to the nature reserve could also officially add the title Laird, Lord, or Lady of Linnhe to their name. Lana could imagine for many rich Americans that alone would be a reason to buy a plot.

When Viola walked over to her, Lana closed her phone. "Can you change my flight?" the younger woman asked. "I want to go home as soon as possible. There's no reason to stay here."

"Sure, no problem," Lana said as her phone began to ring. "Give me a moment, then I'll see if anyone else wants to leave right away." Lana half turned away from Viola as she answered. "This is Lana Hansen."

To her surprise, it was Roger, the curator who had given them a private tour at the Scottish National Museum. "Hello, Roger. What can I do for you?"

At the use of the curator's name, Viola stepped closer and leaned her head forward, obviously trying to listen in.

"Gwen is not answering her phone, but she warned me that her battery kept dying, so she gave me your number, as well. Is Gwen with you now? I need to speak to her for a moment."

"I'm so sorry to have to tell you this, but Gwen is dead."

"What! How could that be? What happened to her?"

Lana stepped away from Viola, feeling increasingly uncomfortable with having her standing so close, and began pacing. "She fell over the railing at Stirling Castle during our visit this morning."

"What a horrible way to die."

"I have to agree with you there. Is there anything we can do for you?" Lana asked.

"No, I just wanted to thank Gwen for sending over the artwork so quickly."

"Do you mean the paintings Presto wanted to sell to you? I got the impression that they hadn't yet been crated up for shipment."

"Yes, well, I'm not certain who did the work, but I just received confirmation from the shipping company that the twenty paintings he earmarked for us have left Seattle and are on their way to bonnie Scotland."

Lana looked automatically to Viola, who was watching her closely. "That is good news. I'll share it with the family," she said before hanging up, wondering whether she would. She didn't think Viola or any of the others would actually be pleased to hear that those twenty paintings were on their way to Edinburgh. Viola would definitely go ballistic; among them were two she'd had restored in the hope of featuring them in her future museum.

When she turned to walk away, Viola grabbed her arm. Her grip was far stronger than Lana expected. "Why did the curator want to speak to Gwen?"

Lana blew out her cheeks, wondering what to say, when the younger woman's nails dug into her skin. "You're hurting me."

"What did he say?"

"He was calling to thank Gwen for sending over the twenty paintings Presto had promised him."

Viola's eyes bulged as Lana's words seemed to sink in. "It was all for nothing!"

Her screams tore at Lana's soul. After releasing her arm, Viola dashed off towards the shoreline.

What a spoiled brat, she thought as she watched the young woman run away. All that crying and carrying on, simply because she didn't get exactly what she wanted. Why couldn't Viola be happy with part of the collection? It was still far better than inheriting none of Presto's artwork.

On the other hand, Viola had spent so much time researching the artists and paintings while dreaming about them filling her museum one day. Lana could imagine she saw them as her children, not as soulless objects decorating Presto's walls.

When Lana headed back to the group, Harry was busy calming his mother down. Zach was still weeping, but his tears had lessened to a stream instead of a waterfall. Terrance and Kurt remained on the sidelines; both looked as if they wanted to be anywhere but here.

"What are we supposed to do now, Lana?" Harry asked.

Lana threw up her hands. "How am I supposed to know? I was hired to get you from point A to point B—I cannot help you with this mess."

"I say we head back to civilization. I need a drink," Zach stated before beginning to walk towards their taxi. Ursula, Harry, and Terrance followed suit.

Kurt had to drag Viola away from the lake. "Come on, kid. All is not yet lost," he said while pulling her towards the awaiting taxi.

After they were all inside, Lana asked, "What do you want to do? We can head straight back to Edinburgh; the house is available to us for three more days. Or would you prefer to go to the hotel on the lake, as we originally planned? It's a twenty-minute ride from here."

She had booked them in at a hotel located close by, so they could come back and visit their properties in the morning—though she doubted her group would want to return.

"I want to go to the hotel. I don't think I can handle driving all the way back to Edinburgh right now. Dad's treachery has worn me out," Zach said. Lana figured he was more interested in their bar than the sleeping arrangements.

"I second that. Though the way I'm feeling right now, I might just drown myself in that lake," Ursula said, her tone grim.

Startled by her words, Harry grabbed his mom's hand. "We're going to get through this, Mom. Once my show sells out, we'll be able to…"

Ursula laughed at her son. "Sold out? We had to cancel eleven shows on your last tour because we didn't sell enough tickets. Don't you get it, Harry? You don't have enough name recognition or talent to fill the halls. Dad was right; you need to take a step back and focus on improving your skills before we waste any more money setting up a tour for you."

Harry's mouth dropped open in shock. Lana's did, too. That was the most rational thing Ursula had said during this entire trip.

46

Drowning Their Sorrows

August 16—Day Five of the Wanderlust Tour in Edinburgh, Scotland

After Lana got her group checked into the hotel, she arranged for a late dinner, knowing they all wanted a drink first. Considering how despondent they were, she wondered whether any of them would actually want to eat later or whether they would rather drown their sorrows in a bottle.

Lana then popped up to her room for a quick shower. *What a day*, she thought as the water washed the stress away. Presto was full of surprises, even in death.

When she came back down to the lobby, feeling clean and refreshed, Lana saw Viola talking to the hotel receptionist. After she thanked the man and walked away from the counter, Lana rushed over to her guest.

"Hi, Viola. Can I help you with anything?"

"No, I've already taken care of it." Viola stalked off towards the double doors leading down to the lake. She had become even more distant and withdrawn since their trip to the Highland Park Nature Reserve.

Curiosity made Lana join the check-in line, in an attempt to find out what Viola had wanted. Unfortunately, the hotel staff was so busy checking in a large group of hikers that Lana eventually gave up, figuring she could always come back later. Now it was time to explore the surrounding nature, before it got too dark to do so.

Lana stepped outside and took in the glorious views of the lake and tree-lined hills. A set of trail markers pointed in three directions, each leading hikers to another part of the forest. Lana chose the path that would take her around the small lake upon which the hotel was situated.

On her way down to the trailhead, Lana passed her group. They were clustered together in lawn chairs close to the shoreline. Two empty bottles and several unopened ones covered their table. She waved at them and walked quickly down the path and away from her guests. She stopped when all she could hear was the water and wildlife. After climbing up onto a half-submerged boulder, Lana lay back on the cold stone and let herself get lost in the rhythmic lapping of the waves and the calls of birds flying overhead.

The meditative sounds helped to clear her mind. Trying to figure out who'd poisoned Presto and pushed Gwen over was doing her head in. Maybe she was looking at this the wrong way. Had the same person murdered Gwen and Presto? If it was the same killer, Ron couldn't have done it. But if Presto and Gwen had been killed for different reasons, then Gwen's death wouldn't automatically mean his release from police custody.

Lana's head was swimming with motives and possibilities. She had originally believed that Presto's family had many reasons for wanting him dead. Yet none were as pressing as she'd originally thought.

So had Ron killed Presto? It was looking more likely. Lana had looked up intellectual property theft and realized it was going to be incredibly difficult for Ron to prove that Presto had stolen his idea. In the world of magic, borrowing acts and "improving" upon them was quite common. And most magicians didn't want to submit their tricks to the US Patent Office because they would have to explain precisely how the act worked, which made it even more difficult to prove it was outright theft.

If Ron had killed Presto, who'd pushed Gwen over the cliff? Had it been a clumsy tourist? Had she been caught in a breeze and floated over? Or had someone stalking Gwen seen their chance to kill her during their trip to Stirling Castle?

Lana skipped a rock along the water's edge, watching it create tiny rings in the moonlight. If it wasn't one of Presto's family members, then she and the police were most likely out of luck.

When her phone's alarm went off, reminding her of their dinner reservation, a flock of birds, startled by the noise, suddenly flew over the lake. Their low-level flight cast fascinating shadows on the water's surface. She watched the play of moonlight until it faded, then stood up, feeling more refreshed than she had in days.

When she went to fetch her group, they were still outside on the lawn, but were now surrounded by a cluster of hotel guests. And no wonder, Lana thought, Ursula and Zach were sloshing their drinks while telling loud stories about their superstar friends.

As she approached, Ursula began telling her audience about how the lake reminded her of filming with George Clooney last summer. Lana let it slide. "It's time to eat, folks. Looks like you need it."

"That's a wonderful idea," Ursula said as she pushed herself off the lawn chair. Instead of rising, she fell over and rolled across the lawn. Zach tried to pull her up, but he managed to land next to her instead. The two burst into giggles, which led to them rolling around on the grass and trying to tickle each other. Zach's shrieks of laughter brought the hotel's owner outside, out of concern for his hotel guests. Once he'd established that all was well, his staff helped the tipsy guests into the dining room's waiting area.

While a waiter went to see whether their table was ready, Ursula's phone began to beep, signaling a new message. After she'd read it, she sprung up out of her chair and began dancing between the tables, narrowly missing several shocked patrons' wine glasses as she did.

"Why are you so happy?" Zach slurred.

"Because my realtor friend is a genius!" she shrieked. "After I texted her about this land fiasco, she begged me to let her sell my house. She's been saying for weeks that it would be perfect for one of her new clients, and she was right! She's already gotten him to commit to paying more for it than I ever dreamed possible, which means I'll be able to buy whatever I want."

Harry looked up to his mother, his eyes glistening. "You sold our house?"

Ursula grabbed his cheeks and pinched them lightly. "Plan B, darling.

I'm going to use the profits to start a magic-themed bed-and-breakfast in a seaside town. Presto's house wasn't the draw—it's his name and reputation. We can still use his props and posters to decorate whatever we end up buying. And I'll make sure there's a podium where you can perform whenever you want. And we'll get other magicians in to help draw an even bigger crowd. With all the celebrities and their entourages passing through, someone is bound to recognize your talent!"

Harry nodded absently, but Lana could see that he wasn't yet over the shock of his mother's news.

Ursula grabbed her son and held him tight. "It's all going to work out, Harry. Once this sale goes through, we can do whatever we want. Don't you see? Dad did get his way, after all. We didn't need his help as much as we thought we did."

47

A Rich Man's World

August 16—Day Five of the Wanderlust Tour in Edinburgh, Scotland

Dinner was a mess because her group could barely stay seated or awake. None of them made it to the second course. After she and the hotel staff helped her guests up to their rooms, Lana returned to the dining room to finish her meal alone.

The ABBA song *Money, Money, Money* looped through her head. She was definitely not a member of the rich man's world, but she knew from her experiences with her wealthiest clients that money could make a person do really crazy things—even commit murder. Especially when one was faced with losing it.

As certain as she had been two days ago that one of Presto's family members had poisoned him, now she wasn't so sure. None of them got exactly what they wanted or expected from Presto, yet they all landed on their feet, regardless.

Yet someone did murder Presto and Gwen—both deaths couldn't have been accidents. One of her guests must be lying about their actions—but which one?

It couldn't have been Terrance, Lana decided. He hadn't expected to be named in the will, meaning it would have made no sense for him to kill Presto. And even less to push Gwen over the side—Terrance gained nothing from her death.

Lana thought about the multimillion-dollar house and flush bank accounts Zach and Ursula had thought they would be inheriting, along with their siblings. Yet as mad as they had been, once they got over their initial shock, both of Presto's children were okay. Ursula had a house to sell, and Zach's network reached out with a helping hand.

Kurt profited from Presto's death, but not by much. Although he no longer had to pay Terrance blackmail, Presto's passing also meant the physician was out of a job. However, if the magician had lived, Kurt would have been unemployed anyway. The one-time bonus he received in Presto's will wasn't enough to kill for. If the gossip columns were to be believed, ten thousand dollars would not solve Kurt's financial problems, not by a long shot.

Only Viola and Harry didn't get what they'd wanted or expected. Viola had been certain she was going to inherit Presto's art collection and Harry his secrets and stage name. Yet both had received a nasty surprise. What would they have gained by killing Presto during that dinner honoring him?

Harry'd had no idea that Presto had already signed an agreement with Raphael, giving the other magician the rights to use his granddad's stage name and acts. Had Harry and Ursula thought that if Presto died before the handover, Harry would still have a shot at both? Ursula did seem to have her lawyer on speed dial; Lana wouldn't be surprised if he was already trying to get the contract with Raphael annulled. *Fat chance*, Lana thought, Presto had signed the sales agreement months before his death. Yet if Ursula's bed-and-breakfast idea took off, he would still have a place to perform and improve his craft. So all was not lost for the young man.

What about Viola? It was possible that she'd thought if Presto died before the dinner ended, she could have prevented the artwork's shipment and could contest the agreements Presto had signed with the two museums. But she was in the same situation as Harry. Given the fact that Presto had signed the sales contracts weeks before his death, it was unlikely Viola would have won that fight.

Although Presto had already sold thirty paintings to two museums, there were eighty remaining that Viola would probably inherit. She could use the rest to start her precious museum—if her aunt Ursula didn't contest Viola's right to keep the artwork.

Were there enough top-quality pieces left in his collection? Presto had said he was selling the better paintings to the museums. Was that why she was so upset—because her idea of opening a museum was no longer feasible?

As much as Viola wanted to be the new museum's director, she wasn't reliant on that position for an income. The trust fund her mother had left her was apparently quite robust, based on her gem-encrusted rings and bracelets. Money was probably not a motive for Viola to murder.

Yet she wasn't satisfied with only part of the collection—she was obsessed with having all of the artwork. *Such a spoiled young woman*, Lana thought when recalling Viola's yelp that "It was all for nothing" after the curator called to let them know the twenty paintings were on their way to Scotland.

She was particularly upset that Presto had sold two of the paintings that she'd had cleaned. Why were they so special? The museum curator made clear during their private tour that Presto's artwork was more a reflection of his taste than a collection containing important works by preeminent painters. But what if he was wrong?

So how much was the artwork really worth? The only thing left on her to-do list was to call Henry & Sons, the art restoration firm that had worked on Presto's paintings. They might be willing to tell her how much he taxed them for.

48

Matching Brushstrokes

August 16—Day Five of the Wanderlust Tour in Edinburgh, Scotland

After dinner, Lana checked her world clock and saw that Henry & Sons was open. *No time like the present*, she thought as she picked up the phone.

After a polite, older man answered, Lana explained why she was calling. He immediately began cursing Viola's name.

"I wish I'd never met her. A Scottish curator has been hounding me for information about two of Presto's paintings. He seems to think they are forgeries! Luckily, we always take photos of the art before and during our restoration work. We will do everything we can to help clarify this misunderstanding, but I want to make absolutely clear that we would never tax a forgery as if it was genuine."

"I apologize for upsetting you. I was with the curator earlier this week, and he did mention his suspicions as a possible reason for not purchasing those two paintings from Presto. That is partly why I am calling—to find out if there was any basis for his reservations."

"I don't understand. Those two were in excellent condition—there was very little for me to do but clean them. I most certainly did not repaint entire sections, as that curator claims. And even if I had, I specialize in matching an artist's brushstrokes. I am a professional, after all."

The man sounded so distraught, Lana felt bad for calling. But she needed answers if she was going to figure out why Viola was so obsessed with Presto's artwork. "How many paintings have you cleaned or restored for Presto?"

"Twenty-one in the last six months. But only a few required a touchup. All of his paintings were really well cared for."

Alarm bells went off in Lana's head. "Wait a second—Viola said they were badly cracked and pieces of the paint had come loose."

"Not at all," the man said, his tone firm. "Otherwise, it would have taken me far longer to clean and restore the works."

Lana's mind raced. Viola had sworn to the Scottish museum's curator that the artwork in question was badly damaged, which explained why it had been extensively retouched. The paintings the curator had seen couldn't be the same ones that Henry & Sons had restored. Why had Viola lied?

"Did you deliver the artwork to Presto's home after you cleaned it?" she asked.

"No, Viola picked them up with a rented van each time."

"Is that normal?"

"No, it was rather unusual, but then again, so was Presto. He was paying us double our normal fee to put his work first, so we were happy to accommodate his wishes."

"Did you know that Viola was having these works cleaned in preparation for display in a private museum?"

His laughter filled the line, and it took him a few seconds to regain his composure. "Excuse me, that wasn't polite. Yes, I knew. That museum idea was a nice way of stroking her grandfather's ego, but it wouldn't have succeeded."

"What do you mean?"

"The pieces she brought in were worth between fifty and one hundred thousand dollars. That's not much, if you are talking about museum-quality work. After she told me what she was planning, I asked to see the inventory list. Frankly, I was surprised she wanted to open a museum with them as the basis—they are all good works, but none are spectacular. There are several important artists represented in his collection, but the paintings are their earlier works, not their masterpieces."

Lana couldn't believe what she was hearing. "So it wouldn't have been enough for a museum?"

"No. Opening a private museum is an expensive endeavor because your target audience is rather small and it costs quite a bit of money to keep the art in good condition. If there is nothing special or unique on display that will attract visitors in droves, then it will quickly go bankrupt."

"Did Viola know what you thought of Presto's collection and her museum idea?"

"Oh yes, I told Viola that I thought it would be a waste of time and money. I even gave her the names of several collectors who might be interested in buying the artwork she brought in, in case Presto wanted to sell to them instead."

"Did your opinion upset her?"

"Not at all. She accepted what I had to say and took the list of buyers with her. We never discussed the museum again, but she did mention that she'd sold several paintings and was grateful for my help."

"Oh, no," Lana moaned. Like a lightning bolt, the truth struck her blind. Thanks to her exhibition about modernizing masterworks, Viola knew artists who could copy masterpieces perfectly. Presto gave her free rein with his artwork, meaning she could have picked up the newly cleaned painting and brought it to an artist, instead of driving it back to Presto's home. Afterwards, it would have been easy for her to replace Presto's painting with the newly created copy and sell the original to an unsuspecting art lover. The tax report from Henry & Sons would have ensured that no one got suspicious about the sale or the work's authenticity. And because he was not really interested in the art, Presto would probably not have noticed that the originals had been exchanged for forgeries.

Yet, even if Viola had stolen from Presto and committed fraud, why would she have killed him or Gwen? Surely that wasn't enough of a reason to off her grandfather. She was independently wealthy; she could have reached an agreement with Presto and paid him back.

Lana thought again about Viola's strong reaction to the curator's concern that the two works she'd had cleaned might be fakes. If Viola had switched out the two paintings with forgeries, the museum's scientific staff would discover her deceit as soon as they ran their tests. Would they try to reach a private agreement with Viola, to avoid dragging Presto's name through the mud? Or would Viola be charged for theft and fraud? Avoiding imprisonment was a strong motive for murder.

But why take such a huge risk in the first place? Nothing made sense. Viola was rich enough to afford whatever she wanted, Lana thought. Was she bored and doing it for the kicks? Or was there another explanation?

49

Another Explanation

August 17—Day Six of the Wanderlust Tour in Edinburgh, Scotland

After her conversation with Henry & Sons, Lana waffled between calling the police or confronting Viola. Lana was convinced that she had switched Presto's art out for forgeries. But had she murdered him and Gwen?

If she called the cops now, they would want to know why she suspected Viola of harming Gwen and Presto. No matter how she looked at it, Lana couldn't believe that Viola would have killed either of them because of the artwork. Money could solve most problems, and based on Viola's spending habits, she had plenty of cash to throw around.

There must be another explanation, Lana decided, but right now she was too tired to see it. She crawled into bed and turned off the light, hoping sleep would bring the answer.

Soon after Lana's mind calmed down enough to let her body fall asleep, her ringing phone pulled her back into consciousness.

"Hello, Lana, I just want to let you know that I'm home, safe and sound." It was Betty, Presto's personal assistant.

Lana stifled her yawn with the back of her hand. "Good morning, Betty. Hey, that's great to know. How was your flight?"

"Oh my, I forgot to check my clock. You sound exhausted. I'll let you go back to sleep."

"No—please don't hang up. How are you doing? Did you talk to your sister about your travel plans, yet?"

"I did," Betty said brightly, "and she wants to join me! She's bored living in that retirement condo; nothing much happens there. I'm going to put my house on the market this week and then we'll start planning our trip. I think Fiji or somewhere tropical will be our first stop."

"That sounds absolutely wonderful!"

"Is Presto's family treating you alright? I do feel bad about abandoning you like that, but I had to get away from them. I hope you understand."

"Don't worry, I understand completely and don't blame you a bit." Lana sidestepped Betty's question, not wanting to have to explain how his children had been cut out of his will or that Gwen had fallen to her death. She needed Betty to first answer a few questions before she broached either of those subjects.

"Speaking of which, since I have you, what can you tell me about Viola's parents? What happened to her mother?"

"Gosh, she and Viola's dad are still married, so far as I know. She's a lovely woman, quite chatty. I think they're back East, but I'd have to check my computer to know for certain. Why do you ask?"

Lana sat up straighter in her bed. "You mean she's not dead?"

"Not that I'm aware of, but I haven't talked to either of Viola's parents in several months. Her dad called last year to give me his new address. They were downsizing from a single-family home to a condo so they could save money. If her mom had passed, he would have told me. Unless it happened more recently. Is that what Viola said, that something happened to her?"

Lana's brow creased. If Viola's parents were rich, why would they need to sell their home to save money? Besides, trust funds were only distributed after a person's death. "So they aren't rich?"

"Heavens, no! Her mother is a homemaker and her dad an insurance agent. That's why he helped her out with college. Viola had a full-tuition scholarship for her first two years, but her parents weren't able to pay for the rest, so Presto ended up footing the bill."

"Are you sure about that?"

"Quite. Ursula was on the warpath when she found out and demanded that he also pay for Harry's education."

When Lana remained silent, Betty added, "I can get you her dad's phone number, if you want. I'll need a few minutes to look it up. But I'm certain we would have heard about it if her mother died."

"No, that's alright. Thanks, Betty." Lana's thoughts were already racing forward. Viola's parents weren't rich, and her mother was still alive. Viola was lying about both, which meant Lana had found her killer.

50

Means, Motive, and Opportunity

August 17—Day Six of the Wanderlust Tour in Edinburgh, Scotland

What do I do now—call the cops or confront Viola? Lana wondered. Considering her guest had probably killed two people, she picked up the phone and dialed 999, the emergency number in the United Kingdom.

After thinking through all the facts, Lana was convinced that Viola had the means, opportunity, and the strongest motive.

There was no trust fund, and she was living far above her means. The sales from Presto's paintings must have been paying for her lifestyle.

Shortly before the dinner honoring him, Presto had announced he was going to sell several paintings to two museums. Lana was certain he had not used the past tense. But from his treachery with Harry, it was clear Presto avoided confrontations at all costs. He must have known if he told Viola the truth—that they'd already been sold—she would have gone ballistic. And it was mere hours before the dinner honoring his career began.

Viola must have poisoned Presto in the hopes of stopping him from selling the artwork that she'd had restored. But when it became clear that she was too late, that he had already signed sales agreements with the two museums, she had another problem to contend with. At the Scottish art museum, Gwen had said the artwork still had to be shipped over. Viola must have pushed Gwen off the cliff, in the hopes of stopping the artwork's transportation to

Scotland. She couldn't have known that it had already been crated and was ready for shipping.

"It was all for nothing," Lana murmured. When Viola had screamed that, she'd thought the younger woman was devastated because she hadn't gotten what she wanted. Yet, what if Viola was devastated because the art was on its way to Scotland and the museum would soon discover the two fakes?

Now there was no stopping the shipment. The museum's staff had already expressed their concern about those two paintings. They would certainly be checked by a curator and unmasked as forgeries. If they hadn't been recently cleaned and taxed, Viola could have said that Presto had purchased fakes and that would have been the end of it. It was well known that he had not had his artwork authenticated before buying it. But now, she was going to be found out. Fraud and forgery carried a heavy jail sentence.

If Lana was right, there was no way out for Viola. Would she try to flee to another country and begin a new life? Or would she stand her ground and deny the charges of fraud and theft to her dying breath? The young woman was so arrogant and self-assured that it was difficult to know which way she'd go.

51

Off-Road Adventures

August 17—Day Six of the Wanderlust Tour in Edinburgh, Scotland

After Lana had been connected to the nearest police station and explained her suspicions about Viola, the officer dispatched a patrol car before telling her it would take at least a half hour for someone to arrive from Glencoe. Considering they were in such a sparsely populated area, Lana was grateful it wouldn't take longer.

She thanked the officer and hung up, wondering what she should do now. Although deep down she knew it would be smarter to wait for the police to arrive before confronting Viola, Lana's desire to hear the younger woman confirm her suspicions about what she was doing and why was overwhelming.

As the first light of dawn broke over the lake, Lana crept down the hall to Viola's door and knocked.

There was no answer.

Lana knocked again, harder this time, and laid her head against the door to listen. A squealing noise drew her attention outside. Someone was attempting to drive a Jeep through the hotel's potholed driveway at top speed, but was apparently not used to the all-wheel traction. When the driver revved the engine again, the wheels caught, and the Jeep surged forward.

Oh, no, Lana thought, *that wasn't Viola, was it?*

When she ran downstairs, the hotel's front door was open, and the owner was outside shaking his fist at the Jeep. "That woman can't drive! She's going to ruin the gear box."

"What woman? Is it my guest Viola?"

The hotel owner turned to Lana. "Yes, it is."

"Call the police! They need to know that the suspect is fleeing. Can I borrow your car?"

The owner looked at her as if she was crazy. "The suspect? What the devil is going on?"

"She's killed two people, and now she's getting away! I don't want to lose sight of her."

The man's face whitened when Lana mentioned murder, but it did seem to snap him into action. After grabbing a shotgun from under the reception desk, he looked to Lana, determination in his eyes. "I'm driving."

As they ran out to his truck, Lana asked, "When did she rent the car?"

"She asked for one last night and said she'd pay extra to have it delivered as soon as possible. But the rental company's owner was at the pub when I called and didn't hear my message until a few minutes ago. He raced right over when I told him how much extra that lady was going to pay him."

Luckily, the hotel owner wasn't afraid to use the gas pedal. Unfortunately, his old truck wasn't as agile or fast as Viola's newer rental, especially on the rough dirt road leading from the highway to his hotel.

"Did she say where she's headed?" Lana asked as Viola's Jeep turned a corner far in the distance.

"She didn't, but last night she asked if there were any marinas nearby where she could charter a boat. I told her that Holy Loch Marina was the closest."

"Let's go there. She must be trying to get out of Scotland via boat. I'll call the police back and let them know where we think she's going."

The driver nodded solemnly and returned his focus to the rough road ahead. Lana picked up her phone to dial, when she noticed they were approaching the asphalted highway. She sucked in her breath, hoping Viola was still in sight.

To her surprise, Viola's Jeep was doing a U-turn and pulling back onto the freeway just as they approached the intersection. When the hotel owner turned to follow, he gunned his engine and his truck smashed into the back of the Jeep, denting both bumpers.

"Whoa, sorry about that. Are you okay?" the man asked as he braked to check whether Lana had been hurt.

"Don't slow down—she's getting away!" Lana pointed to Viola's Jeep, now far ahead of them. When the hotel owner picked up his speed and began actually gaining on her, Viola suddenly turned off-road again and accelerated up the rolling hill bordering the freeway.

"Hold on," the man yelled as he turned to follow. Unfortunately, his truck couldn't handle the incline as well as the Jeep, and their speed slowed considerably. The rocky protrusions and boulders, interspersed between patches of purple heather, made it even more slow going. Lana's heart was racing so fast that she began pounding on the truck's dashboard, willing it to go faster.

Viola was already over the hill and going down the other side by the time they crested it. When gravity took hold of the old truck, propelling it down the rock-encrusted hillside, its owner had trouble keeping control of the wheel. Lana screamed as they rode over a rocky outcrop, the stones lifting them up in the air before they landed hard. The crunching noise that accompanied their fall signaled the end of the man's truck.

Lana panted heavily as adrenaline coursed through her system. When she recovered enough to move, she carefully twisted her arms, legs, and back to ensure none had broken. After she was certain that she was still in one piece, Lana turned to her driver. The man was white with shock and breathing rapidly.

"Are you alright?"

"Aye," was all he could say before he passed out on the wheel.

Lana didn't know what to do. She checked to see whether he was bleeding, but saw no open wounds or visibly broken bones. When she put her ear close to his mouth, she could hear him breathing softly. Figuring it was better not to move him until she knew what was wrong, Lana tried opening the passenger side door.

With a few shoves, it creaked open. She stepped out and looked around. There were no houses or businesses close by, only a single-lane road and Viola's Jeep far in the distance. Lana cursed the rocks, truck, and Viola as the rush of adrenaline and anger exited her body, leaving her feeling tired and helpless.

After dialing the police and explaining both their predicament and Viola's likely destination, she hung up and returned to the hotel owner. Thankfully, he was awake.

"What happened?"

"We took an unexpected turn. Are you hurt? I've called the police, and they are sending a tow truck and ambulance."

The driver nodded as his eyes began to flutter closed again. "It'll take them a while. I think I'll stay here and rest my eyes."

Lana didn't know whether that was a good idea, but she also wasn't certain what else there was to do but sit quietly and wait. If the man had broken anything, her forcing him out of his truck or shaking him awake might make things worse.

She climbed back into the passenger seat and closed her eyes, as well. The adrenaline was well and truly gone. There was nothing they could do now but hope the police had caught up with Viola before she could leave the country.

Seconds later, both were softly snoring.

52

Why Did Presto Have To Die?

August 17—Day Six of the Wanderlust Tour in Edinburgh, Scotland

When a car horn began blaring, Lana woke with a start. On the road below was a tow truck, ambulance, and patrol car. A police officer and two paramedics carrying a stretcher were making their way up to the truck, stuck high up on the hillside.

The officer scratched his head as he took in their position. "It might take us a while to get this truck removed. Are you Lana Hansen, the woman who called us about Viola Craighead?"

The paramedics were already caring for the hotel owner, who thankfully had nothing but a set of new bruises to show for their adventurous ride.

"Yes, I am. Did you find her?"

"Aye, we believe the person you called in about is down there in that patrol car. Could you come with me and confirm it is the woman you suspect of two murders?"

"Of course, I'm happy to do so." Lana charged down the hillside, ready to confront Viola. She only hoped the younger woman wouldn't try to deny that she was behind the forgeries, thefts, or murders.

When she spotted Viola sitting in the back of the police car, her head hung low, Lana sprinted over to her. Another officer was standing close by and must have noticed Lana's determined look because he sprung in front of the

"

door, blocking her from opening it.

The glower that Viola gave Lana through the glass brought a smile to her face. She wasn't going to get away with murder, after all.

The officer opened the door so Lana could better see the arrestee. "Is this Viola Craighead, the woman you called us about?"

"Yes, it is," Lana said. "Why did Presto have to die?" she asked before the officer could close the door.

Viola glared at her, then blew out her cheeks. "What does it matter now? Presto's paintings are going to be tested; there's no getting out of it. It was Presto's fault. If he had told us the truth, instead of what we wanted to hear, we wouldn't have had unrealistic expectations. He promised me the artwork and never mentioned he was considering selling any of it. Otherwise I wouldn't have switched them out for forgeries. And if he had been honest and told me he'd had already signed a contract with that Scottish museum and arranged for the art to be shipped over, I wouldn't have poisoned his drink."

"But why did he have to die?"

"I have no desire to go to prison for theft and fraud."

"Wouldn't he have let it slide? He was your grandfather, after all."

Viola laughed. "Are you serious? You met him. I sold twenty-one of his paintings and made close to a million dollars, even after paying that forger. No, Presto wouldn't have let it slide. He would have done everything in his power to make me and my parents pay."

Lana thought back to the dinner. Presto had carried the heart pills in his jacket pocket, which he'd taken off and left on his throne for most of the evening—meaning anyone could have taken them. And Viola had asked to talk to Ron, right before Gwen went onstage.

"Did you put Presto's heart pills in Ron's jacket pocket?"

Viola jutted out her chin. "Maybe."

"What did you do with the glass? You did make a show of getting him that gin and tonic. You put some of his pills into it, didn't you?"

"I was just giving Granddad a taste of his own medicine," she said and laughed.

She's a cold-blooded psychopath, Lana thought with a shudder.

"Were you sleeping with Kurt?"

Viola crinkled her nose. "No, he's far too old for me. But it was handy having an inside man. I led Kurt on so that I had access to information about Presto's medical condition."

"But why take such an enormous risk if you expected to inherit Presto's collection?"

Viola snorted. "He was so unpredictable, I knew better than to assume he would keep his word. If he didn't leave it all to me, I figured he would have given it to his children to divvy up. I could have easily made the taxation reports disappear and led them to believe that Presto bought a bunch of fakes over the years. None of them cared about the artwork or bothered to see what I was doing with it, so they wouldn't have known which ones had been recently cleaned. But no, Presto had to sell them to a museum, where paperwork was required and it was standard practice to test them before accepting them into their collection. He shouldn't have lied to me."

Lana looked at the young woman before her. There was no trace of remorse in her expression—only angry defiance. As much as she wanted to hate Viola, Lana's heart grieved for this young life gone so very wrong.

53

Baby Names

August 17—Day Six of the Wanderlust Tour in Edinburgh, Scotland

After they'd been questioned by the Glencoe police, the remains of Lana's tour group wanted to head back to Edinburgh. No one spoke during the three-hour ride as they struggled to process Viola's betrayal.

As soon as the Edinburgh police were informed of Viola's arrest and confession, the process to release Ron was set in motion.

Lana arrived at the police station minutes before he was discharged. When her ex-husband walked out of the holding area, Lana rose slowly, unsure how he would react to her presence.

Ron seemed momentarily startled to see her, but as soon as he recovered, he sprinted over and wrapped Lana up in a bear hug.

"Thank you," he cried into her hair. "The police told me what happened with Viola and how you figured out what she'd done. You set me free, Lana."

"No, I did what my boss asked me to do—help the police figure out who killed Presto. I did not do it for you or Candy," Lana said resolutely as she tried to squirm out of his embrace, but he refused to let her loose.

"I'm still grateful, and I'm certain Candy is, too," Ron said before finally releasing her from his grip.

As if called, his new girlfriend burst into the reception area the moment he spoke her name.

"Ronnie!" she screamed as she ran over to him. The intensity of their kiss made Lana blush and divert her eyes.

"Thank you for helping us," Candy sobbed, her arms firmly wrapped around her boyfriend—the same man Lana had once loved.

"I didn't do it for—you know what? You're both welcome." When they began cuddling again, Lana turned to walk away.

Candy grabbed her arm. "If it's a girl, we're going to name her Lana."

Ron's eyes widened as much as Lana's did. "Oh, no. I appreciate the sentiment, but please don't do that," she said hastily. "It's kind of creepy. What about Jennifer or Stacey? Those are nice, neutral names."

Candy nodded, but Lana doubted she had heard her; the younger woman only had eyes for Ron.

Lana looked at the pair, so obviously in love, as jealousy took hold. *Why can't someone love me like that?* she thought. Until she remembered that someone did.

54

London Bridge

August 19—London, England

London Bridge sparkled in the twilight as the Millennium Wheel turned in the distance. Their seats on the upper deck of a riverboat chugging along the Thames were perfectly situated to see both the famous city skyline and the first stars of the evening.

"Ask me that question again," she said as she snuggled closer to Alex.

"Which question?" he asked before kissing her hair.

"The one you asked me back in Seattle."

He frowned in concentration until his thoughts aligned with hers. His smile increased in intensity as he took out his keychain and got down on one knee. Several passengers gasped and pointed when they saw what was going on.

"Lana Hansen, would you move in with me?"

"Yes, Alex Wright, nothing would make me happier." She wrapped her arms around his neck and pulled him in for a kiss as the boat erupted in applause.

Lana lay back in his strong arms as their cruise continued, knowing she'd made the right decision. Moving in together would bring new challenges to their relationship, but none were insurmountable. And being able to spend all of their Seattle time together made it more than worthwhile.

She only hoped that Dotty would be pleased to hear the news.

245

55

Landing On Their Feet

September 9—Seattle, Washington

"What can I do for you, Lana?" Dotty asked as her dogs, Chipper and Rodney, tore through the hallway, racing towards Lana at top speed. Unfortunately for Rodney the pug, the speed was too much, and he couldn't slow down in time. He pushed out his little paws in an attempt to stop himself, but to no avail. He bashed into Lana's leg—tongue first—then looked up at her with his bulbous eyes as if to say "I'm sorry."

"Oh, Rodney. Are you okay, buddy?"

When she scratched at his head, he began to pant and lick her hand, signaling that all was right with the world.

"Boys, let Lana come inside." Dotty shooed Rodney to one side as she picked up Chipper the Jack Russell terrier and walked towards her living room.

Lana handed her friend and boss a folder full of paperwork. "Here is the rental agreement. Alex signed it, as well."

"Oh, that's great. I'll send it over to my property manager and have her get you the keys right away."

Despite Dotty's previous assertions that Lana was free to move out at any time, she still hadn't been certain that the older woman would be truly okay with it. She should have known that there was no reason to be concerned.

246

After Lana had broken the news as gently as she could, Dotty had sprung out of her chair and raced to her in-home office to get her laptop. Moments later, they were looking over several rental properties that Dotty owned, all of which would soon be vacant.

After days of driving around and looking at potential homes, Lana and Alex agreed on a houseboat moored on Lake Union, with a dock big enough to store two kayaks. There was even a fence around it, meaning her cat, Seymour, couldn't accidentally fall into the water. Lana was in seventh heaven.

"Have you talked to Zach recently?" Dotty asked, after she'd made certain that Alex and Lana had signed and initialed each page.

"Zach, as in Presto's son?"

Both Dotty and Lana had attended Presto's funeral in Seattle a week earlier, and she knew that her boss had spent the evening with his family. Lana left after she'd paid her respects to Presto at the graveside service; she'd spent more than enough time with his kin and had no desire to stick around for the wake afterwards. Not that any of his family noticed. Lana figured at least three hundred people attended the funeral, and several media networks covered it live, as well.

"Zach managed to save his production company from bankruptcy."

"How did he pull that off?" Lana asked, stunned to hear Zach hadn't yet gone belly up.

"You know the actor who played Harry Potter—the one with the glasses? Apparently he loves those over-the-top art-house productions. He saw Zach's play, and afterwards they got to talking about his future plans. Apparently they share the same artistic vision, and that actor's committed to funding—and even starring in—Zach's next production."

"That's incredible!"

"And Ursula's bed-and-breakfast reality show is a go. MTV is going to start filming a pilot there next month."

Lana's eyebrows shot up. "How did she land a deal so fast?"

"Apparently her realtor friend knew about an adorable hotel for sale and the deal was complete before Ursula got back to Los Angeles. She invited several of her A-list celebrity clients to stay at there for free the first week they were open. Ursula somehow persuaded them to play all sorts of silly magic-themed games while she filmed them. Her guests gave her permission to put short clips up on YouTube, and they were such a hit that a television producer got in touch right away to sign her."

"That's amazing."

"It really is. Her success got me thinking. Everyone is releasing their own videos, songs, and books these days. The gatekeepers are becoming irrelevant. Maybe we should start filming our tours and posting clips online? We could provide travel tips and show potential clients the places they'd visit with us—kind of like what you do with your Travel Time blog. We might be able to make it into a weekly show. It would be a great marketing tool."

Lana shook her head automatically. "There are some guests, like Ursula, who would love that. But I think most would hate being followed around while they are trying to relax and enjoy their vacation."

"That's a good point. We would have to give the guests a pretty significant discount if we were going to do something like that. I'll have to work out if it would be cost-effective or not."

Lana chuckled, knowing her boss wasn't ready to let this idea go. "We'll see. Anyway, it is great to hear Zach and Ursula landed on their feet, after all. Just as Presto hoped they would."

"Yes, they did. Even Harry is doing well, from what Ursula said. He's been practicing a new act with tricks that don't involve cards for a change, and her hotel guests love it. I wouldn't be surprised if he does end up finding a financial backer for another tour. In any case, he's bound to get more exposure and a lot of practice, because he's performing there five times a week."

"Good for him."

It seemed as if all of Presto's family got what they wanted—with one exception. Only Viola lost out on "her" art and paid for it with her freedom. In six months' time, she had managed to switch out twenty-one of Presto's paintings for forgeries and sold the originals to unsuspecting art lovers. She would most likely be convicted of forgery, fraud, and theft before being sentenced to several years in a state prison.

"Oh—I haven't told you the biggest news! Randy and Gloria are engaged! They're going to tie the knot in Italy a week before Christmas. She wants to get married in the village her parents grew up in."

"I know, isn't it great? Alex is one of Randy's best men, so I found out about it last night."

"That makes sense; they are brothers, after all." Judging from her tone, she was slightly put out that Lana already knew her big news.

"Randy called me this morning to ask for my help," Dotty continued. "He invited several of his mountaineering friends to the wedding, but most have never been abroad, so they want to fly over early and see more of Italy. Randy asked if I could help him arrange a few day trips for them, so he can help Gloria get ready for the wedding. She's a wonderful girl, but she's got one of those dream weddings in her head, and it's going to take quite a bit of preparation to make it happen. Luckily, she's got a big family to help, but Randy wants to be involved, too. Now he's torn between showing Italy to his friends or helping his fiancée."

"Gosh, that is a conundrum," Lana responded, unsure where her boss was going with this.

"He is such an asset to this company. And he's gone through so much these past few years—that crazy stalker, his leg injury, taking on this new job. I was thinking of treating his friends to a three-day tour of Rome, so he can help Gloria get ready for the wedding. Do you think Randy would like that, or am I being too pushy?"

"I think he would be incredibly grateful and his friends would love it."

"Would you consider helping me out with his friends, if Randy agrees?"

"I would love to!" She was more than happy to lead that group. She and Alex had talked about flying over early to explore Italy together, but he had already committed to working that week. Now she could see more of the country before the wedding, without feeling guilty about not doing so with Alex.

"I wonder what the best men are going to wear. You know, the wedding might give Alex ideas," Dotty said as a grin split her face in two.

Lana blushed in response. "I hope not! We haven't even moved in together. Let's see how that goes before we consider taking another major step."

"If you say so," Dotty tittered.

Lana walked back down to her basement apartment, thinking about Randy's upcoming wedding and her imminent move to the houseboat with Alex. *Mrs. Lana Wright does have a nice ring to it*, she thought, before scolding herself. *One step at a time, Lana; one step at a time.*

THE END

Follow the further adventures of Lana Hansen in ***Death by Fountain: A Christmas Murder in Rome***—Book Five of the Travel Can Be Murder Mystery Series!

When Randy Wright's ex-girlfriend is found floating in the Trevi Fountain, Lana Hansen must sleuth out who murdered the young woman in order to set her fellow guide free.
Order it now on Amazon!

Thanks for reading my novel!
Reviews really do help readers decide whether they want to take a chance on a new author. If you enjoyed this story, please consider posting a review on BookBub, Goodreads, or with your favorite retailer.
I appreciate it! Jennifer S. Alderson

Acknowledgments

Many thanks to my wonderful family for their continued support and encouragement. I am also grateful to my editor, Sadye Scott-Hainchek, for her incredible work on this book and series.

As much as I would love to say I thought up the wire-array system used in Presto's Rainbow Walk, it was created by illusion designer John Gaughan for magician David Copperfield's Levitation Illusion. Gaughan's unique wire-array system was patented on October 11, 1994, as US Patent #5354238—some say against Copperfield's wishes.

Having Presto walk over water was my husband's idea—thanks, Philip!

Highland Titles is a real environmental conservation project that inspired my fictitious nature reserve's setup and location. My version is in no way representative of that organization's policies or efforts.

Two incredible trips to Scotland informed my descriptions of places, as well as the choice of locations and murder weapon. I hope my story inspires you to learn more about Scotland and bagpipes!

About the Author

Jennifer S. Alderson was born in San Francisco, grew up in Seattle, and currently lives in Amsterdam. After traveling extensively around Asia, Oceania, and Central America, she lived in Darwin, Australia, before settling in the Netherlands.

Jennifer's love of travel, art, and culture inspires her award-winning Zelda Richardson Mystery series, her Travel Can Be Murder Cozy Mysteries, and her Carmen De Luca Art Sleuth Mysteries. Her background in art history, journalism, and multimedia development enriches her novels.

When not writing, she can be found perusing a museum, biking around Amsterdam, or enjoying a coffee along the canal while planning her next research trip.

For more information about the author and her upcoming novels, please visit Jennifer's website [http://jennifersalderson.com].

Books by Jennifer S. Alderson:

Carmen De Luca Art Mysteries
Collecting Can Be Murder
A Statue To Die For
Forgeries and Fatalities
A Killer Inheritance

Travel Can Be Murder Cozy Mysteries
Death on the Danube: A New Year's Murder in Budapest
Death by Baguette: A Valentine's Day Murder in Paris

Death by Windmill: A Mother's Day Murder in Amsterdam
Death by Bagpipes: A Summer Murder in Edinburgh
Death by Fountain: A Christmas Murder in Rome
Death by Leprechaun: A Saint Patrick's Day Murder in Dublin
Death by Flamenco: An Easter Murder in Seville
Death by Gondola: A Springtime Murder in Venice
Death by Puffin: A Bachelorette Party Murder in Reykjavik

Zelda Richardson Art Mysteries
The Lover's Portrait: An Art Mystery
Rituals of the Dead: An Artifact Mystery
Marked for Revenge: An Art Heist Thriller
The Vermeer Deception: An Art Mystery

Standalone Travel Thriller
Down and Out in Kathmandu: A Backpacker Mystery

Death by Fountain: A Christmas Mystery in Rome

Book Five of the Travel Can Be Murder Cozy Mystery Series

Rome—the city of churches, marble … and murder? For one American tourist, a famous fountain will become her final resting place.

Wedding bells are ringing, and Lana Hansen could not be happier! Wanderlust Tours guide Randy Wright and his Italian girlfriend are tying the knot in Tuscany, right after he and Lana finish leading a tour around Rome.

Unfortunately for Randy, his ex-girlfriend is still convinced they are meant to be together. When she tracks him down in Saint Peter's Square, they have a nasty fight, and Randy threatens to harm her if she doesn't leave him be.

After her body is found in the Trevi Fountain, Randy is immediately arrested. Lana is convinced he didn't do it, yet none of her other guests seemed to have wished the young women ill. With a shortage of suspects, Lana must dig deep in order to sleuth out who really killed Randy's ex-girlfriend—before his visit to the Eternal City becomes permanent.

Available as paperback, large print edition, eBook, and in Kindle Unlimited.

Excerpt from **Death by Fountain**

Chapter 1: Christmas Shopping in The Eternal City

December 17—Piazza Navona, Italy

"Do they have one of those nativity scenes in a larger size? That baby Jesus is way too small." Dotty Thompson's voice crackled through Lana Hansen's telephone speaker, making it difficult to hear her clearly. The wind whipping through the market stalls was not helping matters. As another gust took hold, several of the lighter ornaments flew off of their racks, to the dismay of the many shopkeepers crowding the space.

Lana scanned the cramped stall filled with handcrafted Christmas decorations as she looked for a manger scene that would please Dotty, her boss and the owner of Wanderlust Tours. In addition to decorated glass balls, religious figurines, and miniatures of Rome's most famous icons, this shop also sold a magnificent selection of nativity scenes. Her eyes zoomed in on two planks dedicated to tiny porcelain figurines portraying Joseph, Mary, and the three wise men, as well as cribs made from real twigs and straw, with a baby Jesus resting in each. *Which one would Dotty like the most?* she wondered.

Since arriving in Rome a few hours earlier, Lana and her fellow Wanderlust Tours guide, Randy Wright, had spent most of their time in Piazza Navona's Christmas and Epiphany Market, doing Dotty's holiday shopping. The long, rectangular space was filled with the sounds of shoppers, musicians, happy children, and the twinkly jingle of a wooden-horse merry-go-round. Lights shaped like stars, Christmas trees, and comets topped most of the market stalls. The smell of sugar-coated desserts and hearty bread filled Lana's nostrils.

Luckily, the market was located in one of Rome's most popular tourist spots, considered so thanks to the iconic fountains and buildings that filled the square. In the center of the Piazza Navona rose an Egyptian obelisk, a stone dove with an olive twig in its beak perched on its crown. The gigantic monument rested atop a mass of carved stone, which rose out of an enormous fountain decorated with palm trees, papal symbols, a lion, a serpent, a crocodile, and a dolphin.

Lana knew from her guidebook that it was the Fountain of the Four Rivers by one of Rome's most famous artists, Gian Lorenzo Bernini. Four God-like figures, each representing one of the world's major tributaries, rested on the rocks holding up the obelisk. Staring down at her was the river god Ganges, casually holding an oar as he gazed over the busy market. To Lana, he appeared to be watching the masses of tourists with a mixture of awe and disdain. Water poured out of the rocks and into a large basin surrounding the mythical figures' feet. In the shallow pool, the water appeared to be more green than blue.

Buildings painted in soft yellows and oranges lined one side of the square, contrasting nicely with the Sant'Agnese in Agone, an ivory white church situated on the other. In front of that masterpiece of baroque architecture stood a Christmas tree at least five stories tall wrapped in lights and dusted in artificial snow. Based on the sunny blue skies and mild temperatures, Lana doubted they ever got much of the real thing in this part of Italy.

"Do you see any nativity scenes that are about three feet wide?" Dotty pushed, bringing her attention back to the task at hand. "That would block out the base of my tree."

"No, I don't see anything bigger than a foot," Lana replied. "Besides, how would we get something that big back to Seattle without it breaking?"

"You do have a point," Dotty said, her tone divulging her disappointment.

Lana scanned the cramped stall again until her eyes rested on a manger scene big enough to please her boss, yet compact enough to fit into a suitcase. "What about this one?" She aimed her phone's camera towards the intricate scene, took a photo, and sent it to her boss.

"It's perfect—I can see baby Jesus's face! Add it to the pile," Dotty squealed.

Lana turned to the shopkeeper, already busy packing up their other purchases, and pointed to the nativity scene. "We'll take that one, too."

The man's grin intensified as he carefully lifted the massive object from the shelf. When he rang it up at the register, Lana startled at the hefty price, glad that her boss had given her permission to charge it all to the company credit card.

Randy whispered in her ear. "If Dotty keeps this up, we'll need to take a taxi back to the hotel."

Lana eyed the Christmas decorations, figurines, and nativity scene they had chosen and nodded in agreement. There were at least twenty pieces on the counter that still had to be wrapped for transport.

"I heard that, Randy," Dotty called out. "Get yourself a taxi and I'll pack an extra suitcase so I can get it all back to Seattle in one piece. I do appreciate you doing this for me. Those Italian decorations are so unique, I know they will be the perfect gifts for my good friends and family. I should have planned more time in Rome so I could have shopped for them myself."

"They really do have a gorgeous selection of decorations here," Lana agreed. She had already purchased several hangers shaped like the Colosseum and Saint Peter's Basilica. However, her favorites were the ornaments featuring "La Befana," a big-nosed, broom-riding witch who brings presents to Italian children on January 6. Lana had gotten several for her own friends and family. Like Dotty, she was glad to be able to give them something unique on Christmas Day.

"It's not a problem, Dotty. We're just surprised by the quantity, that's all," Randy teased his boss. "How many friends do you have, anyway?"

"I know it's a lot, but I don't want anyone to feel left out. Which reminds me—could you pick up one more ornament? Something manly—maybe Randy can choose it for me," Dotty said.

"Sure," he said and began scanning the wares for another gift.

"What's going on? Do you have a new boyfriend?" Lana teased, expecting her boss to laugh off her remark.

"Yes, well, I do have a new man in my life, and I want to get him something special."

Lana's mouth dropped open. "Oh, yeah—what's he like? How tall is he? Is he retired? Is he handsome?"

"Hush, child, you're making me blush. He is quite tall and a true gentleman.

You'll meet him at Randy's wedding next week."

"It must be serious if he's flying over with you."

"We are getting pretty close, that's true," Dotty said, her tone noncommittal.

"That's great; I'm happy for you."

Her boss, six times a widower, had been single for the past two years and, as far as Lana knew, had not been on the lookout for a new partner. Lana couldn't blame her. Though all of Dotty's marriages had been happy ones, her husbands did have an unfortunate tendency to die soon after they tied the knot. Not that Dotty was a black widow. In fact, all of her husbands had been killed when she was nowhere near them. Lana wasn't certain how all six had passed, but knew that one had been trampled by elephants in India, another had been knocked off a sailboat during a Seattle storm, and a third had sustained shark bites while diving in Fiji. She hoped whoever Dotty had her sights set on next was luckier and less accident-prone than her other husbands.

Dotty whispered through the phone, "Hey, Lana—how is Randy holding up?"

Lana took the call off speaker and stepped away from her fellow guide. "Randy is a bundle of nerves. But who wouldn't be, a week before their wedding day?"

"I sure hope leading that tour through Naples didn't make things worse."

Lana looked to Randy and considered Dotty's question as she reviewed the ten-day tour in her mind. She and Randy had just completed a fascinating tour of Naples, including excursions to Vesuvius, Pompeii, and Herculaneum. After they'd gotten their guests to the airport this morning, they'd jumped on a train and headed north to Rome.

"He was a bit jittery the first night, but as soon as the tour started, he was in his element. He did a great job guiding, as usual, and was his normal jovial self almost all of the time. If anything, the guests' questions helped keep him distracted from the week ahead. Gloria did call quite a few times with questions about the wedding, some of which he couldn't answer. It is a good thing that he is able to go to her family's village a few days before it takes place. They have so much to get ready before their big day. And by working this tour, he's had time to adjust to the time zone so he won't have to deal with jet lag when meeting Gloria's extended family for the first time."

Randy had told Gloria, when she'd accepted his proposal, that he wanted to make her ideal wedding come true. He didn't realize at the time that her perfect day included getting married in a foreign country. Her dream of exchanging nuptials in the same village that her parents had was incredibly romantic, but did create a few extra hurdles they would not have had to deal with if they had married in Seattle.

"That's true. I'm glad to hear it. Why don't you—" Dotty's voice was momentarily drowned out by barking. Seconds later, she yelled out, "Chipper! Rodney! You leave Seymour alone."

"Dotty? Are you still there?"

"I'm sorry, Lana. My boys are having fun chasing your cat around. But I promise they haven't actually caught him. Seymour is one fast feline," Dotty said, admiration in her voice.

"Don't worry, I know they are just having fun." Lana knew from experience that Dotty's pug and Jack Russell terrier loved to chase after her cat, but that Seymour was always several steps ahead.

"Mary Sue is moving in tomorrow, so she can get used to the boys' routine before I leave."

"That's great. I'm so glad your new tenant is also able to look after our pets while we're in Italy. Is she nice?"

"She seems pleasant enough but doesn't have much spunk. I'll have to work on that. But don't worry, Lana, she could never replace you," Dotty rushed to add.

"You're sweet. I miss our chats, too."

"Hey, thanks a bunch for picking up all of those presents for me," Dotty said. "Treat yourself to a nice dinner tonight—on me."

"That's really generous of you," Lana said as she looked at her watch. "Gosh, we'd better pay for these and grab a cab. It's already three in the afternoon. No wonder my stomach is rumbling."

"You two take care. I'll see you next week," Dotty sang out before hanging up.

* * *

Are you enjoying the book so far? Buy *Death by Fountain* now and keep reading! Available as paperback, large print edition, eBook, and in Kindle Unlimited.

* * *